P9-DCM-446

Bitten by Cupid

LYNSAY SANDS

PAMELA PALMER
JAIME RUSH

AVON
An Imprint of HarperCollinsPublishers

AVON BOOKS
An Imprint of HarperCollins*Publishers*
10 East 53rd Street
New York, New York 10022-5299

"Vampire Valentine" copyright © 2010 by Lynsay Sands
"Hearts Untamed" copyright © 2010 by Pamela Poulsen
"Kiss and Kill Cupid" copyright © 2010 by Tina Wainscott
ISBN 978-0-06-189445-9
www.avonbooks.com

First Avon Books paperback printing: January 2010

Avon Trademark Reg. U.S. Pat. Off. and in Other Countries, Marca Registrada, Hecho en U.S.A.
HarperCollins® is a registered trademark of HarperCollins Publishers.

Printed in the U.S.A.

10 9 8 7 6 5 4 3 2 1

Vampire Valentine

LYNSAY SANDS

Vampire Mirabeau La Roche may think she's prepared for anything this Valentine's Day, but she hadn't counted on evading the enemy by running through the sewers below the city. And in her fluffy peach bridesmaid's dress, no less. She's even less prepared for Tiny McGraw, the red-hot, red-blooded private investigator who's been assigned to help her.

Hearts Untamed

PAMELA PALMER

Ten years after he spurned Julianne's declaration of love and then vanished, Zee's back—only this time he's the one being rejected. Julianne's in desperate straits, and involving Zee could jeopardize his immortality. But he won't take no for an answer—and Julianne's about to discover that her former love is even wilder than she thought . . .

Kiss and Kill Cupid

JAIME RUSH

Kristy Morgan's ability to hear other people's thoughts has never been more than a nuisance—until she hears the notorious Valentine's Day killer plotting to make her his next victim. Kristy's new boss, Adrian, vows to protect her, but because his mind is mysteriously closed to her, trusting him could prove fatal, even if resisting him is starting to seem impossible. With February 14 just two days away, all that's certain is the killer wants her, and he won't be denied . . .

By Lynsay Sands

THE RENEGADE HUNTER
THE IMMORTAL HUNTER

By Pamela Palmer

PASSION UNTAMED
OBSESSION UNTAMED

By Jaime Rush

OUT OF THE DARKNESS
A PERFECT DARKNESS

CONTENTS

Bitten by Cupid

Vampire Valentine

LYNSAY SANDS

Tiny had just raised his hand to knock on the door when a shriek rang out from the other side. The sound immediately had him dropping the bags of blood he carried to charge into the room. He'd taken several steps inside, his eyes quickly scanning the situation, before he came to a confused halt. He'd expected to find that one or more of Leonius's no-fangers had snuck into the church and was attacking someone, or, at the very least, a mouse that had startled someone, but there was neither. The room was filled with women, most of them in white, all peering at him with wide, startled eyes.

"Tiny?" The query was accompanied by a rustle of silk that drew his gaze to Marguerite Argeneau as she disengaged from the small cluster of women to his right. Tiny felt his eyes widen and his mouth drop as he caught sight of the Argeneau matriarch. The woman wore a long gown with a scooped neck, cinched waist, and a full skirt that belled out from her legs thanks to the tulle underneath. It was in every way a gorgeous, traditional wedding gown . . . except that it was a deep blood red color with black trim that made her look like a queen among her ladies-in-waiting dressed in white and pastel gowns. Tiny simply stared at her as she stood before him, his eyes caught by the full, pale breasts on display in the low-cut gown. It almost looked to him as if the dress was trying to push the round globes out of the neckline, as if their perfect presence somehow offended the rich material.

"Tiny?" Her voice was amused this time, and he forced himself to drag his fascinated gaze away from the escaping flesh to raise apologetic eyes to hers. Tiny offered a wry smile and sent out a silent apology he knew she would read, then cleared his throat and glanced around. "I heard someone scream."

"And thought the worst," Marguerite said with an understanding nod. She patted his arm soothingly. "All is well. It was a happy shriek, though with Jeanne Louise, it's sometimes hard to tell."

Marguerite's niece wrinkled her nose at her gentle teasing and excused herself by saying, "I'd just heard Leigh's good news. It took me completely by surprise."

As Jeanne Louise turned back to Leigh to give her a congratulatory hug, Tiny glanced questioningly at Marguerite, wondering what the good news was, but her attention was on the doorway behind him. "Is that for us?"

The question drew his gaze back to the open door and the bags that lay scattered on the hall floor. Much to his relief, none of them appeared to have been damaged by the fall.

"Oh, yes. Bastien asked me to bring them to you gals. I dropped them when I heard the scream," he admitted, turning to head back to the door. Marguerite followed, and when she knelt to help him collect them, he asked quietly, "What's Leigh's good news?"

"She's pregnant again," Marguerite said with a smile.

Tiny's eyebrows rose, and he started to smile as well, but the expression died as he recalled how crushed Leigh and Lucian had been when she had miscarried the first time. If she lost this one as well—

"She's more than three months along. This one should carry to term," Marguerite said reassuringly, proving she still had the bad habit of reading his mind. "They waited until she was past the dangerous stage to share the news. I think she was afraid that announcing it before then would jinx it."

Tiny nodded with understanding. From what

he'd heard, the first miscarriage had been a terrible blow to the couple. He wasn't surprised they'd waited to announce this one.

"Tell her congratulations from me," he said quietly, as they straightened.

"Why don't you tell her yourself?" Marguerite suggested.

Tiny hesitated and glanced to the women, all gathered now at the far end of the room. Terri, Leigh, and Inez all wore traditional white wedding gowns in various styles. Jackie, Jeanne Louise, Lissianna, and Rachel, who were acting as bridesmaids, wore pastels—pink, aqua, and lavender. They all looked exquisite . . . which was the problem. They were gorgeous, and they could read his thoughts. Much as he hated to admit it, not all those thoughts were stellar. He was a man after all . . . and he didn't want to unintentionally insult any of the women with a stray thought that made its way up from his nether regions.

"Ah," Marguerite said with understanding, reading his thoughts as always. She patted his shoulder reassuringly. "It's all right. They are used to mortal men and their stray thoughts."

"But I'm not used to women being able to read mine," Tiny said dryly as he set the blood he'd collected on the table inside the door. "Tell Leigh congratulations for me and tell the others they look lovely."

"Very well," Marguerite said solemnly, but when he turned to retreat from the room, she followed him out into the hall. Knowing she had something else to say, Tiny paused and glanced back in question. Marguerite hesitated, then murmured, "After the recent trouble, it is nice to have so much to celebrate."

"Hmm." Tiny waited, knowing she had more to say.

Finally, she breathed out a little sigh, and simply asked, "You will be careful on this assignment?"

"Geez, Marguerite," he said with irritation. The woman was always treating him like a child who couldn't take care of himself. It was sweet but—

"I know you can take care of yourself, Tiny," she assured him quickly. "And if this were a normal assignment, I probably wouldn't even worry . . . much," she added wryly when his expression turned dubious. She then rushed on, "But this is no-fangers we are dealing with here and—"

"Hang on," Tiny interrupted suddenly as realization struck. "How do you know about this assignment? Lucian said it was top secret. We—" He snapped his mouth shut and grimaced as he realized she'd probably plucked it out of his thoughts. Which was probably why Lucian hadn't given him the full details of the assignment until just moments ago. The wedding was only moments away, and he was supposed to stay in the private rooms until it did, then slip to his seat. Lucian was hoping that would minimize the chance of the wrong person reading his thoughts.

"Actually, I didn't read your mind," Marguerite assured him quietly. "In fact, I'm the one who suggested you and Mirabeau when Lucian mentioned his plan to me."

"*You* suggested Mirabeau and I be given the job," he said slowly, a frisson of alarm sliding through him. Marguerite was well-known for her matchmaking, and the woman didn't do anything without a purpose. He suddenly wasn't feeling so good about this task he'd agreed to do for Lucian Argeneau.

Marguerite rolled her eyes. "Oh, don't look so alarmed."

"Marguerite," he said, the name rolling off his tongue in a low growl. "Everyone knows what happens when you put two people together."

"They find their life mates," she said with a satisfied smile, then rolled her eyes at his expression. "Please don't try to claim you wouldn't like to find a life mate."

Tiny frowned. He was mortal. Human. Non-vampire. And mortals as a rule didn't have life mates. At least he didn't think they did. Certainly the divorce rate among his fellow mortals didn't suggest such was the case. Only immortals had life mates, or what they called life mates. Perfect partners they couldn't read or control so they could live out their long lives in peace and passion.

However, mortals could *be* life mates to immortals. As for whether he'd like to be one . . . Tiny found his gaze sliding back into the room and to the women clustered inside, still smiling and chattering excitedly over Leigh's pregnancy. His gaze slid over all those beaming, very happy faces, then settled on Jackie, his boss and partner at the detective agency. She used to be mortal too, but she'd turned out to be Vincent Argeneau's life mate. Tiny hadn't seen much of the woman he considered one of his best friends since then. The two rarely came up for air, but he'd met them in Vegas and stood in for her deceased father to give her away at their Elvis-inspired wedding a month ago, and he knew she was deliriously happy. Both she and Vincent fairly glowed with their joy. Spending that time with them . . . It had been hard not to yearn for that kind of connection and happiness too. Spending time with any of the immortal couples would make it impossible for anyone not to yearn for that kind of connection. Still . . .

Tiny shifted his gaze back to Marguerite. "So you think this Mirabeau and I . . . ?"

"Mirabeau La Roche." Marguerite nodded with a wide smile. "I think you shall suit each other perfectly."

Tiny arched a doubtful eyebrow at the words as he asked, "Isn't she the gal with the black-and-pink hair?"

"Normally yes." Marguerite nodded. "But not today. I told her no one would think anything of her hair here in New York, but she wanted a more traditional hairdo for the wedding. Besides, she didn't feel her hair went well with the peach gown she is to wear, so I took her to my hairdresser this morning to work her magic for the wedding."

"Hmm," Tiny murmured, his gaze sliding to the women in the room, but he was pretty sure he hadn't seen a peach gown.

"She's helping Elvi get dressed," Marguerite explained, gesturing to a closed door at the opposite side of the room. "You'll meet her soon enough, and when you do . . ." Marguerite hesitated, then sighed, and said, "Our Mirabeau is prickly. She has a lot of defenses. She lost her entire family to the greed and betrayal of a favorite uncle back during the Massacres of St. Bartholomew and finds it hard to trust and love. She's erected a lot of protective walls. You will need to be patient."

Tiny stared at Marguerite blankly. She seriously believed he would be a life mate to this Mirabeau. The idea was both exciting and scary as hell. His life would change forever. God. A life mate. It would mean his days as a bachelor were over . . . and he'd probably have to turn, become an immortal like Jackie had. He'd have to drink blood and . . .

"Breathe," Marguerite said softly, soothingly. "Do not panic. I may yet be wrong. Why do you not just wait and see? Meet Mirabeau, take care of the task Lucian has set the two of you, and allow nature to take its course."

Tiny felt his body inhale deeply, then blow out the air taken in, seeming to breathe out the stress and worry suddenly plaguing him along with it. His eyes narrowed on Marguerite. "You're controlling me," he said, his voice an accusing rumble.

"Just enough to calm you down," she said unapologetically, then beamed at him. "I have great hopes for you and Mirabeau. And if all works out as I hope, I need never worry about losing you to age and time. You will be a member of my family forever."

Tiny's eyebrows rose slightly at the words, and he peered down at the top of her head, his hands automatically rising to pat her back as she suddenly hugged him. He said, "I take it Mirabeau is one of your strays then?"

"She has become like a member of our family over time," Marguerite corrected solemnly as she stepped back. "Thanks to her uncle, she had none of her own."

Tiny felt amused affection curve his lips. "So you adopted her into yours as you're wont to do with strays . . ." Marguerite grimaced at his use of the term *strays*, but before she could comment, he added solemnly, "But I'm not a stray, Marguerite.

I have family . . . And I am very fond of them. I'm not sure I'd be willing to give them up."

Worry flickered briefly over Marguerite's face, but then she smiled. "All will work out. It always does."

"Always?"

"When you live as long as we do, it usually does," she assured him with a chuckle, and gave him a gentle push. "Go on. Check and see how the men are doing. The ceremony will be starting soon, and I'm sure Bastien is making himself and everyone else crazy trying to ride herd on all the details. He's had to arrange, cancel, and rearrange this wedding so many times, I don't think any of us thought it would ever happen."

Tiny smiled faintly at the words but merely nodded and turned to head up the hall. His smile died, however, once he'd turned the corner and was out of Marguerite's sight. His mind immediately played back their conversation as he tried to grasp the fact that she thought he would be a life mate to this Mirabeau gal he was supposed to be working with for the next couple of days. The idea both fascinated and scared the hell out of him. It also absorbed his complete attention so that he practically sleepwalked through the multiple wedding of various members of the Argeneau clan. It was almost a shock when Decker Argeneau Pimms suddenly tapped him on the shoulder, and said, "Our turn to sign," as he nodded toward the front of the church and the open door behind it, where Lucian Argeneau stood gesturing them forward.

The registry room behind the podium where they were to sign as witnesses to the unions was tiny, far too small for everyone to have fit in at once, so they'd decided to do the witnessing in shifts. Half the group went in to sign first, then they shuffled them out a side door while the other half entered from the podium door to do their own signing. It was how they were going to cover their disappearance from the celebrations that would follow. If Leonius Livius or any of his people were watching, they wouldn't immediately realize that anyone was missing from the party, and—hopefully—once they did, it would be too late.

"Ready?" Decker asked as he, his mate Dani, and her sister Stephanie stood up beside him.

Tiny stood at once and ushered the trio ahead of him toward Lucian. It was time to concentrate on the task at hand. His assignment was about to begin, and the chances were about fifty-fifty of its being either a walk in the park, or a dangerous, tension-filled job that ended in a bloodbath. Tiny was hoping for the walk in the park. He had no illusions about his chances against a no-fanger . . . and he was too young to die.

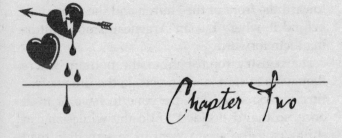

"This is just wrong on so many levels," Mirabeau muttered to herself, instinctively raising the long skirt of her bridesmaid's gown a little higher in an effort to keep it from trailing in the sludge surrounding her. Only Lucian Argeneau would even consider sending a woman into the sewers as an escape route and not warn her ahead of time so she could arrange for a suitable change of clothes.

A skittering sound alerted her to the fact that she wasn't alone. Knowing it was probably rats, Mirabeau instinctively jerked her skirts higher to prevent one of the little buggers from climbing the delicate cloth, but then just as quickly started to lower it as she realized the action left her stockinged legs bare for them to try to climb if they were brave enough. She caught herself before the gown dropped into the inch-deep sewage she stood in and stomped her feet instead to warn off her companions in the dark tunnel. There was no sudden skittering sound of the creatures fleeing up the tunnel; instead, the small sounds stopped altogether, and she knew the rats had frozen and were now no doubt staring at her, their beady little eyes wary or curious. This suggested they were used to and unafraid of humans down here.

"Great," Mirabeau muttered to herself, then stiffened and glanced upward as she heard sounds from the metal trapdoor she'd descended through from the church basement. She listened to the thump of someone dropping onto the cover above, and to the shuffling sound that followed before there was a second thump that was heavy enough to suggest twice or even three times the weight behind it. Mirabeau was frowning over that when a low grinding followed—the sound that of the trapdoor being unlocked.

She raised a hand to shield her eyes as a flashlight beam suddenly shot directly down into her face.

"Sorry." The word was a deep rumble as the flashlight beam was moved away from her.

Mirabeau was just fretting over the fact that she didn't recognize the speaker's voice when it sounded again, this time a quiet murmur that resembled distant thunder. She caught the soft words, "You go first. I'll pull the door closed and lock it behind us."

Those words obviously weren't directed at her and Mirabeau shifted her hand to see who was descending into the sewer to join her. She had only expected one person, her backup for this assignment, who was supposed to be bringing the package they were to deliver. She'd assumed her backup would be a male. There were few female enforcers in the northern states and Canada, and her usual partner, Eshe, wasn't available, so the fact that it was a female presently climbing carefully down the slick metal ladder to join her was definitely a surprise. Mirabeau watched the slim figure in a knee-length dress step off the ladder onto the concrete beside her, then glanced to the second person as he started down the ladder as well. Mirabeau had assumed the third person was merely there to close and lock the trapdoor behind them, but while the man pulled the door closed behind him, he too quickly scrambled down the ladder to join her.

Mirabeau automatically moved back to make more room for the large man. When he stepped onto the concrete and turned to face her, she found herself examining the two newcomers in the light thrown by the flashlight the man carried. He held it pointed down at the ground to prevent blinding her again, which she appreciated, but between her night vision and the flashlight, she could see them both as well as if they were out in sunlight.

The female definitely wasn't her backup, Mirabeau decided. She was little more than a girl and couldn't be more than fourteen or fifteen—a child to most people but a baby to someone who had passed more than four hundred and fifty years herself. The child was slender and flat-chested, with long blond hair pulled up on top of her head. The look merely emphasized the youthfulness of her features and her slender neck.

Mirabeau wondered briefly who she was and why she was there. She looked familiar, but Mirabeau couldn't place where she knew her from. She finally turned her attention to the man. The girl was immediately forgotten. Mirabeau had met a lot of men, both mortal and immortal in her life, but she had met very few who could measure up to this one. He was a good head taller than her own five-foot-ten-inch height. He was also handsome, with dark hair and the sort of rugged features she enjoyed. To add to that, the man was extremely wide, with shoulders a linebacker would envy. That wide chest tapered down to a narrower waist and—from the glimpse she'd gotten as he'd descended the ladder in his dress suit—quite the finest behind she'd seen on a man in a long time. The kind a gal could grasp and dig her nails into to urge him on as he—

"Oh, brother. Not you too."

Mirabeau blinked at the exasperated words from the teenager and turned to peer at her blankly. Not her too what?

"Not *you*," the girl said to her on a sigh, then encompassed both her and the male with a gesture. "*Both* of you. You're both standing there thinking about what it would be like to have sex with each other. You're as bad as my sister and Decker. They're always lusting after each other . . . or doing it." She sighed unhappily, then added, "It's pathetic . . . I swear I'm never having sex or finding a life mate if it's going to turn me into a slavering idiot like the rest of you."

Mirabeau simply stared at the girl, several thoughts striking her one after the other. First, she now knew who the girl was. The reference to a sister and Decker meant this was Stephanie McGill whose sister was Dani McGill, Decker Argeneau Pimms's life mate. The girl was a new turn, having been mortal until this last summer, when she'd been kidnapped by a rogue vampire. Every rogue hunter close enough to be of help had been called in to search for the girl, including Mirabeau and her partner Eshe. The kid had been found eventually, but not before the rogue, a no-fanger, had turned her. Fortunately, Stephanie had turned out Edantate rather than a no-fanger. While Edantates had the slight impediment of being unable to grow the fangs most immortals enjoyed, it wasn't a serious problem now that blood came bagged.

No-fangers, however, had that impediment plus a distressing insanity that led them to perform horrible atrocities on the mortals they all depended on to survive. It was for that reason that no-fangers were always hunted down and killed.

Her second thought was that the kid had managed to read their thoughts. It wasn't surprising to her that Stephanie had read the man's thoughts since Mirabeau had already picked up on the fact that he was mortal. She couldn't have explained how. She'd simply sensed it. But it was rather startling that she'd been able to read Mirabeau, herself. She was the girl's elder by more than four centuries. Stephanie shouldn't have been able to read her thoughts, at least not if she'd been guarding them which, Mirabeau acknowledged, she might not have been doing. She would have to take care to do so, Mirabeau decided, her mind already moving on to the third thought.

While she'd stood pondering the mortal and noting his physical attributes, she'd been vaguely aware that he was doing the same in return. However, from what Stephanie had said, he had been standing there contemplating having sex with her, or lusting after her as the teenager had so charmingly put it. The thought made Mirabeau smile as she peered back at the man again.

After four and a half centuries, she'd been sexually active for a long time, but she'd found the urge to communicate on such a base level waning this

last century. It was good to know she could still
lust after a man, and it was always nice to know
he lusted back. Perhaps after this assignment she
could convince him to—

"Tiny McGraw."

Mirabeau's eyebrows rose at the name. It was one
she'd heard a lot from Marguerite Argeneau. The
woman had mentioned Tiny at least once every
time Mirabeau had visited with her since the
woman's return from California, where she'd first
met the private detective. Frankly, Mirabeau had
grown tired of hearing the name. That thought
slid away as a hand suddenly appeared before her
at waist level. She automatically placed her own in
it, but her eyes widened when her much smaller
hand disappeared inside the catcher's mitt-sized
hand that closed warm and strong over her fingers. The man had huge hands, she noted silently,
and instinctively glanced down to his feet to note
that they too were extremely large.

Jesus, she thought faintly, *the man must have a
mammoth—*

"Oh God! Stop before you make me puke,"
Stephanie gasped, then started making gagging
sounds to the left of them.

Mirabeau closed her eyes, embarrassment
briefly struggling with anger. Anger won out, and
she snapped, "Then stay the hell out of my head."

"I'm not *in* your head. You're practically shriek-
ing your thoughts at me," the girl shot back.

"Er . . . I'm guessing you're Mirabeau La Roche, and you two know each other. Or should I make introductions?" Tiny asked uncertainly.

Mirabeau sighed with disappointment at the sense of loss when he released her hand, but then forced herself to straighten and act like the enforcer she was. "Yes, I'm Mirabeau. But no, Stephanie and I have never met. I do know who she is, though. I've seen her around the enforcer house," Mirabeau explained. She then raised her eyebrows. "I gather you're my backup to deliver the package?"

"Yes, yes, he's your backup," Stephanie interrupted impatiently, then added, "And I'm the package. So can we get moving now? It really stinks down here."

Mirabeau turned narrowed eyes on the girl. She supposed she should have realized what the assignment was the moment she'd recognized the girl. However, she hadn't. Now she stared at her as the true horror of this situation sank in. She was to deliver Stephanie to Port Henry, which meant at least ten hours trapped in a vehicle with this rude, mouthy teenybopper. She should have cottoned onto that sooner. She'd overheard Lucian, Dani, and Decker talking about the girl's future at the enforcer house a couple of times. Lucian had insisted that the girl wouldn't be safe anywhere but at the house with the enforcers around to watch out for her. Dani had insisted that Stephanie be moved, that the girl was miserable there with nothing to do but think of all she'd lost. She needed to have friends, finish high school, and have as normal a life as possible.

Port Henry was obviously the solution they'd come up with. A small town in southern Ontario, it was relatively vampire friendly, with some of the townfolk knowing of their existence and a small group of immortals living there who could help look out for Stephanie. Mirabeau supposed it was the kid's best chance of a normal life. She just didn't understand why she and Tiny had been chosen to deliver her. Where were Decker and Dani? Were they not going to live there with her as well?

"Dani and Decker are going on a honeymoon," Stephanie informed her with a sigh, obviously still reading her thoughts.

"When did they get married?" Mirabeau asked with surprise. Decker was an enforcer, and—having to depend on each other for survival as they did—all the enforcers were a pretty tight group. If Decker had gotten married, she not only should have known about it, but she definitely should have been invited to the wedding and was insulted at the possibility that she hadn't been.

"No, they aren't married. This is a prewedding honeymoon. Once they get the worst of the 'new-mate hormones'—as Dani calls them—out of their systems, they'll plan the wedding and join me in

Port Henry. Until then, that Elvi woman and Lucian's brother, Victor, are going to put me up and keep me safe."

Mirabeau peered at the girl, judging her expression. She didn't seem upset by this turn of events. Rather, there was an almost excited gleam in her eyes, and Mirabeau dipped briefly into the girl's mind to see that, to her way of thinking, she would be like a border in Elvi's bed-and-breakfast, and for all intents and purposes she would be free to do as she wished. The thought was heady stuff for a teenager, her first taste of freedom. Mirabeau decided it wasn't her place to disabuse the kid. She knew Elvi Black, now Argeneau, had lost a daughter of her own sometime ago and suspected the woman would mother the girl and get all in her business. She also knew without a doubt that Victor Argeneau was not going to leave the kid unsupervised. However, she didn't want a sulky Stephanie for the rest of this assignment so kept her mouth shut.

She also didn't believe for a moment that Dani McGill had abandoned her sister to travel around working off "new-mate hormones" with Decker. Mirabeau knew that Leonius Livius, the rogue no-fanger who had turned them, was interested in recapturing both sisters. That being the case, she suspected the "new-mate hormones" story had just been a cover to keep Stephanie from worrying about her sister. Mirabeau suspected Lucian had convinced Dani to be bait in a trap to try to catch the no-fanger, and Dani, desperate to see her sister safe, had agreed so long as the girl was somewhere safe and out of the way.

Recalling that Stephanie could read her mind, Mirabeau killed that thought as soon as it occurred, just as she had the thought that Elvi would be more a guardian than a landlady in Port Henry. While she pushed both thoughts aside quickly, Mirabeau did decide she would have to check into the possibility of a trap once this assignment was done and see if they needed help with it. Leo was a tricky bastard who had gotten away from them twice already. If she could help keep it from being three times, she was in.

The rustle of paper drew her attention to Tiny, to see he had pulled a notepad from his pocket and was now leafing through the pages. When he paused with a satisfied murmur, she moved closer and peered at the page he was shining the flashlight beam on. It was a hand-drawn map of the sewers, she saw, noting the church marked clearly on the page as the starting point and the veinlike blue lines running away from it. A path had been marked in red, and it looked pretty convoluted. It seemed Lucian was determined to make it as difficult as possible for anyone to follow them without being noticed. Some of the turns appeared to be close together, and others seemed to bend back the way they'd come. Anyone attempting to follow them would have to stick pretty close to keep from losing them.

She didn't know why Lucian had gone to all that trouble when he and the others were in the church registry office, where the secret passage leading to the basement and the entrance to the sewers was. But then it occurred to her that the wedding party couldn't linger in the registry office too long without drawing attention. If Leonius or one of his people had dared to sneak into the church for the ceremony, they might become suspicious at the long delay. They might start reading minds, or notice that Stephanie hadn't come out of the registry room.

While Lucian was unreadable to most, the entire wedding party had been in the room when Mirabeau entered to sign as a witness to the ceremony for Marguerite and Julius. The others had watched silently as Lucian had taken her arm once she'd finished signing and ushered her to the secret panel, explaining that her partner was in the second group of witnesses and would soon join her with the package. While some of the others in the wedding party were older and harder to read, an equal number were new turns, easily read whether they wished it or not. It wouldn't take long for someone to figure out where Stephanie McGill had disappeared to, she realized, and decided they had wasted enough time. They needed to get moving.

Tiny appeared to be thinking along the same lines, for he was already closing the notepad and slipping it back into his pocket. He shined his flashlight up the tunnel, saying, "We'd better get moving. We go this way past three offshoots and turn right at the fourth."

Mirabeau lifted her skirts a bit and nodded as she turned in the direction they were to head. "I'll lead. Stephanie, you're in the middle. Tiny will bring up the rear."

"Do you need the flashlight?" Tiny asked, then smiled wryly when she turned back to him. She guessed her eyes were glowing bronze in the darkness as they caught and reflected what light there was down there because he muttered, "Right. Of course not. Lead the way."

Deciding he was smart for a mortal, Mirabeau turned away and started up the tunnel, careful to keep her skirts out of the sewage surrounding them.

They walked in silence, Mirabeau leading them through two of the turns into offshoot tunnels before it occurred to her that if there was trouble, it was likely to come from behind and that perhaps leaving Tiny, who was mortal, to guard their back wasn't the smartest move. Aside from the fact that she thought it would be a shame for such a fine-looking mortal male to die, she figured Marguerite would be upset if she let it happen. Unfortunately, Mirabeau suspected Marguerite would be upset if she insulted the guy too. The woman was pretty fond of him. The problem was that mortal males could be so touchy about their manhood and appearing strong and capable. She was going to have to come up with a lie to get him to trade places with her.

When they had reached the third offshoot, Mirabeau paused and turned back.

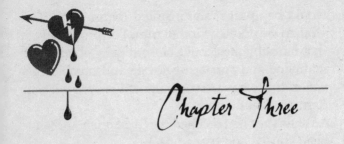

Chapter Three

Tiny was considering Marguerite's suggestion that he might be a life mate to Mirabeau. Now that he'd met the woman in question, he found the possibility a fascinating one. He was trying to recall all the reasons he shouldn't feel that way when Stephanie suddenly stopped in front of him. His nerves immediately on the alert for a possible threat, he glanced to Mirabeau to find she'd stopped and was walking back toward him. Tiny relaxed when he saw her expression. She looked neither grim nor urgent with warning. In fact, Mirabeau's expression was almost pained, and her words stilted as she said, "I was thinking . . . perhaps it would be better if you lead the way after all. It is very dark in here, and you have the flashlight."

Tiny glanced down at the flashlight in his hand,

then back to Mirabeau. He had no doubt she was lying about the reason for wanting him in the front. He had spent enough time around immortals to know his weak little beam wasn't needed by them to see. Hell, he thought, it was probably as bright as daylight in there to the two females. He just didn't understand why she suddenly wanted him in the lead.

"She's worried you'll get yourself killed at the back of the pack, and Marguerite would never forgive her. She's spooked herself with visions of you being attacked from behind and beheaded or something," Stephanie said with a teenager's amusement, answering the question he hadn't asked. "She's just crap at coming up with a lie to get you at the front of the group."

Mirabeau scowled at the girl, then glanced to Tiny. "It did occur to me that I would have a better chance of hearing if we were approached from behind, and since that's where the trouble is most likely to come from—"

"Enough said," Tiny interrupted, managing not to visibly wince at the reality behind her words. Despite her efforts to ease the blow, his ego had taken a hit. At six-seven and two hundred eighty pounds of pure muscle, he wasn't used to being considered the weak member of the herd. In fact, it was only recently that he'd been forced to face the fact that he was . . . at least among immortals. For ten years, Tiny's partner had been a female who was mortal like him. Jackie had been a tiny little thing, and while he'd always known and respected that she could handle herself, he'd still been the brawn in the partnership. But when Jackie had met Vincent and gone off to be his life mate, Tiny had found himself partnered with Marguerite Argeneau for a European case, and his vision of himself had been altered with a vengeance. That little lady, nearly a foot shorter and less than half his weight was beautiful, sweet, and could tuck him under her arm and run down the road as if he weighed no more than a child. And Tiny didn't doubt for a minute that either of the two delicate flowers of womanhood before him could do the same thing.

He was still big and brawny, but Tiny was the fragile one who needed looking after. How depressing was that? Tiny pondered the question as he started to ease around Stephanie to get to Mirabeau's side, but quickly forgot it when Mirabeau suddenly gave a choked cry of surprise.

He instinctively jerked his flashlight upward at the sound, flashing the beam in her face and blinding her briefly. Tiny saw her eyes squeeze shut against the light and instinctively started to lower the beam but paused as he glimpsed the figure behind her. It was a man, shorter than Mirabeau, just the top of his head and squinting eyes showing over her shoulder. They were not an immortal's eyes. The man was a mortal like Tiny, but much dirtier, he noted, taking in the scruffy, unwashed hair and dirt smudged across the man's forehead. A homeless guy, then, he deduced, probably someone who lived in and wandered the sewers, not much of a threat to Mirabeau. Or at least, he shouldn't have been, but the guy was presently holding Mirabeau by the hair that had been swept up on the back of her head in a bun and tugging her head back at what looked to be an uncomfortable angle.

Tiny hesitated, expecting Mirabeau simply to take control of the man's mind and make him release her, but instead, she reacted in what he suspected was a purely instinctive move and raised her knee to shoot her foot back at the man in a blow that probably would have taken out his kneecap if she'd finished it. Unfortunately, Mirabeau's long gown got in the way, caught her up, and made her lose her balance and her footing. Her eyes and mouth shot open with surprise as she began to fall. Tiny tried to get around Stephanie to save her, but arrived just in time almost to be knocked to the ground by her flailing legs as she crashed to her bottom in the tunnel.

Tiny managed to save himself by grabbing at the wall beside him. Then he started to reach for Mirabeau, but paused and raised the flashlight beam at a groan from the mouth of the tunnel. The circle of light lit up the man, revealing his dirty clothes and matted hair, as well as the fact that he now held what appeared to be half of Mirabeau's hair in his hand. For one moment, Tiny thought the fellow had scalped her, but then recalled Marguerite saying they had done something to cover the fuchsia tints in Mirabeau's hair and realized this was what it had been. They must have put extensions or something on, he thought, as he quickly flashed the beam toward Mirabeau to see that while the sides, freed from the bun, now hung down over her shoulders in a pure, dark color, there were pink tips sticking out in every direction on the back of her head.

Her attacker didn't seem to realize he'd merely removed some of her extensions. The man was gaping at the clump of hair he held with horror, but the moment the flashlight beam hit him, the fellow squinted and turned his attention from the hair he held to the source of the beam. When he did, Tiny shifted the flashlight so that the circle of light included his large frame and simply murmured, "Boo."

That was all it took. As usual—at least among mortals—his size alone made an impact and persuaded the man that he didn't want to mess with him after all. Releasing a startled squeak of alarm, the fellow dropped the hair, quickly shuffled backward, and turned to hurry away, almost immediately disappearing into the darkness.

Tiny waited until the sounds of the man's departure grew faint, then moved to help Mirabeau. She was floundering around in the water, trying to regain her feet, but was hampered by her gown, which was thoroughly soaked. It kept tripping her up and unceremoniously sending her back to sit in the sludge. Stephanie, he noted, was simply watching it all, her mouth agape and eyes full of horror. He supposed it was what Mirabeau was floundering around in that had caused the reaction. He tried hard not to think of that himself as he murmured, "Here," and handed Stephanie the flashlight.

The girl managed to gather herself enough to take it from him, and the moment she had, he shifted carefully around Mirabeau, managing to avoid her flailing legs, and get behind her. Tiny then simply hooked his hands under her arms and hefted her quickly to her feet.

"Thank you," Mirabeau muttered, the sound a sort of breathless growl as she got her feet under her. Tiny waited to be sure she had her footing, but then let his hands drop and took a quick step away from her. He didn't mean to offend, but couldn't help himself. The smell down here was bad enough when just walking through it, but Mirabeau had stirred it up with her struggle, and the odor seemed to have intensified and attached itself to her at a concentrated level. The woman he had spent a good portion of the walk lusting after smelled like a backed-up toilet. It tended to dampen his ardor a bit. Probably a good thing, he decided. After all, they had a job to do.

Retrieving the flashlight from Stephanie, Tiny flashed it over Mirabeau and winced at the state of her dress. If he hadn't seen her in the wedding party back at the church, he would have thought it was a peach top paired with a long brownish black skirt rather than a peach dress. The gown was definitely ruined. He wasn't the only one to notice. Mirabeau was gaping down at herself with a horror that surpassed Stephanie's. She glanced around furiously, and growled, "Where is he?"

"He's gone," Tiny said, thinking it was probably lucky for the guy that he was. "It was just some homeless guy. He took off when he got a look at me."

He wasn't surprised when, rather than look relieved, Mirabeau appeared disappointed by this news. He suspected she'd wanted to throttle the man for grabbing her and causing the state she now found herself in. He simply waited patiently as she stared at him with impotent fury, wondering if she would take out her rage and frustration on him . . . and if he would let her. In the end, she merely cursed and looked at her mud-covered hands with disgust. Tiny was about to offer to sacrifice his suit jacket for her to wipe her hands on when she managed to find a small patch on the front of her skirt that had escaped the soaking. He watched in silence as she wiped her hands on it, then forced an encouraging smile when she again glanced his way.

The sight of it made her sigh, and say, "I guess we should get moving."

"Yes, I guess," he agreed quietly.

Mirabeau nodded, then moved toward the tunnel entrance on his left, only to pause as the skirt of the gown wrapped itself around her legs. She nearly lost her balance again, and Tiny immediately reached to steady her, but she waved him off and managed to keep her balance on her own. She then glanced down at the gown with distaste.

"You might as well," Stephanie said quietly. "It's ruined anyway."

Tiny knew the kid was reading Mirabeau's mind again, but wasn't sure what she was suggesting until Mirabeau suddenly bent, grabbed up the hem of her dress, found one side seam and began to rip it apart. She split it all the way up, well past her knees, then quickly tore sideways, ripping away the bottom three-quarters of the skirt all the way around. Once finished, Mirabeau was wearing a dress that only covered her to midthigh.

"It's a little short," she judged as she straightened and tossed the detached material aside. She then added wryly, "But I can move more easily, and I won't be restricted if I need to fight."

"Yes," Tiny agreed absently, barely aware of

growling the word as he took in her stockinged legs. The skirt now started where the tops of her stocking seams ended. Every time she shifted, it flashed a tantalizing hint of flesh. The stockings themselves were black net and covered what appeared to him at that moment to be nearly a mile of leg.

Jesus, the woman is all leg, he thought. And fine legs they were too, muscular, but still slender and feminine, tapering down to tiny little ankles.

"It's my own fault," Mirabeau commented with self-disgust as she peered down at herself. "I should have checked that the offshoot was empty before turning my back to it."

"Didn't you hear him approach?"

Stephanie asked the question in an innocent voice, but Tiny suspected she was taunting Mirabeau. It made him frown at the teenager. The girl obviously had a chip on her shoulder, but then he supposed she had earned it. She'd been through a great deal this last year. Fortunately, Mirabeau didn't seem to suspect the question was a jab at her. She merely frowned toward the offshoot and shook her head.

"Come to think of it, no I didn't." She moved to the mouth of the tunnel on his right and peered into the darkness. "He must have already been standing here just inside the entrance to the tunnel and simply waited when he saw us approaching.

He would have seen the flashlight from a good distance."

"Waited for what purpose?" Stephanie asked curiously. "What did he want? Besides your hair?"

The last was added on a burble of amusement, but Mirabeau just shrugged and swung back toward them. "Who knows? He wasn't right in the head . . . which is why I couldn't control him when he grabbed me, but I caught enough of his chaotic thoughts to know that he thought we were rats."

"Rats?" Tiny asked with amazement, finally managing to tear his eyes from her legs.

Mirabeau nodded silently in the beam of light he lifted to her face.

"Talking, human-sized rats?" Stephanie asked doubtfully.

"He couldn't see us in the dark, just the flashlight beam," Mirabeau pointed out, then added, "And from what I got from his thoughts, he's always suspected there were mutant human-sized rats down here. In his mind even the little rats talk to him."

"Oh," Stephanie murmured, and Tiny echoed her comment in his head, as his gaze shifted past Mirabeau to the tunnel the little madman had disappeared down. He kind of felt bad now for scaring the poor bastard. The guy needed help.

"Well . . . I guess we should keep going," Mirabeau murmured suddenly, but she didn't move except to glance the way they'd come, then back down the tunnel she stood in front of. Knowing she was no longer sure where he would be safest, at the front of the party or the back, Tiny made up her mind for her and slid past her. He shined the flashlight down the tunnel and followed the beam, moving slowly at first until he was sure Stephanie and Mirabeau were following him.

Mirabeau might be concerned about someone's following them, but so far there had been no sign of that. He was more concerned about running into more underground crazies wandering the sewers. While Tiny felt bad for them, he didn't feel so bad that he was willing to risk one of the girls getting hurt.

Mirabeau paused when Stephanie did and glanced expectantly toward Tiny. He had the map out again and was peering at it, running his flashlight around the area, then peering at the map again, his eyebrows drawing together in a way that made her uneasy. Eager to keep moving and get the hell out of the endless tunnels, she shifted impatiently, then grimaced as her skirt shifted with her. The damned thing was drying and attaching itself to her as it did. So were her panties . . . and it was damned uncomfortable.

"What is it?" she asked finally, as Tiny repeated the map-checking and area-scanning deal again. She moved around Stephanie to his side to peer at the map.

"I think we took a wrong turn."

"What?" she gasped with disbelief, her eyes scanning the map. Much to her relief there was a tunnel offshoot on the map just as there was here in the tunnel. Relieved, she said, "No. It was two offshoots after the last turn, then this one we take. We passed two offshoots since the last turn, so we take this one."

"Yes," Tiny agreed patiently, then pointed out, "But according to the map there should be another offshoot across from this one and—" He raised the flashlight to shine it over the wall opposite. "No offshoot."

Mirabeau stared blankly at the solid wall, then at the map, but it didn't suddenly change. Cursing, she took the map from him and, using her finger, silently backtracked on it, counting off the offshoots they'd passed between each one they'd taken, trying to see where they had made a wrong turn. She retraced their steps all the way back to where she'd been grabbed and fallen.

"Crap," she breathed unhappily as she stared at the map.

"What?" Tiny asked, leaning close to peer at the map as well.

"Everything seems fine," she said quietly. "From what I can tell, we took the right turns according to the map. The only thing I can think is . . ." Mirabeau fell silent and simply pointed to the two tunnels side by side.

"That was back near the beginning, the third

turn," Tiny murmured thoughtfully, looking at where she pointed, then he straightened slightly. "That's where that guy—"

"Yes," Mirabeau interrupted on a sigh. "I'm thinking we may have taken the wrong tunnel. If they're right next to each other, we might have gotten a bit turned around after the attack."

Tiny cursed and glanced back the way they'd come. Then he sighed, and said, "We'll have to backtrack. See if that's where we—"

"But that was hours ago," Stephanie protested, moving up beside them to peer at the map as well. "Look, it's practically all the way back at the beginning. I am *not* slogging back through these tunnels just to start over again. Besides, what if you're wrong, and we just counted off wrong at one of the other turns?"

"We didn't count off wrong," Mirabeau said quietly. "We've both been counting. It has to be that we took the wrong tunnel at that stop."

"Well, then, maybe the map is wrong," Stephanie argued desperately. "People make mistakes, even Lucian must make mistakes once in a while." Her desperation turning to rebellion, she crossed her arms, and snapped, "I am *so* not backtracking. You'll have to knock me out and carry me because I am *not* walking back all that way only to start again. I'm tired and hungry and sick to death of this stink. I want a shower and a bed and blood. I just want out of here," she ended with frustration.

Silence filled the tunnel as Stephanie snapped her mouth closed. She was sulking. Mirabeau didn't much care so long as she did it silently. Her mind was taken up with the words "shower and a bed and blood" all of which she rather wanted herself. They hadn't been in the tunnels for hours, maybe an hour and a half, and she suspected that had they taken the right tunnel, they would have been out of the sewers long ago.

"A bed?" Tiny asked quietly. "It's only a little after midnight, Stephanie. That's the middle of the day for you now, isn't it?"

The teenager clucked with disgust. "We aren't vampires, Tiny. Heck, I don't even have fangs, and I don't stay up all night and sleep all day. As long as I avoid the sun, I can stay up during the day. Besides, there's nothing on television at night, just old movies and crappy shows selling crappy gizmos." She sighed. "I usually go to bed by midnight or so."

When Tiny glanced her way and raised an eyebrow, Mirabeau merely shrugged. She herself usually stayed up nights and slept days. However, she hadn't had much sleep today. There had been too much to do to get ready for the wedding. She wouldn't mind a nap herself. Blood sounded pretty good too. As for a shower, Mirabeau thought she'd kill for one just then . . . and a change of clothes. Dear God, she wanted out of those sewers as well, and she was not riding ten hours in an SUV in sewage-soaked clothes.

That thought at the forefront of her mind, Mirabeau handed the map to Tiny and turned back the way they'd come.

"Where are you going?" Stephanie snapped with dismay, hurrying after her. "I told you, I'm not walking back through the tunnels."

"And yet you're following me," she pointed out dryly and wasn't surprised when the teenager stopped abruptly.

"Only to tell you I'm not going," she said shrilly, as Mirabeau continued up the dark tunnel.

"Fine. You stay here and sulk. But we passed a manhole to the surface a few minutes back, and I'm using it to get the hell out of the sewers," Mirabeau said calmly.

"Really?" The excited and surprised squeal was followed by the tapping of the girl's shoes on the concrete as she hurried to catch up to her. Mirabeau had expected as much.

Tiny followed more quietly so that she nearly missed the sounds of his approach before she heard him murmur, "What's the plan here?"

Mirabeau sighed to herself and paused. They were supposed to be partners, but she wasn't used to having mortal partners, or even male ones for that matter. Eshe usually thought pretty much along the same lines as she did, so that they rarely disagreed or even needed to discuss matters. The other woman would have been leading the way to get out of the sewers, but she suspected Tiny was going to have a problem with it. He was probably one of those by-the-book guys.

"The plan," she said quietly, "is to get out of here, check into a hotel, shower this crap off, get us all a change of clothes and food, catch a nap, then find the SUV before dawn to head out of the city."

"Yay!" Stephanie squealed happily and did a little dance on the concrete.

Mirabeau felt her mouth twitch but managed to keep from smiling, and said solemnly to Tiny, "Lucian provided the name of the parking garage on the map. It should be easy to find topside. If it's as far away as I suspect it is, we can take a taxi and wipe the driver's mind when he drops us off."

Tiny stared at her silently through the gloom for so long, she was positive that he was going to balk and insist they stick to the plan Lucian had given them; but, much to her surprise, he nodded, and simply said, "There doesn't appear to be anyone following us, and it beats driving ten hours in these clothes."

Mirabeau relaxed and allowed a smile to curve her lips, until he added, "Now we just have to worry about there being a hotel within walking distance."

She frowned over the words briefly, then shook her head. "You can't walk a block without tripping over a hotel in this town. There has to be one close by."

Despite the brave words, Mirabeau was worried that the offshoot they'd wrongly taken had led them to a part of New York City that didn't have any hotels. With that worry on her mind, she led the way back to the ladder to the surface that they'd passed sometime ago. Tiny offered to go up first and see if he could open the manhole at the top, but Mirabeau merely shook her head and began to climb. She suspected they had special locks or something on manhole covers to prevent people from messing with them and a little muscle might be needed to get it open. Tiny had a lot of muscle . . . for a mortal, but she had more.

"Can you tell where we are?" Tiny asked, as she got the cover open and eased it upward to look out.

Mirabeau took a moment to peer around as much as she could. They were near a corner, but a parked van blocked the street signs from her view.

"Where are we?" Stephanie said impatiently.

"I'm not sure, but there's a hotel across the street," Mirabeau answered. She noted that the driver of the van was off-loading trays of what appeared to be food and fresh vegetables. She supposed it was easier to make deliveries at night when the streets weren't so congested. Turning, she peered at the duo at the foot of the ladder. "Come on. We'll check into the hotel, then sort out where we are."

Stephanie was halfway up the ladder behind her before the last word had left Mirabeau's mouth. Smiling wryly, Mirabeau shifted the manhole out of the way and quickly climbed out to crouch on the street before Stephanie trampled over her to get out. Tiny was right behind the girl and helped Mirabeau shift the manhole back into place before they straightened and moved to the side of the road. Traffic was slower at night in New York, but it wasn't nonexistent, and they had been fortunate to climb out when they had. They'd no sooner stepped up onto the curb than a taxi came flying past.

"Maybe you girls should wait here and let me go in and rent the room," Tiny said quietly, ushering them away from the curb.

Mirabeau shook her head at once. "I'll get the rooms. If anyone has realized that you're missing too, they might figure out that you're with Stephanie and try to track your credit cards."

"The same is true of you," Tiny argued with a frown.

"Yes, but I don't need to use a credit card," Mirabeau pointed out dryly, and started up the sidewalk toward the front of the hotel.

"Just a minute," Tiny said, catching her arm. "Maybe this is a bad idea after all. You two are pretty memorable in the state you're in. If anyone comes around asking questions—"

"They won't find any trace of us in the memories of the people we encounter," she finished quietly.

Tiny met her gaze briefly, then nodded. Mirabeau actually felt the relieved breath Stephanie exhaled. The girl needn't have worried. Though they were out of the sewers, their stink was still all Mirabeau could smell. They'd brought the stench with them, and she was determined to get rid of the stink if it was the last thing she did. She wasn't going to change her mind about a stop at the hotel.

Turning, she led the way to the hotel entrance, slipping quickly into the doorman's mind as he approached—no doubt to stop them entering. She watched his face go blank and his eyes shift away as they passed, then turned her attention to the people in the lobby. Much to her relief, it was late enough that there were few people around. A gentleman sat reading a newspaper on one of the sofas. He started to raise his head to glance their way but simply lowered it again once she touched on his thoughts. He would not look up again until they had left the lobby. A young, overly made-up blond clerk stood at the desk. Her eyes went from sleepy to horrified and back to sleepy as Mirabeau approached and slipped into her thoughts. Then the woman began to tap on her keyboard, took two keycards out of a drawer full of them, ran them through a machine, tucked them in a small cardboard holder, and scribbled a room number on it before handing it to Mirabeau, all without lifting her eyes from the keyboard.

Mirabeau took the packet and turned to lead the way to the elevators, her eyes sweeping the lobby one more time to be sure she hadn't missed anyone. That was when she spotted the small store in one corner of the lobby.

"What is it?" Tiny asked, when she paused.

Mirabeau hesitated, her eyes slipping to the girl at the counter once more. A quick read of the clerk's mind made her frown and sigh. Continuing forward, she murmured, "Nothing. Let's go."

The elevator doors opened the moment Mirabeau pushed the button. She stepped on board and hit the button for their floor, then glanced to Tiny as he followed Stephanie on board. She noted the way he glanced worriedly back at the lobby as if suspecting she had sensed trouble. Not wanting him to worry about nothing, she admitted, "I just noticed the little store in the lobby. It had clothes and other things in there, and I thought maybe I could get a change of clothes for all of us, but the girl at reception didn't have a key. Only the hotel manager and the store owner do, and neither of them is around the hotel at this hour."

"Oh." Tiny relaxed. He then cleared his throat, and asked carefully, "So, we aren't paying for the hotel room?"

Mirabeau's eyebrows rose at the question. His careful tone suggested he wasn't too comfortable with the idea, and she frowned over the matter, then shrugged and said, "When we get to Port Henry, I'll call Bastien, and he can send someone to take care of it."

Tiny nodded, his shoulders easing even farther in his suit jacket, and Mirabeau found herself staring at him curiously. Most people wouldn't have troubled themselves about borrowing a hotel room for a couple hours without paying for it, but she already knew from the countless tales Marguerite Argeneau had told her about this man that he had a thread of honor as strong as steel running through him. She found it somewhat refreshing.

"More like stupid," Stephanie muttered. "It's not like they'd notice. Obviously, no one's using the room she gave us."

"Rooms. I got us a suite," Mirabeau murmured, scowling at the girl. It was bad enough she kept reading her thoughts, but insulting Tiny just wasn't on in her books. The mortal was putting his life at risk to see the girl safely to Port Henry. A little gratitude wouldn't go amiss.

"Whatever," Stephanie mumbled, obviously still caught up in her own thoughts, but she also looked a bit chagrined, so she obviously got the silent reprimand in Mirabeau's thoughts.

"Am I missing something?" Tiny asked quietly, drawing her gaze again.

"Nothing important," Mirabeau assured him, as the elevator doors opened.

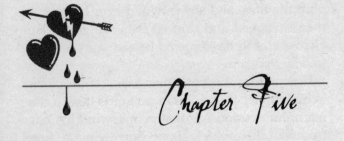

The suite was two normal hotel rooms connected by a living/dining area, with a dining table and chairs at one end and a couch, chair, and television at the other. It wasn't very grand, but then the hotel wasn't exactly one of the grand ones either.

It would do for their needs, Mirabeau decided as she glanced over their accommodations.

"I get this room," Stephanie announced peering into the bedroom on the right. She then turned and arched an eyebrow as she asked, "Which one of you gets the other and which one takes the couch?"

"Nice try," Mirabeau growled, tossing the packet of room keys on the dining table. "You and I get that room. Tiny gets the other."

"No way. I'm not sleeping with you," she protested at once. "You probably snore."

Mirabeau scowled, her patience snapping, but

before she could blast her, Tiny said lightly, "I wouldn't be so hasty. Your options are Mirabeau in the second bed in your room, or me . . . And I *do* snore." When Stephanie opened her mouth, probably to protest further, he added, "It's that or we go find the SUV right now and head out as we are. You can't be left alone until we get you safely to Port Henry. There's still a chance Leonius or one of his men could find us."

Stephanie snapped her mouth closed, then huffed, "Fine. Mirabeau then. But I'm telling Lucian how awful you two are as bodyguards." She whirled away, adding, "I'm taking a bath. A long one. You both stink, and I can't stand it anymore." On that charming note, she stomped into the bathroom of the room she was to share with Mirabeau and slammed the door behind her.

Mirabeau growled and started forward, murder on her mind, but Tiny caught her arm. When she turned furiously on him, he said soothingly, "You can use my bathroom."

"She—" Mirabeau began, but he interrupted.

"Is a teenager who was kidnapped, subjected to who knows what horrors, and turned against her will. In the process, she lost her whole family except her sister and she's now losing her, at least temporarily, while she's hidden away in some podunk town in southern Ontario."

Mirabeau found a smile tugging at her lips at his words. "Podunk?"

"Her word," he said wryly.

Mirabeau nodded. She hadn't paid attention to what they were discussing but had been aware that Tiny and Stephanie had chatted quietly as they'd traveled through the tunnels. It seemed that the girl had been airing her grievances, and she did have more than her fair share. Stephanie had been through a lot, Mirabeau acknowledged, and forced herself to relax. She took a deep, cleansing breath, then murmured, "You're very patient with her."

"I'm a patient guy." He grinned, and Mirabeau found herself relaxing completely and grinning back. The moment she did, Tiny patted the arm he'd grabbed, then stepped away. "Go on. Take a bath in my room. Take as long as you want. I'm going to go out and see if I can scrounge up some food for us."

Mirabeau bit her lip as she watched him walk to the door, suddenly worried about his being on his own. She didn't think anyone had followed them, but there was a slight possibility they had, and she didn't like the idea of his being alone if that were the case. She also knew saying so probably wasn't the smart thing to do. The guy wouldn't appreciate her fretting over him as if he couldn't take care of himself, so instead she said, "Don't you want to at least shower or something first?"

"And get back into these stinky clothes?" Tiny asked dryly, pausing at the door. He glanced back to peer at her and smiled faintly. "Don't worry about me. I'll be fine. Take a bath, then maybe talk to Stephanie."

"Talk to her?" Mirabeau asked with dismay, forgetting her worry for him. "What about?"

"About what she's been through," he said quietly. "Other than her sister, you can probably help her more than anyone."

"Me?" Mirabeau squeaked with disbelief. "What makes you think I—?"

"Because you lost your entire family at a young age too, didn't you?" he said quietly. "Of anyone, you should understand at least part of what she's going through."

Mirabeau felt herself closing up. It was as if something was squeezing tight around her. The slaughter of her family was a subject she never allowed herself to think of. She supposed Marguerite had told him about it for some reason or other, but she didn't appreciate it and didn't know how to respond other than to say almost resentfully, "Her family is still alive."

"But she can never see them again. She can never enjoy their love and support again," he pointed out quietly.

"She has Dani," Mirabeau insisted grimly.

"Not at the moment, she doesn't," Tiny said, then added quietly, "Talk to her. She's as alone and lonely as you."

This time Mirabeau didn't stop him from leaving but simply watched the door close behind him while a small storm of emotion rolled through her. *Alone and lonely? Where the hell had he gotten that idea?* And there was a vast difference between Stephanie and her. While the girl couldn't, or at least shouldn't, approach her family now that she'd been turned, she at least knew they lived, could check on them from time to time and reassure herself of their happiness. However, Mirabeau's entire family—mother, father, and three brothers—were all dead, along with the once-favored uncle who had killed them. She had no one, she thought, turning to enter the room Tiny was to use.

She had entered the bathroom before acknowledging that that wasn't really true. She had the Argeneaus. Mirabeau had been seventeen when her family had been killed, and Lucian had taken her to stay with his sister-in-law, Marguerite, afterward. That fine lady had taken her under her wing. As if sensing that treating her like a daughter would be too painful and would simply remind her of what she'd lost, Marguerite had offered her a combination of love and friendship that an aunt might offer a niece. She had opened her home and made her welcome in her family, and Mirabeau had eventually come to be treated by the whole clan as a dear family friend and offered all the love and support she could wish . . . but lovely as that was, it could never replace the family she had lost and simply made Mirabeau uncomfortable. While she was always included in special celebrations like Christmas or weddings, those events always reminded Mirabeau of her own lack of family . . . and she supposed that was something Stephanie would have to go through as well.

Sighing, she turned on the shower and quickly stripped off her ruined clothes to step under the hot spray. She turned under the showerhead, rinsing away the worst of the muck coating her, then grabbed the hotel soap, her mind on what she could possibly say to Stephanie to help her through this. Unfortunately, there wasn't anything anyone could really say to make it better for the girl. Even Mirabeau herself could only let her know she understood and perhaps take her under her wing as Marguerite Argeneau had done for her.

The problem was, Mirabeau wasn't sure she was any good at that kind of thing. She hadn't had a lot of practice. Other than Eshe and the Argeneaus, she hadn't really opened herself up to anyone since the deaths of her family, and her opening up to the Argeneaus was wholly Marguerite's doing. The woman was like some irresistible force. If she decided you were family, you were family, and that was that. It was futile to resist. As for Eshe, it had taken a good couple of decades of working together for her to open up and allow herself to be true friends with her. Mirabeau just didn't like to care about people; it meant pain should you ever lose them.

She stepped out from under the shower and

wrapped herself in a towel, but then simply stood there frowning, both at her own thoughts and the fact that while she had soaped and scrubbed every inch of her skin, she still didn't feel clean. She also didn't know how she could possibly help Stephanie. The girl was angry and resentful and hurting ... much as Mirabeau had been after the loss of her family ... and still probably was if she was honest with herself. She had never really healed from her loss but simply refused to acknowledge it. That being the case, she hadn't a clue how she was supposed to draw the girl out and help her.

Tiny was giving her way too much credit in thinking she could, Mirabeau decided as she stared at the empty tub. She decided that perhaps a soak in a steaming hot bubble bath would make her feel clean. It might also relax her enough that she could come up with something to say that might help Stephanie.

Glancing around, she spotted the small hotel-sized bubble bath on the counter and grabbed it up. Mirabeau dumped almost the entire contents of the small bottle into the tub and began to run a bath. She would soak and think.

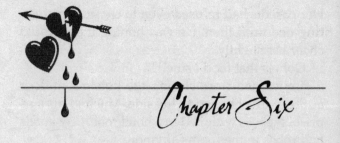

Tiny returned from his hunt for food with several bags in hand. One held sandwiches, chips, and various soft drinks, the others held loads of tourist wear. There were T-shirts, tank tops, joggers, and jackets all in various sizes and all saying I ♥ NEW YORK or something else about the city. It wasn't ideal, but he thought what he'd found was better than the clothes they were wearing and hoped the women would agree.

In one of the clothing bags, there was also a selection of temporary tattoos. They were for Stephanie. As they'd walked through the sewers, the girl had been complaining about all the things she couldn't do now that she had been turned, and tattoos had been high on the list. It seemed she'd planned to get one as soon as she turned eighteen.

Her parents had refused even to consider her getting one until then. He was hoping these would cheer her slightly.

"Ooh, is that food I smell?"

Tiny turned from closing the hotel-room door as Stephanie hurried to his side. Much to his surprise, she was wrapped in a hotel robe. Few hotels had robes in the rooms anymore.

"I called down to the desk for the robe. Most hotels have them to purchase. They'll put it on the room bill," Stephanie explained absently as she began plucking at the bags he held. "What is this? You found clothes too?"

"I found a twenty-four-hour market. It's amazing what they carry in those places," he murmured, as she urged him toward the table. The moment he set the bags on it, she started poking through the contents. While she'd at first been interested in the food, she now ignored that bag and began dumping out the contents of the others to sort through them.

"Nice." She held up a black tank top with NYC on it across the breasts. Tiny had picked it up thinking of Mirabeau. It had seemed her style, and he hoped it was her size. He could actually imagine her in it. Apparently Stephanie read the thought in his mind and dropped it on the table. "It would look better on her anyway. I don't have the boobs for it."

Tiny sighed to himself, thinking it might be nice to be an immortal if he could then guard his thoughts from others. It was bad enough having every adult immortal he encountered in his head, but even worse to have Stephanie in their sifting through his sometimes less than PG-13 thoughts. He would definitely need to start editing his own thinking around the girl.

"Hey! What are these?"

Tiny glanced to the girl to see that she'd found the tattoos. Clearing his throat, he said, "I thought you might have fun with them. I know they aren't the same as getting a real tattoo, but that just means you can change them as you like and won't be stuck with one you might get tired of."

"That's true, I guess," she murmured, leafing through the sheets of tattoos. "How come they're all hearts and lovey-dovey stuff?"

"It's Valentine's today, kiddo," he pointed out, then realized that wasn't true. While the wedding ceremony had taken place on Valentine's Day—an effort he suspected to be sure the men never forgot their anniversary—it was now past midnight and February fifteenth. Shrugging, he added, "That's all they had besides I ♥ NEW YORK tattoos, and I didn't think you'd be interested in them."

"No," she agreed with a grimace, then brightened. "I'm going to show Mirabeau. Where is she?"

"My bathroom," Tiny guessed, and when she quickly headed in that direction, warned, "She's probably in the tub."

But he was too late. Like all immortals, the kid

could move fast. By the time he even started the warning Stephanie had already passed through his room, and burst into the bathroom. He winced and moved into his bedroom as he heard Mirabeau squawk, curse, and ask something about the girl's having any boundaries.

"Sorry." Stephanie's voice sounded deflated, and there was misery on her face as she turned toward the door, muttering, "I used to talk to my mom all the time while she was in the tub. I guess I wasn't thinking."

He caught a glimpse of Mirabeau as Stephanie shifted to leave the room and saw that she was now biting her lip, regret on her face. He smiled to himself when she suddenly said, "So did I."

He'd known she could handle the kid and wasn't at all surprised when Stephanie paused and turned back uncertainly to ask, "Really?"

He saw Mirabeau nod solemnly and was just thinking it would be all right when Stephanie said, "They had baths in your day?"

That had definitely been the wrong thing to say. The kid didn't seem to be able to say anything to Mirabeau that wasn't insulting, and he wasn't surprised to see Mirabeau's eyes narrow, though he was surprised that he was managing to keep his eyes on her face. Fortunately, only her head and upper shoulders were sticking out of the sea of foamy bubbles in his bathtub.

"Can you say *anything* that isn't insulting?"

Mirabeau asked grimly. "Did the turn somehow eradicate your manners? Or maybe your mother never taught you any."

"She did too," Stephanie said at once, her voice high and harsh. "She was a good mom."

"So what's your problem?" Mirabeau asked.

"What's *your* problem?" Stephanie countered, and stomped out of the room, slamming the door behind her. Tiny stepped out of her way as she passed and watched her go with a sigh. His head came back around to the bathroom door, however, when he heard sloshing water in the bathroom. Mirabeau was getting out of the tub, he realized. Not wanting to get caught eyeing the door, he busied himself emptying his pockets in preparation for stripping to take his own bath. When he finished, he moved out to retrieve the 3X T-shirt and joggers he'd bought for himself as well as the black tank top, a medium-sized T-shirt, and the medium-sized joggers he'd bought for Mirabeau.

He was carrying them into the bedroom when the bathroom door opened and Mirabeau appeared, wrapped in a towel. The sight brought him to a dead halt. It wasn't that she wasn't covered at all the important points, but he couldn't help but be aware that she was completely naked beneath the towel.

She paused on spotting him and her shoulders sagged as she said wryly, "I guess I didn't handle her as well as you'd hoped."

Tiny couldn't seem to drag his eyes away from their inventory of the naked flesh visible above and below the towel, but did manage to murmur, "Well, she was kind of rude."

"I was probably ruder at her age," Mirabeau admitted wearily, then noticed the clothes he held and started forward, her expression brightening. "You found clothes?"

She said it in a tone of voice he would have only expected from an offering of a designer original, but he completely understood her happiness. He'd been pretty thrilled himself when he'd spotted the clothes in the store.

Tossing the clothes for him on the bed, he offered the others to her. "I guessed you were a medium, but wasn't sure which you'd prefer. I thought probably the tank top, but it is winter, so—"

"Cold doesn't bother me," Mirabeau assured him, choosing the tank top as he'd hoped.

Her words made him wish he'd brought the short shorts as well. She probably wouldn't have worn them, but he could fantasize.

"These are great," Mirabeau said happily as she took the joggers as well. When she caught his wry expression she laughed, and pointed out, "They don't stink and cover more than a towel."

"Yeah, that's what I thought," he admitted, his eyes dropping to run over the back of her legs as she spun away and headed for her own room.

"I rinsed the bath, it's ready if you want to take

your turn at it," she said, then slipped through the door and out of sight. Tiny sighed as the door closed behind her. He supposed it had been too much to hope that the towel might slip or something. Ah well . . . He would shower to wash the stink away, then eat some of those sandwiches he'd brought back. While he was hungry, the thought of eating in his present state just made him want to gag.

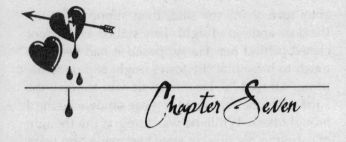

Stephanie was sitting cross-legged on the far bed when Mirabeau entered the room they were to share. She supposed that meant the nearer bed was hers and dropped the clothes on it, then whipped off her towel and grabbed up the joggers to pull them on, aware that Stephanie was watching her. She wasn't self-conscious about her body. The nanos her kind had in their bodies had been programmed to fight illness, repair injuries, and keep them at their peak condition. Peak meant young and healthy, and she knew she looked her best. Or perhaps it was just that after so many years she'd been naked in front of so many people for one reason or another that it didn't bother her anymore. Mirabeau didn't know or care why it didn't bother her. She didn't even really think about the fact that she was naked until Stephanie spoke.

"You don't shave your legs," the girl said with surprise. And then her eyes widened with sudden alarm, and she asked, "We can shave and wax our legs, can't we? The nanos don't just make it grow back within minutes or anything, do they?"

Mirabeau paused and glanced down at her legs, which were sporting a soft feathering of hair that, until Stephanie had spoken, hadn't bothered her. Now she worried about it and thought she would have to pick up a razor or something on the way to Port Henry. She would need to shave before seducing Tiny, and Mirabeau was growing more and more determined to do that once this assignment was over. Aside from being attractive physically, she was starting to find him very attractive in personality as well. She'd known he was a good man from the stories Marguerite had told her, but his empathy and patience with Stephanie were really making an impression on her. She wasn't the patient sort herself. Never had been. Perhaps that was why the trait in him was so attractive to her.

Pushing that thought aside, she glanced at Stephanie, and said, "Of course we can shave. It doesn't grow right back. Hairs are strands of dead cells or whatever, nanos don't bother with them."

"Oh." Stephanie looked relieved, and asked, "So why don't you shave?"

"I do, I just haven't bothered in a while," she muttered. Mirabeau had started shaving along with every other woman in the world when it had become popular. But it had been so long since she'd been interested in dating or anything of that nature that she'd stopped bothering.

"What's it like?" Stephanie asked, as Mirabeau finished donning the joggers and reached for the black tank top.

"What?" she asked absently as she pulled the top on over her head.

"Being so old?"

Mirabeau turned on the girl with exasperation as she tugged the tank into place. Before she could snap at her, however, Stephanie said quickly, "I'm not trying to insult you, I just mean, you know . . . what's it like to live so long?"

Mirabeau forced herself to relax and shrugged. "I don't know. It just is. I guess you'll find out in time."

"Yeah, in a century or so," Stephanie said dryly, then fell silent and watched as Mirabeau moved to the mirror over the dresser to run her fingers through her damp hair, trying to bring some order to the tangled strands.

It was an impossible task without any sort of brush, Mirabeau decided, scowling at her reflection and wondering if she could remove the remaining extensions or if had to be done by a hairdresser. It had hurt like the devil when the fellow in the sewers had ripped out that clump of extensions, but she'd checked and didn't appear to have been snatched bald back there. Perhaps she could just yank out the remaining extensions as well.

"Does it ever get better?"

"What?" Mirabeau asked with distraction.

"The pain of losing them?" Stephanie said quietly, and Mirabeau was just wondering if she meant her hair extensions, when the girl added, "Tiny told me you lost your family too, and I . . . It hurts so much sometimes, and I can tell you still hurt, and I . . ."

Mirabeau stopped messing with her hair and turned to peer at the girl. There was real agony on her face, which made panic well up inside Mirabeau. She wasn't good with emotional stuff. In fact, she generally avoided situations that involved it like the plague. However, Stephanie was hurting, and there was no one else there to help her. Swallowing thickly, she moved to the side of Stephanie's bed to sit on the edge . . . and stared at her briefly before reluctantly raising a hand to set on the girl's leg in what she hoped was a comforting touch. Clearing her throat, she said, "It does hurt, and I am hurting right now because your situation reminds me of my own, and it hurts me at holidays and special occasions too, but it eases a bit, gets easier to bear . . . and you do have Dani for those holidays."

Stephanie swallowed and nodded solemnly. "You don't even have that, do you?"

Mirabeau felt her throat close up. She grimly swallowed away the lump and tried desperately to change the subject by asking, "Do you want me to put one of your tattoos on for you?"

Stephanie hesitated, eyeing her silently, and Mirabeau knew the little brat was wading through her thoughts. It made her wonder how the hell the kid kept doing that. She was a new turn. New turns couldn't read even mortals as a rule. It was a skill they had to learn. She shouldn't be able to read at all yet, let alone someone as old as Mirabeau.

"Really?" Stephanie asked, sitting up a little straighter and pleasure twitching the corners of her mouth. "I know Dani can't read minds yet, but I thought that was just her."

"No, it's not just her," Mirabeau assured her quietly, relieved to have the subject changed and the kid looking less weepy. She didn't know what she would have done if the girl had turned on the waterworks. Seeing that she was pleased by her unusual ability, Mirabeau added, "You seem to be a special case. A natural reader. It's rare."

Stephanie grinned and held up the sheet of tattoos she had been clutching. "Which one do you want?"

Mirabeau blinked. "I didn't mean I'd put a tattoo on me. I meant I'd put one on you for you."

"Oh I know," Stephanie said with a grin. "But I don't want you to mess it up. We'll do you first. That way we can figure out what we're doing."

Mirabeau gave a small, disbelieving laugh at the words. "So we experiment on me so that we don't mess up when we put on yours?"

"Exactly," she said, her grin widening farther.

Despite herself, Mirabeau chuckled, but then sighed and shook her head as she glanced over the tattoos Stephanie held. "Fine. Give me Cupid then."

Stephanie's eyebrows rose slightly. "Why Cupid?"

"Because he's an archer, and so am I," she said simply.

"Really?" Stephanie asked curiously as she began to prepare the tattoo.

"Yes. My mother trained me as a child, and I've kept it up over the centuries. I actually prefer the bow and arrow to a gun—much quieter and easy to see if you've hit your mark. Besides, our bodies can push out bullets given a little time, but they can't force out the larger, heavier arrow. So if you hit a bad guy with an arrow, he isn't likely to get up again unless you remove the arrow for him."

Stephanie seemed impressed. "Can you teach me archery?"

"We'll see," Mirabeau murmured, unwilling to make a promise unless she was sure she could keep it.

"That's a good policy," Stephanie said solemnly, then raised the tattoo and asked, "Where do you want it?"

"My arm," Mirabeau answered at once. She sat silent and still as Stephanie set to work transferring the temporary tattoo to her upper arm, her concentration on watching what she was doing. She was taken by surprise when Stephanie suddenly said, "I do have Dani, but she's kind of wrapped up in Decker right now. Sometimes it feels like I lost her too."

Mirabeau frowned. The entire situation was rather difficult. She knew Dani was doing her best by the girl, but with Leonius out there needing to be caught and having just met her life mate in Decker, Mirabeau didn't doubt the woman would have trouble fulfilling Stephanie's probably exaggerated need for attention. Anyone would.

Finally, she cleared her throat, and said, "It's true she's wrapped up in her own life at the moment. Dani also has to deal with all this stuff, you know. She's going through every single thing you are."

"But she has Decker," Stephanie said unhappily. "And if they get married and have kids, she'll have her own family. She won't need me anymore."

Mirabeau sighed. "She will always love you and need you in her life, Stephanie. If she's preoccupied now, it's just temporary. Besides, you too will someday meet your life mate and start a family of your own."

"So will you," Stephanie said quietly. "Do you think the loss will ease a bit then?"

"I don't know, it might," she said quietly, though the truth was she didn't think she'd ever have a life mate and children, and the very thought that she might almost made her nauseous though she couldn't have said why.

Stephanie was silent as she finished with the tattoo, but then sat back, saying, "There. It's done. Look at it in the mirror."

Mirabeau stood and moved to the mirror to examine her new temporary tattoo. It didn't look too bad. It was just the black silhouette of Cupid on her arm. She could live with it.

"It kind of matches my outfit, doesn't it?" she muttered, peering at herself in the black joggers and tank.

Stephanie choked out a laugh. "You hate it."

"No," she said at once, but then smiled wryly, and admitted, "I've just never been much into body art. It's fine though. Nice."

Stephanie laughed with open disbelief, then looked her over and sighed. "I hope I have a figure like yours someday so a nice man like Tiny follows me around with his tongue hanging out."

"He isn't following me around with his tongue hanging out," Mirabeau said, amused.

"No, but if you could hear his thoughts . . ." She rolled her eyes, fanned herself, and added, "Oooh la la."

Mirabeau laughed at her hamming, but was pleased at the thought that Tiny might find her attractive. She hadn't taken the time to read his thoughts herself but thought perhaps she should. If he was as interested as she was, it boded well for her intention to seduce him. She would just have to be careful not to accidentally control his mind in bed if she got too excited. Marguerite would probably be upset if she did.

"So, am I going to continue to grow, or am I going to be stuck looking fourteen forever?" Stephanie asked suddenly, still peering enviously over Mirabeau's figure.

Mirabeau's eyebrows rose, surprise sliding through her. The girl had been turned about six months ago. She would have expected her to know the answer to those kinds of questions already.

"Well, Dani doesn't know much about it," Stephanie pointed out, reading her mind without apology. "Every time I ask her a question, she has to go ask Decker, then they get distracted and its hours or sometimes even the next day before I get my answer, so I just stopped asking her."

"Hmm." Mirabeau almost asked why she didn't ask someone else, but then realized the only other female usually at the enforcer house was Sam, who was also a newly turned life mate likely to get distracted when she went in search of the answer. Mirabeau herself was probably the first unmated female immortal Stephanie had been around long enough to ask the questions.

"Right," she said calmly, moving back to sit on the bed again, determined to answer any questions she could. "You'll grow so long as you continue to feed regularly. Once you reach your peak adult condition, you'll stop aging and look somewhere between twenty-five and thirty forever."

Stephanie considered that. "How often is regularly?"

Mirabeau hesitated, then said, "It's best to feed in small bouts about every three hours until you're about twenty-five."

"Like a baby," she said with disgust.

"Basically, yes," Mirabeau said with amusement, then noted the girl's pallor, and asked, "When did you last eat?"

Stephanie grimaced, but reluctantly admitted, "Before we left for the wedding."

Mirabeau glanced at the clock. It was almost two o'clock now. Well past time the girl fed again.

"Lucian said there was blood in the SUV," Stephanie said helpfully. "We can feed before we leave in the morning."

Mirabeau was silent. Lucian had told her that as well as he'd ushered her to the secret panel in the church. The SUV would be the easiest source of blood at the moment, especially since Stephanie had no fangs. The simplest thing would be to head out as soon as Tiny had finished his shower, retrieve the SUV, feed, and head out of the city. It was probably the safest thing to do as well.

"No," Stephanie protested at once, reading her thoughts. "You said we could nap. Surely I can wait a couple of hours? I'll have twice my usual dosage when we get to the SUV." The wheedling tone of voice and the fact that she called it *dosage* suggested the girl usually had trouble feeding. Mirabeau supposed she shouldn't be surprised. Raised as a mortal, the girl was no doubt having trouble getting past the fact that she was having to drink blood at all. She probably resisted it and had to be urged to drink the stuff. Mirabeau suspected she would resist less now that she knew it was necessary for her body to mature properly. No girl wanted to be flat-chested forever.

"Okay, I did say you could nap before we left," she said soothingly. "I'll run over and pick up the SUV while Tiny showers. You can have some blood, we'll all nap, and head out in the morning as planned."

Mirabeau started for the door, but paused before she reached it as she recalled where she'd put the keys Lucian had given her. Without a purse on hand or a pocket in the bridesmaid's dress, she'd merely tucked them into her bra. It was a handy-dandy little naturally made pocket she occasionally utilized in a pinch. However, the bra was now on the floor in the bathroom where Tiny was showering.

"So wait until he's done with his shower," Stephanie suggested, then held up the package in her hand. "You can give me my tattoo while we wait."

Mirabeau returned to the bed and sat down. "So which one do you want?"

"The heart," Stephanie said, handing her the tattoos.

Mirabeau took them from her, frowning when she saw the jagged line across it where some of the tattoo had been scratched away.

"I altered it a little," Stephanie said quietly. "It seemed more suitable."

Mirabeau stared at the heart, realizing that once applied it would look broken, just as the girl's heart was at the moment, and as her own had been since she was seventeen. She just hoped Dani's presence and the fact that her family hadn't died might help Stephanie heal faster than she had . . . or hadn't, as the case may be, she acknowledged unhappily.

Chapter Eight

Tiny shut off the water and stepped out of the shower with a pleased sigh. It was extremely nice to feel clean again. While he hadn't taken a tumble in the sewer as Mirabeau had, his clothes and even his skin had carried the stink of those tunnels by the time they'd gotten out of them. It had been a relief to strip off the clothes and even more of a relief to be able to wash away whatever stench had clung to him. He was looking forward to pulling on clean clothes, even if they were tourist wear. Clean tourist wear beat a smelly Armani suit any day, though he'd enjoyed the designer suit before his stint in the sewers and regretted the loss of the expensive item.

The thought of those clean clothes on his mind, Tiny quickly toweled off, wrapped the wet towel around his waist, and headed out of the bathroom. He stepped into the bedroom on a cloud of steam, but stopped abruptly when he spotted Mirabeau pacing its length. She whirled midpace at his arrival, relief covering her face.

"Oh, thank goodness," she muttered, hurrying forward and pushing past him to get inside the room he'd just exited.

Eyebrows rising, Tiny turned to watch her snatch up her discarded gown and lacy underthings to rifle through them quickly.

"What is it?" he asked, when she cursed and dropped the destroyed clothes with disgust.

Sighing, she glanced over, and admitted, "I was going to go get some blood from the SUV for Stephanie. The keys were tucked into my bra when we started out through the sewers, but they aren't here." She scowled unhappily. "They must have fallen out when I took that tumble in the sewers."

"Hmm," Tiny murmured, his eyes sliding over her in the new clothes. The black joggers had NYC down the side seams, they were a bit large and riding low on her hips, while the black tank with NYC across the breasts was hugging her curves lovingly. *I did good*, Tiny decided. She looked sexier in the outfit than he'd thought possible . . . and the keys had been lucky to be nestled between her breasts for even a few minutes.

A disgusted cluck from Mirabeau made him

force his eyes away from her body to her face as she sighed unhappily, and said, "I guess I'll have to call Lucian and tell him. He'll have to send out someone with keys or send a new SUV altogether." She gave an exasperated huff. "God, he's going to be so pissed. It completely defeats our having snuck out of the church the way we did and sloshing through the sewers. Leonius or one of his men could follow whoever delivers the keys and—"

"We don't have to call Lucian," Tiny said quietly, and Mirabeau turned startled eyes his way.

"We don't?" she asked hopefully.

He shook his head. "I can get us into the SUV and get it started without keys."

"You can?"

She was peering at him now as if he were a god. It made him smile wryly. While he liked that she was looking at him like that, it would have been nice if it were for a different reason than that he could help her avoid calling Lucian, he thought, then admitted, "It's one of many more dubious skills I possess. I had something of a shady past before Jackie's father took me under his wing and taught me to be a PI. If not for him, I think I probably would have become a criminal. Fortunately, he caught me while I was still young."

Much to his surprise, the words made Mirabeau's mouth widen into a full-fledged smile. Moving toward him across the bathroom, she chuckled, and admitted, "That touch of shadiness just makes you even more attractive."

Tiny felt his eyebrows rise and smiled. He was certainly attracted to her and had hoped it was returned, but while Marguerite was hoping they were life mates, and Stephanie had made a comment or two about their lusting after each other, he hadn't really seen any evidence of it from Mirabeau before then. He couldn't seem to take his eyes off her, but she had been all business up until that moment, so he said, "More attractive? You *do* find me attractive then?"

"Oh, yeah," she assured him huskily, glancing down and running one finger lightly along the bare skin just above the towel around his waist.

Tiny sucked in a breath, his stomach jumping and his body along with it. He wasn't at all surprised to see his towel tenting outward as little Tiny came to roaring life. Neither was he surprised that Mirabeau's smile had widened even farther and now had a satisfied edge.

Her eyes were beginning to glow with what he knew was evidence of her own desire when she lifted her face to his again, and her voice was a soft growl as she said, "After this assignment is done, we'll have to do something about that."

Tiny was already reaching for her, and her words didn't stop him from drawing her forward to press against his chest and other less flat parts.

"Why wait?" he growled, then covered her

mouth with his. He kissed her with all the desire he'd been experiencing since joining her in the tunnels. His mouth was demanding, and even though he was getting a response, he knew she was holding back, that her sense of duty was struggling with her own desire, and she wasn't giving him all of herself.

Breaking the kiss, he began to nibble his way across her cheek to her ear, and whispered, "We're on a break right now. Stephanie's safe and probably sleeping, and we have a couple hours before dawn . . . consider this a dinner break."

Mirabeau pushed him away so swiftly, he thought at first he'd somehow offended her, but then she kept pushing, urging him away from the bathroom door and backward across the bedroom to the king-sized bed. Tiny felt it bump up against the back of his legs, then Mirabeau was pushing him back onto it and climbing on top of him to straddle his toweled hips.

"Dessert, not dinner," she whispered, and bent forward to kiss him. This time she unleashed all the passion he'd suspected she was holding back . . . and more. She was like molten fire, pouring over him, her mouth melting into his, and her body plastering itself to him like warm wax. Her hands caught and pinned his to the bed, and she slid her tongue into his mouth and did things that had him groaning and thrusting his hips upward against her.

Mirabeau's own hips were not still. She was shifting and rotating on his groin, her breasts pressing against and rubbing across his chest as she did, the combination sending his excitement through the roof, so that it seemed to vibrate through him in waves, growing stronger with each reverberation. Growling low in his throat, Tiny tugged at his hands, managing to catch Mirabeau by surprise and pull free of her hold. They were immediately everywhere, trying to touch all of her at the same time, first sliding up her sides, then covering her breasts through the cloth of the thin cotton tank top she wore then shifting to slide beneath it to touch her bare skin.

Christ, I've never experienced this kind of passion before, Tiny thought faintly, as his fingers slid over the hot skin of her stomach. It felt like they were both burning up; she was almost feverishly warm to the touch, and he was burning up from the inside out. He wanted to feel all of her against him. He wanted her naked flesh pressing down on his everywhere, and he wanted to thrust his body into hers and bury himself in her moist heat. But that would bring an end to it, and he wanted this never to end.

Mirabeau moaned when Tiny's hands found her breasts under her tank top. She was immediately hit by wave after wave of almost unbearable pleasure. Wanting more of it, she broke their kiss to rise up on him and cover his hands through the cloth and squeezed his hands encouragingly. She then opened her eyes and met his gaze as she let her hands drop to the hem of the top he'd bought her. Tiny licked his lips and watched as she slowly tugged it up and off over her head, revealing a perfect, porcelain torso. His own darker, suntanned skin stood out where he covered and caressed her breasts, and Tiny didn't think he'd ever seen anything quite so lovely.

"You're beautiful," he whispered, letting his hands drift away from her breasts to clasp her by the sides and enjoy the full view of her from the waist up.

The words brought a smile to her lips, and she let the scrap of black cloth drop to the bed beside them, then reached down to run one finger down his chest toward the top of the towel. She shifted her hips over him then, closing her eyes and groaning as a shaft of pleasure shivered back and forth between them.

Tiny couldn't resist anymore and returned his hands to cover her breasts. When he did, Mirabeau opened her eyes to peer at him. Her smile becoming a grin, she bent forward, pressing into his caress until her mouth was just above his. Her tongue slid out and she licked his lower lip, then caught and sucked it between her own lips. She tugged and sucked at it gently, letting it slip from her mouth, and murmured, "Mmm, delicious. I'll have to thank Lucian for assigning you to be my backup when I next see him."

"Marguerite," he corrected automatically and tried to claim her lips again, but she pulled back slightly, her expression frozen.

"What?" she asked carefully.

Tiny hesitated, suspecting he maybe should have kept his mouth shut. Wishing he had, he reluctantly admitted, "Marguerite is the one who suggested we work together on this assignment."

As he'd feared, that announcement definitely ruined the mood. A pail of cold water couldn't have had more of a shocking effect on Mirabeau. Horror immediately covered her face, and she jerked upright, all signs of passion gone as she asked sharply, "Marguerite suggested you be my backup?"

He nodded slowly.

"But Marguerite only interferes when she thinks—" Her words died, and she stared at him, the horror on her expression growing exponentially. It seemed she wasn't pleased at what it meant, that Marguerite thought they might be life mates.

He met her gaze for a moment, then asked huskily, "Can you read me?"

Mirabeau sat back slightly on his hips, rocking back a bit as if he'd hit her, but after a moment her shoulders straightened, and her gaze shifted from his eyes to his forehead and concentrated there. He knew without a doubt that she was trying to read him and simply lay still, waiting. When he spotted the flash of fear shoot across her expression, Tiny knew instinctively that she couldn't read him, and that, rather than being pleased, the knowledge terrified her.

Even having seen her expression, Tiny wasn't prepared when she suddenly slid off him and climbed off the bed. She was at the door before he could even think to speak.

"What about the SUV?" he asked desperately as she started out of the room. The minute the words were out of his mouth, he felt shame claim him that he'd allowed himself to forget her intention to get blood for the girl. Judging by the way Mirabeau halted and her shoulders bowed, she felt much the same way as she was reminded of the reason she'd been pacing his room in the first place.

She stood silent and still in the doorway for a moment, but then released a long sigh. Mirabeau didn't even glance back when she finally said, "It won't hurt Stephanie to wait a couple of hours this one time. She's probably asleep anyway. We can leave at dawn and feed her when we get to the SUV as planned. I'll wake you."

Tiny sighed as she left the room and closed the door. While he'd been reluctant at the idea of being a life mate when he'd realized what Marguerite was up to in suggesting he accompany Mirabeau for this assignment, he'd gotten over that in a hurry once he'd met her. But it seemed Mirabeau would need more time to adjust to the idea. While she wanted him, it seemed it wasn't enough to get past whatever fears she had regarding finding a life mate.

Marguerite was right, Tiny realized as he peered down at the aching tent pole his erection had become. He was definitely going to have to be patient with Mirabeau if he wanted her. On that thought, he lay back on the bed with a sigh to wait for his towel tent to fold.

Stephanie seemed to be asleep when Mirabeau returned to the room they shared, so it startled her when the girl suddenly whispered, "I know you're afraid of letting people in again because it hurts to lose them as we have, but surely it's worth it? You don't wish you'd never known or loved your family, do you?"

Mirabeau stilled, shocked by her words, and to hear them from a girl who was so young. Such insight and wisdom from a kid was rather unusual, but then Stephanie was proving to be an unusual kid.

"Dani said that to me a while ago," Stephanie admitted quietly. "And she's right. I have to not be afraid to care for people again. I would miss out on a lot of good stuff. We both would."

Mirabeau heard Stephanie moving and glanced over in time to see her finish turning onto her side away from her. It seemed it was all the girl had to say, which should have left Mirabeau to crawl into bed and go to sleep for the few hours she had until dawn. However, while she crawled into bed, she didn't sleep. She lay there thinking about the fact that Marguerite had set her up, that she couldn't read Tiny but wanted him with a desperation she hadn't experienced for anyone else in all her more than four hundred and fifty some years, and that meant he was probably her life mate. She also thought about what Stephanie had said. While the idea of caring for anyone again was terrifying, did she really want to miss out on what they could share just to avoid hurting later?

All those thoughts ran around and around inside her head as the night crept past. It was all so scary and confusing that Mirabeau was actually relieved when she saw predawn light through the crack in the curtains. She still didn't know what she was going to do about Tiny, but it was a relief to get moving and have something to do besides lie there fretting over things.

Chapter Nine

"Want a bite?"

Mirabeau jerked her head back a little with surprise as Tiny raised what he'd called a chili cheese dog in front of her face. Frowning, she murmured, "I don't eat foo—" The last word died on a gasp of surprise as Tiny suddenly pushed the food forward, catching her on the upper lip and the bottom of her nose.

"Nice one, Tiny," Stephanie laughed between bites of her cheeseburger.

Scowling at the pair of them, Mirabeau pushed away the dog Tiny was still holding out to her and wiped the warm chili from her nose. However, her scowl was replaced with surprise when she licked her lip to clean it and a savory, spicy taste exploded on her tongue. Mirabeau couldn't contain the murmured "Mmm" as she swallowed the bit of flavorful food.

"Good thing I got you one too despite your claim not to want anything, huh?" Tiny teased, lifting a second plate with a chili dog off the tray he'd brought to the table and setting it before her.

Mirabeau hesitated, she really didn't eat much anymore. She indulged on occasion to keep Jeanne Louise company, but she rarely bothered otherwise, food had become boring over time. This chili stuff, however, was not boring at all, she thought as she watched how Tiny carefully picked up his own hot dog smothered with the thick chili and bit into it. Perhaps she'd simply been eating the wrong foods, she thought as she emulated his actions.

"Or maybe Tiny's your life mate and your taste buds, along with your libido, have come back to life like Decker's did," Stephanie said dryly.

Mirabeau paused midbite to scowl at the girl, but she couldn't hold the expression. Her mouth was alive with the wonderful combination of flavors she'd bitten into. Her eyes involuntarily closed as she savored the explosions taking place in her mouth. Chili dogs definitely rocked, she decided, and wondered how it was she'd never had one before.

"Try an onion ring," Tiny urged, holding a round breaded object out to her.

Mirabeau accepted the odd item, turned it curiously in her hand, sniffed it, and then took a careful bite. Her eyes widened with surprised pleasure as an entirely different flavor filled her senses. *Damn, that's good too,* she acknowledged, and smiled when he slid a smaller plate with a mound of rings in front of her. He'd bought two of those as well, she noted.

"How about a chocolate shake?" he said next, and a thick-looking, creamy drink was set before her as well.

This time Mirabeau didn't hesitate to try the offering and as the cold, creamy, chocolate slid across her tongue and down her throat, she understood what he was doing.

"You're trying to kill me with pleasure," she said on a sigh.

"If that were the case, you'd be naked, and I'd be eating this off your supine body," Tiny growled. He then leaned toward her and licked away a drop of chili that rested on her upper lip.

Mirabeau swallowed thickly, her eyes finding and locking on his until Stephanie groaned, and muttered, "Oh, gross. Get a room."

Mirabeau saw the chagrin flicker in Tiny's expression and knew he'd forgotten the girl was there, just as she had for those few seconds. She shared a wry smile with him, then, as if by agreement, they both turned their attention to their food and began to eat, trying to pretend that the moment hadn't happened.

Unfortunately, Stephanie wouldn't let it rest, and asked, "Are you two going to get together after you get me to Port Henry, or what?"

Mirabeau gave her a quelling look, but the girl wasn't willing to be quelled.

"Oh, come on, he's your life mate, right?" she said, waving a french fry around as she spoke.

"You don't know what you're talking about, Stephanie," Mirabeau said sharply. "Eat your food. We have to get going."

"Oh please, even if I couldn't read your thoughts, anyone could see you two are hot for each other."

"Enough Stephanie," Tiny said quietly. "Now eat your food. We're already very late getting you to Port Henry. We really shouldn't have stopped here."

And they shouldn't have, Mirabeau acknowledged. By now the people in Port Henry had probably called Lucian in a panic that they hadn't arrived . . . and there wasn't a darned thing they could do to reassure them that everything was all right. Mirabeau hadn't had a cell phone when she'd left the church, and Tiny's phone had gone missing. He suspected it had been lifted while he was shopping for clothes and food. He'd told her as much as they'd made their way to the SUV in the predawn light.

Mirabeau had considered stopping to use a pay phone to call in, but one of Lucian's last instructions had been not to make contact in any way but through Tiny's cell phone unless it was an emergency. He'd said Tiny's cell was set up specially to be untraceable, while calls from any other phone wouldn't be. He was determined no one was going to figure out where Stephanie was, and he was the boss, so there was nothing she could do to soothe any worries anyone might be having.

And they would be worried, she thought unhappily. By her guess, between getting lost in the tunnels and their stop at the hotel to clean up and rest, they were probably at least five or six hours behind schedule, which meant they should have arrived in Port Henry about three or four hours ago. Instead, they were half an hour southwest of Toronto, eating quite the most delicious food she'd ever enjoyed in one of the ugliest, dreariest-looking diners she'd ever seen. Tiny had picked it after several hours of Stephanie's whining that she was hungry. He'd called it a truck stop and said they always had the best food.

Mirabeau had to admit the food was indeed good. They just really shouldn't have stopped to get it, and had Tiny not been so obviously exhausted from driving all the way up from New York, she would have said so. However, the man had been yawning and wiping his weary eyes for the last hour they'd been on the road, and she'd decided a break was probably smart. She planned to offer to take over driving when they returned to the SUV he'd managed to get them into and get started that morning, all with nothing more than a hanger they'd taken from their room and a screwdriver they'd gotten from the handyman at the hotel. It had been rather impressive to watch him in action. But then he was impressive just to look at, she acknowledged.

"All done? Shall we go?" Tiny asked, and Mirabeau glanced down at her empty plates wryly. So much for not eating. She'd pretty much inhaled the offerings he'd brought her.

"I need to go to the bathroom," Stephanie announced, slurping the last of her own shake, a pink one that smelled of strawberries.

"You take her to the bathroom, and I'll get the SUV started," Tiny suggested, getting to his feet.

"Hey, I'm not a kid. I can take myself to the bathroom," Stephanie protested, scowling at him.

Rather than point out that Mirabeau was to be with her to ensure she remained safe, Tiny grinned, and teased, "I thought you girls always went to the bathroom in packs?"

"Sexist," Stephanie muttered, but amusement was tugging at her lips as she got to her feet.

They were pretty quick in the bathroom, but Tiny was quicker. He'd started the SUV and pulled it up to the door to collect them when they stepped outside.

"I was going to offer to drive," Mirabeau murmured as she climbed into the front passenger seat after closing the back door behind Stephanie.

"That's okay. I'm good. The break refreshed me," he assured her.

Shrugging, Mirabeau settled in the seat and did up her seat belt as he started out of the parking lot. They were back on the highway when Stephanie suddenly leaned forward between the two front seats to ask, "What's your real name, Tiny?"

Mirabeau glanced at him, curious about the answer to that herself, and caught the amusement tugging at his lips as he asked, "What makes you think it isn't Tiny?"

"Because no one but a pair of spazzes would name their kid Tiny," the teenager assured him dryly.

"Spazzes, huh?" Tiny chuckled, and then said, "Well as it would happen, my given name is Tinh." He spelled it out, then added, "Tiny is just what everyone has always called me, like Billy instead of Bill."

"Tinh?" Stephanie said with amazement. "What kind of name is that?"

"Vietnamese."

"You aren't Vietnamese," she said, then asked uncertainly, "Are you?"

"No," he said with a smile.

"Then why did your parents name you that?"

"My father was a soldier in Vietnam," he answered patiently. "He was injured while on recon. He's pretty sure he would have died where he fell had he not been rescued, and nursed back to health by a friendly named Tinh. Dad was never sure if that was his last name or first, but when he married mom and they had me, he named me after the man who had saved his life."

"Oh," Stephanie murmured. "I guess that was cool."

"I always thought so," Tiny agreed.

"I guess it's a good thing you didn't end up a little guy though," Stephanie commented. "They would have been dooming you to a life of teasing and bullying, naming you that if you were little."

"My being little was never very likely," Tiny assured her. "My mother is five-ten, and my father is my size."

"Hmm." Stephanie grunted, then sat back in her seat. "I'm going to watch the end of the movie I started before we stopped to eat."

Mirabeau glanced over her shoulder to see the girl putting earplugs into her ears and hitting the play button on the DVD player in the back of Tiny's seat. She then turned back to face front, but found herself unable to keep from glancing at the man driving. Finally, she asked softly, "They're still alive then? Your parents?"

"Oh yeah," Tiny assured her. "Both retired and spoiling the grandbabies my little sister has given them . . . and cursing me for not giving them more yet," he added with a wry smile.

"You're close to them," she realized, the thought troubling her.

"Yes," he admitted, then glanced sideways at her, and added, "they'll like you."

Mirabeau held his gaze for a minute, then turned away to look out the window as she tried to settle the sudden quandary in her mind. She had only been considering her own point of view when it came to their being life mates. The risk it would be to open her heart up to him and possibly lose him at some later date as she had her family. She hadn't considered what he might have to give up to be her life mate. That perhaps he wouldn't be willing to give it up for her.

"Tell me about your family," Tiny said suddenly.

Mirabeau glanced at him sharply, then away, muttering, "What do you want to know? They're dead."

"Yes," he said quietly. "Marguerite said that your uncle killed them. Tell me how . . . and why?"

Mirabeau stared out the window silently for a moment, but she didn't see the vehicles or landscaping they were passing. Her mind took her back to France in 1572, a mad time in the country.

"My father and uncle were turned in the thirteenth century by a rogue," she said finally. "Fortunately, they were new turns and had committed no crimes so were spared when the rogue was hunted down and killed."

"Like Leigh's friend Danny?" Tiny asked.

Mirabeau nodded silently, then cleared her throat and continued. "They were very close before the turn and for a while afterward, but then my father met my mother. She was his life mate, and they became wrapped up in each other as life mates tend to do. My uncle and father drifted apart while my parents had my three brothers and me in quick succession."

"In quick succession?" Tiny asked with surprise. "I thought you had to wait a hundred years between children?"

"Well, yes, but I mean they had my eldest brother right away in 1255, and then as soon as the hundred years were up, had my second brother and so on. They didn't leave extra time between each. I was born in 1555, almost a hundred years to the day after the youngest of my brothers was born."

"Ah," Tiny murmured.

"Anyway, they were happy. We all were, but apparently my uncle was not. He hadn't yet found his life mate and was jealous of my father, who had my mother and us children, as well as wealth and a title. He wanted all of it . . . including my mother. I guess he thought the St. Bartholomew Massacres would be a good cover for his getting it all."

"I'm sorry," Tiny interrupted gently. "Marguerite mentioned the St. Bartholomew Massacres to me, but I'm not sure what it was exactly."

Mirabeau frowned, wondering how something that had always figured so large in her own life was unknown to most of today's mortals. It was such a turning point in her life that it was difficult to accept that it meant nothing to others. Shrugging that aside, she explained, "St. Bartholomew Massacres were basically a mess. There was some history behind what happened, but the final straw that appeared to light the fury was when the Catholic Marguerite of Valois, the sister of the King of France, was married to Henry of Navarre, a Protestant. The population of Paris was very Roman Catholic, and equally anti-Huguenot. French Protestant," Mirabeau explained before he could ask what a Huguenot was. She then continued, "Over the next six days after the wedding, several events conspired to stir things up, but the end result was that on August twenty-third, the gates to the city were closed, and a Roman Catholic mob began to hunt down and slaughter Protestants in the streets. Thousands were killed, including women and children."

"And your family was in Paris?" Tiny asked with a frown.

"No. And they were Catholic, not Protestant, and they died in late September not August. However, even up to October of that year, there were similar outbreaks of such attacks in cities and towns all over France. Even the hint of Protestantism was enough to mark a family for death.

"I don't know if my uncle planned what he did ahead of time and the St. Bartholomew Massacres simply offered a convenient cover, or if their

eruption spurred him to action, but he planned
to claim we had been suspected of Protestantism,
had been chained in the barn, and burned alive."

"Nasty bastard," Tiny said grimly. "His plan
went awry, obviously." And when she glanced
at him in question, he pointed out, "You're still
alive."

"Oh, yes." She frowned and peered out the
window again, then admitted, "But I'm only alive
because I was a rebellious seventeen-year-old
who snuck out of the castle to drink wine in the
stables with a very handsome stableboy named
Fredrique."

She glanced over in time to see Tiny's mouth
twitch with amusement and wished she could
smile too, but even all this time later she didn't see
the humor in it. "My uncle had arrived for dinner.
After dinner, he and my father and brothers went
out to view a new horse my father had purchased.
My uncle's men must have been waiting and taken
them by surprise, slaughtering them the moment
they entered the stable. By the time I snuck away
to meet Fredrique, there was no one around in the
stables, and I thought they'd already returned to
the castle." She pursed her lips and added bitterly,
"And my uncle *had* returned to the castle . . . to get
my mother.

She closed her eyes briefly, then continued, "We
were in the loft drinking; Fredrique was trying to

steal a kiss when my uncle dragged my mother into the stables to show her what he'd done. The headless bodies of my father and brothers had been lying in the stall beneath us, covered with a thin layer of straw the entire time Fredrique and I had been drinking above. He showed them to her and demanded she be his life mate."

"Hang on," Tiny said with amazement. "Be his life mate? How could she be his life mate? She was your father's life mate. And where were his men?"

"He must have sent his men away, intending to deal with my mother and me himself." Mirabeau said, then grimaced, and explained, "As for her being his life mate, my uncle could not read or control my mother either. She could have been a life mate to either brother, but chose my father."

"Smart lady," Tiny muttered.

Mirabeau sighed. "Perhaps, but I think that is what really drove him mad. That had she but chosen him, he would have had all that my father did."

"I see." Tiny nodded solemnly. "Yes, that must have been hard for him to bear. I'm sorry. Go on."

Mirabeau took a breath herself and swallowed down the pain that always rose in her when she thought on these events. She hadn't told the tale to anyone since Lucian had come upon her that night, and she'd sobbed the story to him. She found, though, that this time it hurt much less and wondered if it was the passage of time, or because it was Tiny she was finally telling it to. It did still hurt, and tears were crowding her eyes, but she was nowhere near sobbing with the agony of loss she'd suffered.

Mirabeau glanced down, noticed his large hand covering her own on her leg, and wondered when Tiny had put it there, but then she cleared her throat and continued, "My uncle told my mother that if she agreed to be his life mate and backed him up in the story that a roaming group of Roman Catholic vigilantes had killed my father and brothers, he would let me live."

"Bastard," Tiny muttered again.

Much to Mirabeau's amazement, she actually felt a smile twitch at her lips at the angry word and the support behind it. But the desire to smile died quickly as she continued, "I thought my mother would agree. I was silently begging her to, thinking we would find a way to escape later and tell the truth . . . and I really think she would have had she not spotted me peeking out from the hayloft. She straightened then, her expression determined as she said, 'No.'

"My uncle was furious. "Not even to save your daughter?" he raged with disbelief, and she suddenly looked serene and stared right at me as she said, "My daughter can save herself. You will not be able to kill Mirabeau. She is strong and brave. She will escape you and carry word of what you have done to the people who can do something about it."

"She was telling you what to do," Tiny murmured quietly.

"Yes," Mirabeau agreed.

"What did your uncle do?" he prompted, when she didn't immediately continue.

"He roared, 'I will slaughter her in her bed where she even now lies sleeping,' and pressed his sword to her throat, but my mother just smiled at me reassuringly over his shoulder, and said, 'You may try. But I vow you will not succeed, and much as I love my daughter, I will not spend one moment even pretending to be your life mate. I shall never let you touch or think of me in that way.'"

When Mirabeau fell silent as she recalled that moment, Tiny squeezed her hand and asked in a hushed whisper, "And so he killed her?"

Mirabeau shook her head and used her free hand to wipe away the tear that had escaped her. "No. She killed herself."

"What?" he asked with amazement. "But how? Why?"

Mirabeau shrugged. "The why is because while he couldn't control her, and they were both immortals, he was still male and stronger. He would have raped and tormented her first, and I would have tried to save her, endangering myself. She knew all this, and so . . ." Mirabeau took a deep breath. "The moment the last word had left her lips, she caught his hand holding the sword and jerked it toward herself while throwing her head forward, beheading herself on the steel edge."

"Jesus," Tiny breathed, then shook his head faintly. "I wouldn't even have thought that possible. The strength needed to do it, both physically and just in fortitude . . ."

"We are strong," Mirabeau said simply, though she had found it all rather shocking at the time. She had never imagined anyone doing that either, but her mother had been like Marguerite, a strong woman capable of doing whatever she put her mind to. And, Mirabeau supposed, her mother had probably seen little to live for with her life mate lying dead at her feet. Finding a life mate was a rare thing, and life could be so lonely when you moved through it without one.

Pushing that thought aside, Mirabeau admitted quietly, "I started to scream when she did it. Fortunately, Fredrique covered my mouth, and my uncle didn't hear what little sound escaped over his own frustrated roar. We stayed where we were while he ranted madly, but when he left to go find me, we slipped out of the loft. I told Fredrique to make himself scarce and mounted a horse and fled. My uncle's men were camped in the woods outside the castle walls. They mounted and gave chase when I raced through their camp. I think they might have caught me had Lucian not suddenly appeared. He and my father were both horse enthusiasts and had become good friends. He'd been heading to La Roche to see the new horse. He arrived just as my uncle's men were about to overtake me."

"And he took care of them," Tiny said quietly.

"Yes," Mirabeau agreed quietly. "As well as my uncle."

Tiny nodded and allowed several minutes to pass in silence, then asked, "What are we going to do about being life mates, Mirabeau La Roche?"

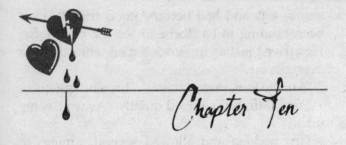

Chapter Ten

Mirabeau glanced at Tiny as panic and shock coursed through her. She hadn't expected the blunt question, and responded harshly. "What do you mean? I never said we were life mates. What makes you think—"

"It was obvious you couldn't read me in my room when you tried," Tiny interrupted quietly, then added, "You're eating too, which is another sign. And I'm pretty darned sure I was enjoying some of that shared pleasure in my bed this morning or last night or whatever it was."

"You two did it last night?" Stephanie squawked.

Mirabeau turned sharply to see the girl still wore her earplugs. Her confusion as to how she could have heard their conversation must have shown because Stephanie rolled her eyes.

"I don't need my ears to hear your thoughts," she said overloudly thanks to the movie sound track playing in her ears.

"Yes, but we were speaking what you heard," Tiny muttered.

"And you're thinking as you speak," she pointed out dryly, then shook her head. "Honestly, this life-mate business makes complete idiots out of adults. I mean, Dani's a doctor, for God's sake, and she's been pretty brainless since meeting Decker. Now you two." She shook her head again and turned her concentration to changing movies as she muttered, "Never gonna let myself get into that state. No sir."

Mirabeau flopped back in her seat with a sigh. Honestly, teenagers were a pain. She was amazed her parents had been willing to have more than one, let alone not take very long breaks between them . . . like maybe a millennium or something. Certainly her time so far in this kid's company was making her think a person had to be insane to want children. Sure, they were all cute and cuddly when they were someone else's baby, but that was when you could send them home. Spend twenty-four hours with them, and there were messy diapers, burping up on you, and the endless crying . . . then they grew up into smart-ass teenagers.

"I don't know who you think you're fooling, Mirabeau," Stephanie said with amusement. "I can read your mind, remember. I know you like me."

Mirabeau grimaced but didn't argue the point. Despite all the smart-ass comments, she *did* like the kid. Stephanie reminded her of herself when she was young. She'd bite her tongue off before saying that out loud though, she realized, and grimaced again as Stephanie began to chuckle in the backseat, positive she'd heard it anyway.

"So?" Tiny prompted after a moment.

It figured he wasn't going to let the subject go, Mirabeau thought unhappily. The problem was she didn't know what they were going to do about it. In truth, she knew that what Stephanie had said last night was right. While losing her parents and brothers had hurt horribly, she would never have dreamed of missing out on the years she'd had with them to save herself that loss. So, did she really want to walk away from what she could have with Tiny just to be sure she never suffered the pain of possibly losing him? *Something that may never happen*, she reminded herself. After all, she could die first, or they might die together.

However, while she thought she might be willing to go forward with it and be his life mate, there was more than just herself to consider here. Tiny too had a choice to make, and he was the one who still had family to lose. Not that he would have to give them up at once, but eventually, he would have to break away from them to prevent their noticing that he wasn't aging.

"What do *you* want to do about it?" she asked finally, rather than answer.

"I really don't know, Mirabeau," Tiny admitted with a wry smile. "A little more than twenty-four hours ago I stood in that church in New York and told Marguerite that I had a family, one I wasn't willing to lose even for the bliss of a life mate, but now . . ." He shook his head, and said with bewilderment, "They seem so far away when I'm with you. I love them, but . . ." He turned to peer at her briefly, then returned his gaze to the road, and said, "Twenty-four hours ago, to me you were just the gal with the black-and-pink hair. How could you become so important so quickly?"

Mirabeau had no idea. She had no idea how this life-mate business worked, just that it did, that she was showing all the symptoms of it, and that the longer she spent with him, the more she wanted to take that risk.

The sign warning of the approach of the off-ramp that led to Port Henry appeared ahead, and Mirabeau stared at it, rather surprised. She hadn't thought that much time had passed since they'd left the restaurant, but then she supposed she'd been a bit distracted with their conversation.

"I guess we'll have to leave this talk for later," Tiny murmured, putting on his blinker to take the off-ramp. "After we leave Port Henry, we'll stop somewhere and discuss it."

Mirabeau nodded at the suggestion but suspected that if they stopped anywhere the least bit private, they wouldn't get much talking done. Even somewhere very public wasn't likely to stop them from consummating their relationship if they were inside the SUV. Once the assignment was over, there would be nothing to stop them except themselves, and life mates weren't known for having a lot of restraint. She'd heard it said that new life mates were like drug addicts, constantly jonesing for a life-mate fix, and she finally understood the comment. She was jonesing for Tiny, very aware of his scent and the heat coming off his body, wishing she could sit closer, run her hands over his chest and legs, nibble at his ear ... She didn't much care that he was driving. The only thing really preventing her doing all of that was Stephanie's presence and the fact that they had been charged with getting her safely to Port Henry. But once that was out of the way ...

Mirabeau squirmed in her seat and licked her lips in anticipation.

"What are they doing here? I would have thought they'd be on their honeymoon now," Tiny murmured as he parked the SUV behind the Victorian house. Elvi and Victor Argeneau, one of the couples whose wedding she had stood up for, had just come out of the back door and were crossing the deck toward the driveway. Apparently the couple had flown back and beat them to Port Henry.

"They probably wanted to be here to welcome Stephanie," Mirabeau murmured, undoing her seat belt and opening her door.

"Are we glad to see you," Elvi announced, rushing forward to clasp Mirabeau's hands as she stepped out of the SUV. "We were really starting to worry. We expected you hours ago."

"We got a little turned around in the tunnels, then had a couple of unscheduled stops," Mirabeau muttered apologetically.

"Well, at least you're here now," Elvi said with a smile, her gaze shooting to Stephanie as the girl climbed out of the back of the SUV. Releasing Mirabeau, she moved to clasp the girl's hands, and said, "And you must be Stephanie. I saw you at the wedding, but we didn't really get to meet. I only found out afterward that you were the special guest Lucian had asked about staying with us."

"He probably didn't want anyone to read your mind and figure out where Stephanie was," Tiny said as he came around the vehicle to join them.

"That's what he said," Elvi acknowledged, her gaze still on Stephanie who—much to Mirabeau's surprise—had shifted rather close to her, like a shy child attaching herself to a parent's or older sibling's side on meeting strangers.

"Well . . ." Mirabeau hesitated, but then glanced back toward the SUV, wondering if they were to head out right away to report to Lucian in Toronto. She doubted they were to risk calling from the house, and the sooner she got it done, the better. The minute she'd made her report, she would be free to do what she wanted . . . or whom she wanted, she thought, her eyes sliding to Tiny. At least she could until another assignment came up.

"You aren't leaving already, are you?" Stephanie asked, sounding alarmed.

"Of course, she isn't, dear," Elvi said at once, slipping between them to put an arm around each female and urge them toward the house, leaving Tiny to follow with Victor. "Mirabeau and Tiny need to check in with Lucian. And then we'll have a nice meal, and they can rest after the long journey before deciding what they'll do next."

Mirabeau felt her eyebrows rise at the words "deciding what they'll do next." It seemed such an odd thing to say considering the woman didn't know them or the situation they were presently in.

"Lucian said not to call using anything but Tiny's cell phone, and we lost that in New York," she explained quietly, as they crossed the deck to the back door. "It's why we couldn't call ahead to explain that we'd be late."

"We have a safe phone," Victor assured her, pulling the door open and holding it for all of them to troop inside.

Mirabeau followed Elvi through an open kitchen with a breakfast counter, then into a large dining area with a beautiful fireplace.

There were three people seated at the table—a very pretty blond woman, and two men, one dark and one blond. All three rose at once to greet them as Elvi said, "This is my best friend Mabel, her life mate DJ and a dear friend of ours, Harper." She gestured to each in turn as their group came to a halt and spread out a bit in the dining area. "And this lovely young lady is Stephanie, who will be staying with us for a while." She beamed a smile at the girl, then added, "And Mirabeau and Tiny, who were kind enough to see her safely here and miss out on the wedding party after the ceremony."

"You didn't miss much," DJ, the darker male, assured them as he moved forward to shake hands. "There was no drunkenness or bawdy jokes, just a bunch of dressed-up people wishing they could go home and get naked."

"DJ" Mabel shook her head, but she was smiling at the man, obviously not really upset by his words.

"Well it's true," DJ said, unrepentant. "What's the first thing we did when we could finally leave and go back to our hotel room?"

"Dear God, they're everywhere," Stephanie muttered.

Knowing she was talking about new life mates who couldn't seem to do anything but "lust after each other or do it" as she'd put it earlier, Mira-

beau turned her back to the group to give a warning look to the girl and heard a horrified gasp
behind her.

"Child, what happened to your hair?"

Mirabeau turned back around, a hand going
self-consciously to the back of her head at that
exclamation from Mabel, but the woman hurried
forward and immediately turned her around to
get a better look at it.

"What on earth," Elvi's friend breathed, and
Mirabeau felt her plucking at the hair left on the
back of her head.

"A homeless guy ripped some of her extensions out," Stephanie said helpfully, and Mirabeau didn't miss the amusement in her voice as
Elvi and Mabel crowded around to examine the
damage.

"Well, we'll have to fix that for you," Mabel decided firmly.

"Yes," Elvi agreed, and began to urge both
Mirabeau and Stephanie out of the dining room
and toward a winding staircase in the front foyer.
"Come along. Tiny can call Lucian while we fix
your hair."

"Yes, you can't go around looking like that. I
thought you'd been scalped when I first saw it,"
Mabel said from somewhere behind her, then
asked, "Are there supposed to be pink patches in
your hair, or is that a result of the extensions?"

"She had fuchsia tips before Marguerite took

her to the hairdresser," Elvi explained in a hushed tone.

"Oh, my, well . . . that's . . . interesting, child," Mabel responded weakly, and Mirabeau felt a bubble of laughter at the back of her throat. It was obvious the woman wasn't sure what to make of it, but then despite her youthful looks, Mabel was somewhere in her early sixties and probably not into the new styles. Of course, Mirabeau was even older still, but had been born immortal and had never looked or even really felt old. These two ladies were new turns who had been gray-haired and grandmotherly before their turn. Which was probably why Mabel had called her *child* when Mirabeau was actually her elder. The woman hadn't gotten used to the idea that, at least physically, she was now a young woman.

"Here we are," Elvi said cheerfully, steering them into a large room with a king-sized bed and sitting area. "This will be your and Tiny's room while you're here."

Mirabeau was blinking at the announcement, when Mabel explained, "Marguerite told us she felt sure the two of you were life mates when she had Lucian put the two of you together to bring Stephanie here. And it's obvious she was right."

"It is ?" Mirabeau asked with dismay, sure she hadn't said or done anything that might give away her feelings for the mortal.

"You don't have to say anything, dear," Elvi said

gently. "Your thoughts are pretty loud. They must be. Mabel and I haven't quite got the hang of reading thoughts yet. We can barely read mortals, and only then with a lot of effort, but you and Tiny are like a pair of radios playing at top volume."

"And you're broadcasting a porno station," Mabel announced with a grin. "Every time you glance his way, your mind is undressing and doing delicious things to him, and he's no better."

"I told you you were screaming your thoughts," Stephanie said with vindication.

Mirabeau merely closed her eyes and wished she were dead.

"You can hear her thoughts then too?" Elvi asked with surprise, and Mirabeau opened her eyes to see Stephanie nod.

"I can hear you too, and everyone downstairs," she admitted.

"Even Harper?" Mabel asked with a frown.

"Yes."

"Well, aren't you clever?" Elvi said, rubbing the girl's shoulder. "That must be a special talent then, because Harper is apparently quite hard to read."

"Really?" Stephanie asked, standing a little straighter under the praise.

"Yes indeed. Even Victor has trouble reading him since he lost his mate." She sighed unhappily, and explained, "He and the other boys found life mates while here the summer before last. But Harper's didn't survive the turn."

"Hmm," Mabel muttered, urging Mirabeau to sit on the bed so that she could fuss with her hair. "And that was a shock, I can tell you. We were all worried about Alessandro's mate because she is in her eighties, but she came through with flying colors. Instead, Harper's life mate, who was young and seemingly in good health, was the one to have trouble. It seems she had a bad ticker no one knew about. She died before the nanos could get to her heart to repair and strengthen it."

Silence filled the room for a moment, then Mabel announced, "I think I can get these out, but we're going to have to move to the bathroom to do it."

Mirabeau immediately found herself ushered to the bathroom.

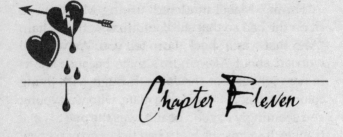

Chapter Eleven

"Would you like a drink?" Victor asked, as the women disappeared upstairs.

Tiny nodded. The chili dog had been delicious but a bit salty, and he'd been parched for the last half hour of the drive. "Thank you, that would be nice."

"Alcohol or coffee?" Victor asked, moving around the counter toward the kitchen half of the room. When Tiny hesitated, he added, "You're off duty now. Alcohol is all right."

"Alcohol it is then," Tiny murmured, thinking a beer would hit the spot.

"I'll get us a couple beers," DJ offered, reading his mind.

As the other man got to his feet, Victor nodded. "Grab me one too, please. I'll get glasses."

DJ opened a door off the kitchen and headed

downstairs to where the beer was apparently kept, and Victor busied himself in the kitchen, leaving Tiny alone with the man they'd introduced as Harper.

"You're Mirabeau's life mate," the other man said quietly.

Tiny nodded slowly. "It would seem so."

"Congratulations," Harper said quietly. Then he asked, "How's your health?"

"Good," Tiny answered, a little bewildered by the question.

"Your heart?" he asked.

Tiny felt his eyebrows rise, but said, "Strong as a bull according to my doctor after my stress test last month."

Harper's lips twisted into a bittersweet smile. "Then don't let your fears of the future hold you back. Being a life mate is a rare and wondrous thing. Grab on to it, and don't let go. You won't regret it."

He then stood and left the room with a nod, leaving Tiny staring after him with bewilderment.

"Harper lost his life mate and is having a rough time of it," Victor murmured, coming back into the dining area. "He's right though. Don't let fear prevent you from accepting the happiness you and Mirabeau could have."

"I won't," Tiny murmured, and knew it was true. While he did have concerns about what it would mean in regard to his family, he just couldn't resist the pull of his attraction for Mirabeau. Accepting the empty glass Victor held out, he murmured a polite, "Thanks," and thought that, while he preferred beer straight from the bottle, he'd drink from the glass to be polite.

"Actually, I prefer the bottle too," Victor said wryly, obviously having read his mind again.

Tiny smiled faintly, but once again thought it might be nice to be immortal and be able to guard his thoughts from others.

"I was trying to be a good host, but"—Victor took back the glass he'd just given Tiny, and said wryly—"this way there are no glasses to clean up." He swung away to return the glasses, adding, "The phone's there on the counter. The handset is cordless, so if you want privacy, take it out on the deck."

"Thanks," Tiny said again, and moved to collect the phone.

"It looks like you have two Marguerites," Mirabeau murmured, as Mabel and Elvi moved away to examine the various shampoos and conditioners they had between them, trying to decide which one would be best for Mirabeau's "stressed" hair now that the extensions were out. They were a delightful pair—amusing, caring, and loving, and had both been fussing over Stephanie as they'd worked, asking her questions and drawing her into the conversation.

The girl rolled her eyes at Mirabeau's words, but

she suspected it was for show. She sensed that the girl was secretly pleased.

"Here we are. We've decided this one is the best bet," Elvi announced, holding out a matching set of bottles, one holding shampoo, the other conditioner. "Do you want to wash it in the shower or just at the sink?"

"The sink is fine," Mirabeau murmured, and immediately found herself with a woman on each side, determined to help her do it at the bathroom sink. Unused to the fussing herself, she was relieved when the chore was done and she could dry her hair and use some gel to return it to its usual spiky state.

"My," Mabel murmured, as Mirabeau finished and presented herself for inspection. "That style is really quite attractive on you, dear. The fuchsia tips are really quite striking. I like it."

"Yes, it's quite nice," Elvi agreed. And then her eyes shifted past Mirabeau, and she smiled, and asked, "What do you think, Tiny?"

Mirabeau glanced over her shoulder with surprise. Her own eyes widened as she saw Tiny standing in the doorway.

"I think Mirabeau always looks beautiful," Tiny said solemnly. "But I like this style best. It suits her."

Elvi beamed at the man, and said, "I knew you were an intelligent man the moment I met you in New York, Tiny McGraw."

Much to Mirabeau's amazement, he actually blushed at the compliment, which just seemed to please Elvi more. Chuckling softly, the woman caught Mabel and Stephanie each by an arm and began to usher them out of the bathroom. "Well, our work here is done, girls. Why don't we leave these two alone for a bit and go have tea? Stephanie, do you like white chocolate strawberry cookies?"

"I don't think I've ever had them," Stephanie murmured, as Tiny stepped out of the way to allow them to exit the bathroom.

"Oh, well then, you're in for a real treat. They're divine," she said, as they headed through the bedroom. "We stopped and picked up a bunch on our way home from the airport."

"She got cheesecake too," Mabel announced dryly, then told Stephanie in conspiratorial tones, "You'll find that Elvi has something of a sweet tooth."

"So do I," Stephanie said with a grin.

"Oh, brilliant," Elvi crooned happily. "We shall get on like gangbusters!"

Mirabeau glanced to Tiny and shook her head wryly as the door closed behind the trio. "They are going to spoil her rotten before Dani can get here to collect her."

"She's been through a lot and deserves a little spoiling," Tiny said mildly, then added, "And so do you."

Mirabeau found her breath hitching in surprise and her heart melting a little at the words. It had been the exactly right thing to say. Mirabeau started across the room with every intention of kissing him for saying it, when he suddenly held up a phone.

"Lucian wants to talk to you."

"Lucian?" She stared at the phone with amazement. "You've been on the phone with him all this time?"

He grimaced and shook his head. "I tried calling, got a busy signal, had a beer with the boys, and tried again."

It had obviously been a long beer, Mirabeau thought, and wondered if "the boys" had been gently prodding him about her just like the women had been prodding her about him. Shaking her head, she sighed and took the phone. "Hello?"

"So Tiny's your life mate," were the first words growled in her ear.

Mirabeau stiffened, then scowled at the phone before saying pleasantly, "Would this be a business call, or pleasure, Lucian?"

"Business," he barked. "Is he or isn't he your life mate?"

Mirabeau grimaced, but snapped, "Yes."

There was a hiss as if he was sucking in air, then Lucian cursed. "Goddamn that Marguerite. She's going to make my life miserable. I was already shorthanded when it came to enforcers, and now I'll be one shorter."

"Well, you're the one who let her convince you to put us together," she pointed out with exasperation. "You could have said no."

"And stop you from meeting a possible life mate?" he asked with outrage. "Not likely, little girl."

Mirabeau found her lips reluctantly curling into a smile. He hadn't called her *little girl* since the death of her family.

"I'm walking you down the aisle," he announced firmly. "Your father would have wanted it."

"There's no walking yet," she gasped, glancing worriedly at Tiny. Dear God, they hardly knew each other, and Lucian had them marrying. "And you haven't lost another hunter. I'll stay the night and tomorrow, then head back as soon as the sun sets, ready for work."

"The hell you will," Lucian snapped.

"I will," she insisted.

"Don't bother. You'd be useless to me anyway. Stay in Port Henry for a while and work Tiny out of your system. That's an order," he added firmly. "And tell Tiny it's an order for him too. Jackie has already agreed and—" He paused abruptly, and Mirabeau heard the murmur of a woman's voice in the background. She only realized it must be Tiny's boss, Jackie, when Lucian's muffled voice said, "All right, all right," before growing louder again as he told her, "Jackie says to tell Tiny she's very happy for him and to take as much time as he needs."

Mirabeau hesitated, her eyes sliding to Tiny and back to the phone, then she asked uncertainly, "What if he doesn't want to?"

"Oh, he wants to, little girl. I already asked him. Enjoy." The last word was followed by a click as he hung up.

"Good-bye to you too," Mirabeau muttered, hitting the button to kill her end of the call. Sighing, she peered at Tiny, cleared her throat, and murmured, "He said we should stay here for a while."

"I heard," he admitted, then asked quietly, "is that all right with you?"

She smiled crookedly. "It doesn't seem like I have much choice. He's my boss, and it's an order."

"That's a cop-out," Tiny said quietly. "Do you want to or not?"

Mirabeau swallowed and avoided his eyes. "I . . . I can't read you . . . and I want you."

"I already knew that, Mirabeau," he pointed out gently. "The question is, are you ready to have a life mate?"

For one minute, she struggled with the question, reluctant to admit that she was, but that was young Mirabeau briefly raising her head and all her fears with it. She wasn't that poor, broken girl anymore. She was an immortal woman, and he

was her life mate, and it didn't matter what she
knew or didn't know about him, or anything else.
The fact was the nanos knew they would be good
together, and as all immortals knew, the nanos
were never wrong. He was her future. Mirabeau
realized suddenly that all the fears she'd been experiencing were just leftover gifts from her uncle's
actions. He'd definitely taken enough already. She
wasn't letting him take Tiny from her too.

"Yes," she said finally, her voice firm and her
chin rising defiantly. "I'm ready."

Tiny started to reach for her, but she stopped
him with a hand on his chest. "What about you?
Are you ready to be my life mate Tiny McGraw?"

"I shouldn't be," he said solemnly. Sliding his
arms around her waist, he drew her closer, managing to press their hips together despite the hand
she had between them, as he whispered, "We
hardly know each other."

"That's true," Mirabeau murmured, as he bent
and pressed a kiss to her forehead.

"I don't know what you like and don't like, what
your beliefs are, religiously or politically, or even
if you want children." He punctuated each point
with another kiss, one to the side of her eye, one to
her cheek, and one to her ear.

Mirabeau murmured something of an agreement, although it sounded more like a moan to
her as her body began to respond to his nearness
and touch.

"We should really talk," he murmured, running his lips across her cheek to press a kiss to the side of her mouth. "Get to know each other."

"Yes," she breathed, forgetting to hold him away and slipping her arms around his shoulders instead. The moment she did, Tiny cupped the back of her head and met her gaze solemnly.

"We'll talk later," he promised.

"Later," Mirabeau agreed, just before his mouth covered hers. His kiss was hot and demanding, and Mirabeau moaned as her body came to roaring life. She then gasped as he caught her by the behind and lifted her up before shifting his hold to her thighs so that her legs shifted around his waist. Mirabeau instinctively hooked her ankles around his back, then gasped and bit his lip as he began to walk across the bedroom, and their bodies rubbed together, bringing on an almost painful need.

When he reached the bed, Tiny set her down on her feet, then quickly and methodically stripped off the tank top she wore. Just as she was reaching to remove his own top, he gave her a push that sent her dropping back onto the bed. He then immediately bent and caught the waistband of her joggers to tug them off quickly. Once he had her naked, Tiny paused to look her over, one hand sliding gently along her heated skin, making her eyes droop to half-mast and her body shiver with pleasure. Mirabeau reached for him then, wanting to feel him on top of her, but he withdrew with a chuckle and straightened, leaving her to watch as he stripped off his own clothes.

As she watched first his T-shirt, then his own joggers hit the floor, Mirabeau traced the outline of his body with hungry eyes and knew it would be a long time before they had that talk . . . a very long time. Perhaps after their first child . . . or the second, she thought, as he came down on top of her, his body firm and hard. And then his mouth covered hers and his hands began to move over her and she stopped thinking altogether and put her trust in the nanos.

LYNSAY SANDS is the national bestselling
author of the Argeneau vampire series as well as
more than thirty historical novels and anthologies
known for their humorous edge. Visit her official
website at *www.lynsaysands.net*.

Hearts Untamed

PAMELA PALMER

Julianne dropped to her hands and knees on the red throw rug, heart racing, perspiration damp on the back of her neck as she yanked boxes from beneath Serenity's bed. She hated this. *Hated* sneaking from one room to the next, a thief in her own home.

Above all, she hated the one who'd put her up to it. *Melisande.* Melisande, with her cruel eyes and terrible truths, who'd appeared a month ago and turned Julianne's world upside down.

Again.

She lifted the wooden lid of a small, flat chest and rifled through the contents with guilty, shaking fingers. Serenity was like a mother to her. She didn't deserve to have her things torn through like this, but Julianne had no choice.

Melisande had demanded that Julianne find and steal a necklace, a rare bloodred moonstone on a silver chain. A necklace hidden somewhere within the mansion that housed the Alexandria Therian enclave. Julianne's home.

And if Julianne failed? Or if anyone learned what she was up to? She and whomever she spilled her secrets to would forever disappear from this world, just as her parents had twenty-one years ago.

They would die. It didn't matter that the Therians were essentially immortal. With the right power, any life could be destroyed.

And Julianne had no doubt Melisande possessed that power. With a flick of her hand, she'd driven Julianne to her knees in pain. With the blink of an eye, she'd appeared and disappeared. With the ease of a wraith, she'd infected Julianne's dreams and stolen her thoughts.

Her threats were all too real.

Julianne's only hope of saving those she loved was to find that necklace before Melisande lost the last of her patience. And to hope that once Melisande had what she'd come for, she'd leave Julianne in peace.

A hope she feared was all too slim.

Voices sounded on the stairs. Julianne's pulse skittered. *Serenity*.

She couldn't get caught because she couldn't explain. Her heart began to thud in her chest. In about thirty seconds Serenity would walk in the room.

Julianne tore through the boxes with badly shaking fingers, pushing things this way and that. Serenity's treasures were simple things. A miniature portrait from hundreds of years ago. A leather wristlet. Yellowed, disintegrating letters. For the most part, Therians were simple people, little different from humans anymore, other than the fact that they didn't age.

They hadn't always been like this. Long ago, the Therians had been the shape-shifters—each possessing the power of an animal, each capable of changing into that animal at will. There had been dozens, maybe even hundreds of different Therian animal lines at one time—wolves, bears, snakes, horses, and any number of predatory cats.

But that way of life had come crashing down millennia ago, when they'd been forced to mortgage their power to save the world. Only nine shape-shifters remained. Nine who still possessed the raw, potent power of their animals. The Feral Warriors. The other Therians lived and worked among the humans, hiding from the deadly draden at night, but otherwise living their long, long lives much as the humans did their far shorter ones.

As Julianne had expected to live her own life. Though all Therians looked thirty, Julianne actually was. She'd graduated from George Washington University seven years ago and taken a job as a physician's assistant to an Alexandria allergist. A fairly normal existence.

For a normal Therian.

Until a month ago, when Melisande arrived carrying the devastating news that she wasn't normal at all.

Footsteps sounded in the hallway, the soft click of Serenity's heels. *She was out of time.* A bead of perspiration rolled between her breasts as she shoved the boxes back under the bed and sprang to her feet, running for the closet. She wrenched open the closet doors just as the bedroom door opened behind her. Her breathing was harsh and uneven.

If only there were someone she could share her awful burden with. *Zeeland.* Once upon a time, Zeeland had been the keeper of all her secrets.

The thought of him brought a harsh longing that raked at her chest and burned the backs of her eyes.

"Hi, Jules. What are you looking for, babe?" Serenity's voice, as always, rang warm and loving.

Julianne glanced over her shoulder at the slender blonde. Guilt curled her fingers, but she fought to keep her voice light and natural, fought to present a calm façade. "Your mint green blouse. I'm in a mint green mood today."

"Sorry, doll. It's at the dry cleaners. Cambria has one about the same color. Or grab anything else you want. What time do you have to be at work?"

"Nine." Julianne snatched a blue blouse. "Guess I'd better get moving." She threw Serenity a smile that trembled at the corners of her mouth, and escaped into the hall. How long could she keep this up?

How long before Melisande lost patience with her for not finding the necklace? How long before Serenity or one of the others figured out something was wrong and started demanding answers she couldn't give, endangering them all?

At least Zeeland wasn't here. As badly as she wished he was still in her life, at least she didn't have to worry about him being harmed by Melisande, too.

He hadn't been in her life for ten years. Not since that horrible, humiliating night.

She'd come to Alexandria, Virginia, twenty-one years ago as an orphaned nine-year-old. Serenity had taken on the task of mothering her, but it was Zeeland who'd taken on the role of protector and best friend. He'd helped her recover from her grief and find the strength within herself to move past it.

But as she'd gotten older, her feelings for him had changed. Grown. He'd become her first crush, and eventually, her first love.

Ten years ago, at the age of twenty, she'd made the terrible mistake of telling him she wanted him to be the one to take her virginity.

He'd been horrified.

Even now, her skin turned cold and clammy at the memory of that night. Of the look of disgust that had contorted his handsome face.

He'd ordered her away from him, and she'd fled to her room. The next morning, he was gone. He'd left for the British enclaves without ever saying good-bye. Without ever contacting her again. Others heard from him, but she never did.

The pain of that night had dulled. But as hard as she tried, she couldn't stop missing him. She couldn't stop the aching need for his strength by her side.

Julianne returned to her room long enough to dress for work, chills skating over her flesh as they did whenever she entered her room.

Her bedroom, the one place that should be her refuge, had become the place she feared the most. It was here that Melisande came to her. Every few days, she appeared. And it had been three days since her last awful visit.

Ready for work, Julianne escaped her room. As she descended the stairs, she heard Grayson's voice roar through the house as he strode into view.

"I have news!" Broad-shouldered with sandy brown hair, Grayson had the physique of a bear and the easy good nature of a poorly behaved Great Dane.

"A little louder, Gray," Cambria called from the

kitchen. "They might not have heard you down in South Carolina."

Grayson ignored the teasing admonition. "Zeeland's coming home!"

Julianne froze on the bottom step, grabbing for the railing.

Half a dozen voices exclaimed in pleasure and joy.

"When?" Serenity's excited voice called from close behind Julianne.

Julianne pulled herself to one side, her limbs stiff with shock, as she let Serenity pass.

"Tomorrow," Grayson replied. "He just called."

Tomorrow. Julianne uncurled her fingers from the rail and forced her feet forward. Stumbling into the foyer, she grabbed a set of car keys from the bowl and escaped into the sunshine. *Shit, shit, shit.* For ten long years, though she'd dreaded the confrontation, she'd desperately longed to see Zeeland again.

But not now. Not now.

No one had ever known her as well as Zeeland had. No one had ever seen her as clearly.

And never had she had so much to hide.

Chapter Two

A rap sounded at the door the next afternoon, the sound Julianne had been dreading. Tension raced up her spine.

"The guys just called," Cambria called through the door. "Zeeland's plane was on time. They'll be here in about fifteen minutes."

Julianne's pulse threatened to run away from her. "Thanks, Cam. I'll meet you downstairs." As she heard Cambria's steps retreat down the hall, she buried her face in her hands.

Zeeland is coming home.

Her skin flushed with old, bitter humiliation, butterflies fluttered excitedly in her stomach, and a harsh longing wrapped itself round and round her heart until the pressure was almost too much to bear.

A dozen times since yesterday, she'd debated running away to another enclave until Zeeland's visit was over. Or even just hiding in her room with the door locked. But with Melisande hovering over her life, her room was no refuge.

And she knew Zeeland much too well. He was as stubborn as an ox and as determined as a jungle cat hunting prey. If he decided he wanted to see her, no locked door stood a chance against him. Nor could she flee anywhere that he wouldn't find her.

If he wanted to find her. A very big *if.*

No, there was no choice but to grit out his visit and hope he paid her little attention. The hardest part was going to be pretending to be indifferent herself.

She dressed quickly in a sleeveless turquoise sheath she'd picked up at Lord & Taylor's a couple of months ago with Serenity and Cambria, then sat at the dressing table and applied her makeup with a light, nervous hand. Therians might live forever, but they kept up with the fashions and took pride in good grooming. Especially when they were expecting company, as they were tonight.

Cambria and Serenity had been cooking all day, preparing for the impromptu welcome-home dinner for Zeeland. According to Cambria, a few of the Feral Warriors might even make an appearance. Though all Therian males tended to tower over their human counterparts, the Ferals were the biggest, the strongest, and without a doubt, the least civilized of the race. Things tended to get interesting when the Ferals appeared.

But the only one she both longed and dreaded to see was Zeeland.

Pulling the elastic band out of her hair, Julianne let the dark waves tumble around her shoulders. She grabbed her hairbrush and was nearly finished brushing out her hair when she felt that all-too-familiar trip of power.

Her breath caught. Fear rippled along the surface of her skin as an unnatural, pine-scented breeze blew through her room, raising the hair on her arms.

In the dressing-table mirror, Melisande appeared behind her, a ghostly figure of a woman.

Julianne shot to her feet and whirled, backing away from her nemesis.

"Melisande." The name shot from her throat, a low burst of air.

The spiritlike woman floated before her, glowing a faint reddish orange. Petite and slender, Melisande dressed like a warrior of old in a brown tunic and tan leggings, a knife strapped at her waist. Her face was deceptively delicate and pretty, framed by golden blond hair pulled back in a long braid.

She looked sweet and harmless to anyone who

didn't notice the brittle look in her eyes or the cruel twist of her mouth.

For a thousand years, the Therians had believed Melisande's race, the Ilinas, extinct. For a thousand years, they'd been wrong.

"The moonstone, Julianne." Melisande's eyes snapped with warning.

Once, Julianne had demanded to know why the woman needed it. She'd been told the Queen of the Ilinas was ill and in need of the stone to heal her.

Julianne lifted her hands, palms out. "I've looked everywhere. Over and over. Give me a hint, Melisande. Anything to narrow the search."

Melisande scowled. "It's somewhere in this house. I can feel its power, but not its source." Melisande stepped . . . *floated* . . . closer. "You're useless, little sister. Worthless. But you will find that moonstone."

Melisande's bright blue eyes gleamed with threat. "I'm giving you one more day, Julianne. When I return tomorrow, you'll give it to me."

Julianne stared at her, a dull quaking beginning deep inside, half fury, half fear. "You're not listening. I've looked everywhere. *It's not here.*"

"It's here! If I could search for it myself, I would."

But she couldn't because the Ilinas were determined to keep their existence a secret. From what little Julianne had been able to ascertain, the Ilinas had faked their extinction a thousand years ago in order to hide from a dangerous enemy, to protect their race. And they would kill to keep that secret.

Something Julianne's mother had failed to do when she'd told Julianne's father her true heritage. That she was half-Ilina. They'd both paid for that bit of honesty.

Julianne would never tell anyone. *Ever*. She would never endanger the people she loved in that way.

Melisande's small hand clenched around the hilt of her knife. "If you haven't found the moonstone by tomorrow, you'll feel my wrath, little sister." Her voice turned low and terrible as her lip curled nastily. "Tomorrow, one of your friends will die."

Julianne jerked as if she'd been hit, her jaw dropping. "You can't do that! They don't know anything. I've told them nothing. I've kept them safe!"

"Then find the moonstone!"

Julianne felt her own lip curl back, fury washing away the fear that had ridden her for a month. An odd tingling sensation began to flow through her limbs.

She glared at the Ilina. "Retract your threat, or I'll do nothing more to help you."

An ugly smile formed on the spirit woman's face. "You would threaten me?"

"The only reason I was willing to help you was to save my friends. If you're going to hurt them anyway, I'll do nothing more to help you. You can find that moonstone yourself."

Melisande's mouth compressed, her eyes beginning to narrow as the tingling in Julianne's body grew worse. She felt as if her blood had become carbonated and was beginning to fizz in her veins like champagne.

Melisande made a sound of disgust.

Julianne lifted her hand . . . and stared.

Her fingers looked as mistlike and insubstantial as Melisande's. She gasped, her eyes widening with horror. The last of her doubts about her heritage died as she stared at her traitorous flesh.

"Why is this happening?"

The cruelty and anger had drained from Melisande's expression, replaced by a look of resignation. "Violent emotion apparently triggered the change in you. When you were young, I had hoped you had too little Ilina blood ever to turn to mist. I'd hoped you could live your life free of any knowledge of us. But I felt the power in you spark to life at your maturation. I feared it was only a matter of time. And I was right."

"You've been watching me?"

"All your life. As I did your mother."

"Why?"

"It is my job to eliminate all threats to the secret of the race." She held out her hand. "You must come with me, little sister."

Julianne stared at that small, mistlike hand. "You'll kill me."

"You will merely abide in the Crystal Realm for a time."

"Where I'll die. Don't play me for a fool, Melisande. The Ilinas may have been out of sight for a thousand years, but we haven't forgotten you. And everyone knows no corporeal being can live long in that place."

Her gut cramped with fear. She'd become a true threat to them. "Tell me how to change back, Melisande." Her words were half demand, half desperate plea. "Tell me how to keep this from happening again so I don't give you away."

Melisande's jaw clenched and unclenched, a debate clearly raging in her eyes.

"Julianne?" Cambria's voice called through the door. "The guys just pulled up. Zeeland's here!"

Melisande flicked her hand. Pain pierced Julianne's flesh as if she'd been hit with a dozen darts, sharp needles of misery that stole her breath and made her eyes water.

Was this it then? Her death?

But before the thought could turn to terror, the pain began to fade. Her hands returned to flesh and blood.

Melisande's face turned hard. "Control your emotions, little sister. This is not over."

A cool, pine-scented breeze blew through the room, and Melisande was gone.

Julianne sank onto the stool behind her, at once furious and terrified. As the last of the pain disappeared from her body, she wrapped shaking arms around her middle and stared at the place where Melisande had stood.

What am I going to do?

The knock sounded again. "Julianne?"

"I'll be right there," she managed, barely controlling the quaver in her voice. She clutched the dressing table, afraid she was going to be sick.

Zeeland. Why now? Why had he decided to return *now?* As much as it would hurt, she could only hope he still harbored the disgust he'd felt for her that last night, that he'd continue to ignore her as he'd done for ten years. Because if he didn't, how was she ever going to keep him from seeing the turmoil inside her and demanding its source?

Outside, she heard the slam of car doors and the glad shouts of welcome.

Zee.

Her stomach a mass of nerves, Julianne pushed to her feet and moved stiffly to the closet to find a pair of heels to go with her dress. For ten years, she'd dreamed of this day. For ten years, she'd dreaded it.

But all her reasons for both—embarrassment, hurt, love—no longer weighed against the fear that now consumed her life.

It no longer mattered how Zeeland felt about her—whether he was glad to see her or tried to keep his distance. It was of little consequence now whether he still saw her as the child he'd possessed only brotherly feelings for, or as a woman he might someday desire.

Only one thing mattered.

Getting him out of here. Sending him back to Britain.

Keeping him, and all those she loved, alive.

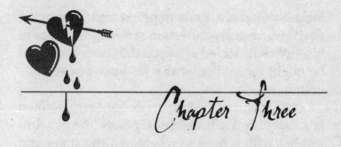

Chapter Three

Zeeland had not changed at all.

Julianne stilled halfway down the stairs, her hand gripping the wooden railing until her knuckles turned white. He was even more handsome than she remembered, his short dark hair framing a classic face that could be as still as an evening lake or, as now, charmingly expressive as he returned the greetings of the Therians gathered around him.

His shoulders were broad beneath the navy blazer and striped dress shirt, his waist trim, his legs long as he stood among the tallest of the men in the room.

As she watched, he looked up. As if feeling her gaze on him, he turned unerringly toward her.

His dark brown eyes zeroed in on her. His gaze

locked onto hers, grabbing hold and burrowing deep. Warmth and affection softened the lines of his face as he stared at her, dashing any hope that he might ignore her, or that he'd maybe even forgotten her.

Love for him rushed up inside her, tearing down her carefully built defenses, nearly overwhelming her with a need to race down the stairs and into his arms as she used to do as a child. But she couldn't give in to the need. Not this time.

If his anger with her was gone, as it seemed to be, she was the one who would have to force the distance between them. The last thing she could afford was for him to get too close. To see too much.

She was going to have to pretend he no longer meant anything to her. Even if it was the greatest lie ever told.

Julianne tore her gaze from Zeeland's, focusing on herself, on the pounding of her heart, and on the need to get her feet moving down the stairs even though part of her longed to turn and flee back to her room.

Panic rose, constricting her throat. How could she face him? How could she hide how she felt about him? How could she keep him from knowing anything was wrong when *everything* was wrong?

Out of the corner of her eye, she saw him start forward. Toward her.

Her pulse careened, her breathing turned shallow and erratic.

Clearly there would be no delaying this reunion. She pulled her mask of friendly indifference tight around her and held on fast.

Julianne.

Zeeland started toward her. As she'd stood on the stair, as still as a statue, her brilliant turquoise gaze had met his, not with pleasure and welcome but with a wary guardedness. Something clenched deep inside him, twisting until it hurt.

Where was his Julianne, his Sunshine? Where was the bright-eyed sprite who'd always flown into his arms with a glad cry whenever he returned?

The woman who descended the stairs was a stranger, her back ramrod straight, her steps measured and controlled.

Too controlled. He hadn't seen her in ten years, not since before she'd come of age. Yet even from here he could see the stiffness in her step.

He pushed past his friends without a word of apology, drawn to her by the same invisible force that had drawn him to her from the day she'd arrived at the house twenty-one years ago. As if he'd always known her. As if she'd always been a part of him.

Why had he stayed away so long?

He'd forgotten how bright her eyes were. He'd

forgotten how strongly his body reacted to the mere sight of her. Goddess, but he'd forgotten how much he missed her.

For ten years, she'd haunted him, her soft beauty stealing into his thoughts at the most inopportune times. For a decade, the memories of her smile and her laughter had remained tucked like precious gems deep inside his heart.

Where was that smile now? That laughter?

He'd run into Ryland in London yesterday and asked about her, as he always did. He'd asked if her music still rang through the house at all hours. Ryland's offhand comment that she'd developed a sudden fondness for Beethoven had sent his heart plummeting and a hundred warning bells ringing in his head.

Ryland hadn't seemed to understand the significance of Beethoven. Zeeland doubted anyone but he ever had. If Julianne was playing Beethoven, something was wrong. Seriously wrong.

He'd wrapped up his business in London and gotten on the next flight to D.C.

Zeeland reached the stairs, meeting Julianne as she reached the bottom step.

She smiled at him, but the smile was a pale imitation of a Julianne smile and didn't reach her eyes. Her gaze almost connected with his, but not quite. As if she focused not on his eyes but his cheek.

Goddess, but she was beautiful. Her skin creamy

perfection, her nose small and straight, her eyes a brilliant turquoise framed by long, dark lashes.

Her scent wrapped around him, a sweet scent that had always reminded him of honeysuckle in the rain. A scent that had haunted his dreams and now wove itself into the very fabric of his flesh, into every drop of his blood, heating him. Hardening him.

Coming back was a mistake.

"Hello, Zeeland. Welcome back." She said the right words, even injecting an appropriate level of warmth into them, but the words fell flat on his ears. They were lies. An act. She wasn't glad he was here at all.

He felt as if she'd plunged a knife through his chest. But what had he expected? That he could return whenever he wanted, and she'd be happy to see him?

Yes, dammit.

Instead, she was treating him like a stranger. Was she punishing him for staying away so long? For never once calling her? Never writing?

Ah, shit. He'd hurt her. Of course he had. Why hadn't he ever considered what it would do to her when he'd left so abruptly? Right after she'd offered him her virginity.

"Julianne." He clenched his hands into fists to keep from reaching for her, because that part of him that had always been tuned to her sensed she was on the verge of bolting. "I'm sorry."

Her smile faltered. "For what?" Genuine confusion lit her eyes. She didn't seem to know.

He studied her, looking past the beauty his eyes had craved, seeing the smudges of dark circles under her eyes and the paleness beneath the flush staining her cheeks. Beneath the pretense of calm, he sensed tightly controlled emotion, though what that emotion was, he couldn't tell. It was more than simple anger. Much more. His instincts sensed . . . fear.

Dammit. How long had she been like this? Why had no one told him? Could no one else see it?

Why had he stayed away so long?

"I hear you've been playing Beethoven again," he said softly.

Her gaze jerked fully to his, her eyes flaring open, her ripe mouth widening with dismay. Need slammed into him hard, tightening his body and squeezing his heart. A need to sweep her into his arms and hold her close. To protect her as he'd done since she was nine. A need to taste that sweet mouth and make love to her as she'd begged him to that fateful night ten years ago.

She wrenched back control, her gaze falling to his cheek. "It's just music," she said defensively.

But he knew better. They both knew better.

"You know you can tell me anything, Sunshine," he said quietly. The desire to touch her was almost a physical ache centered right in the middle of his chest. A desire that was so much more than physical.

She smiled that painfully false smile. "Thanks, Zeeland. I appreciate that, but I'm fine. Really. It's nice to have you back." She sidestepped him, dismissing him.

He shoved his hands in his pockets to keep from grabbing her arm to keep her from escaping. This wasn't the time or the place. They had an audience, he realized belatedly. The whole damned enclave was watching them with sharp interest. Julianne was hardly going to confide anything to him here.

But sooner or later, she was going to tell him everything. That was a promise he made them both.

The moment Julianne left his side, the others surged forward to surround him again.

Grayson slapped him on the back with a laugh. "Come on, Zee." Gray's hair was as short as Zeeland's own, the spider tattoo at the corner of his eye wiggling between the sudden smile lines. "You should see the spread we've got laid out. A true welcome feast. I don't know about you, but I'm starving."

"Your timing is perfect, Zeeland." Serenity hooked her arm through his, her eyes warm. "Tomorrow night is the big Valentine's Day party for the enclaves, and it's our turn to host."

Grayson laughed. "Another captive streamer-hanger. Tell you what, Serenity. Zee and I will be responsible for fetching the beer. How's that?"

Serenity rolled her eyes. "And it'll take you all day to do it, I'm sure."

Gray shrugged. "Hey, these things can't be rushed."

Zeeland caught a flash of turquoise rounding the corner and knew Julianne had made her getaway. For now. The Valentine's party would be a nuisance. The more people in the house, the harder he'd find it to get her alone.

But get her alone he would.

His eyes narrowed with determination. Like the hunter he was, he'd back off for now and let her believe she was safe. He'd enjoy being home again, among his friends.

But the moment he found the right opportunity, he'd spring. Soon enough, he'd get to the bottom of the mystery that had become Julianne.

Nothing was going to stop him.

Especially not Julianne.

Leaning back in his chair at one of the dining tables several hours later, Zeeland regaled the others with tales of his life with the British Guard. While his tablemates leaned forward, listening intently to his stories, his own attention remained elsewhere. On the music wafting in from the grand piano in the living room.

Julianne's music.

Not Beethoven tonight, but Vivaldi. She wouldn't play Beethoven in front of him. But not even Vivaldi was safe from the emotions that must be wreaking havoc inside her.

Her musical gift was as rare and fine as any he'd ever heard, weaving her heart and emotions into a brilliant, visceral tapestry. A tapestry he sometimes thought only he could see. Tonight was a prime example. Could no one else hear the anguish in the music flowing around them? Could no one else sense the fear?

The sound of it seeped into his flesh, tearing at him until he felt as if he'd bleed from the plaintive cry of Julianne's heart. Not since she was nine had he heard such anguish torn from those keys.

She'd been sent to them from the New York enclave after her parents disappeared in an apparent Mage attack. For two weeks, she'd shed no tears, but she'd played the enclave's piano incessantly, pouring her grief into her music. Beethoven. Only Beethoven.

Even then, she'd had an extraordinary ability to weave the music. From the start, he'd heard the depth of her grief in her music.

She'd had no one her own age, for children were rare among the immortal Therians, so he'd befriended her and found a delightful and precious friend in return. He'd watched her grow up, watched her turn from a cute child into a beautiful young woman. A woman he'd eventually come to desire.

She'd been eighteen the first time he'd realized it. Eighteen when his love for the child began to morph into something altogether different. Altogether inappropriate. She was seven years too young.

Therian law forbade the young from entering into the highly physical, carnal world of their elders until they were twenty-five. A not-unreasonable demand as most Therians lived for millennia.

For two years, he'd played the role of best friend as his desire for her had grown. And as her own for him had blossomed. When she was twenty, she'd come to him, raw desire burning in her virgin's eyes, and told him she wanted him to be her first. That very night. She couldn't wait another five years.

He'd sent her to her room with barely contained control, then lain awake all night in a fever of need, imagining her beneath him.

The next morning, he'd packed his suitcase and returned to Scotland, where he'd trained with the Therian Guard years before. He'd known he wouldn't survive another night in that house with Julianne, let alone five years.

But he hadn't stayed away five. He'd drunk himself into a stupor the night she turned of age, but he hadn't come home.

Now he was furious with himself for leaving her unprotected from whatever had hurt her this time.

"Hey, Squirt!" Grayson called into the living room, using the name for Julianne only he used. "How about some show tunes?"

Serenity rose, signaling the end of the meal. The half dozen with kitchen duty started clearing tables while the others sauntered into the living room, most gathering around the piano.

Zeeland stayed back, propping a shoulder against one of the ornately carved pillars holding up the high ceiling, where he could watch the pianist without crowding her. Yet.

With the others pressing around her, she dutifully switched to livelier music, holding her heart and emotions at bay. The music, while beautifully played, rang flat and false. As false as her smile.

No one else seemed to notice.

Hell, from the way the men were watching her, he suspected she could play nursery-school ditties, and they wouldn't notice.

From out of nowhere, a fist of raw jealousy punched him in the gut. His hands clenched as the primal need to rip out their throats barreled through him. They had no right to look at her that way. She wasn't . . .

Wasn't what? Old enough?

With a slam, he remembered she was. And had been for more than five years.

The thought of what that meant nearly brought him to his knees. Five years, she'd been of age. Sexually active.

And Therians were nothing if not sexually active. Unlike humans, Therians saw neither need nor desire to be monogamous.

Conception was rare. Having different partners increased the likelihood that a female might conceive. And taking a mate was even rarer. The mating bond between two Therians was more than a mere promise. It was a physical bond that could never be broken. No one in his right mind willingly bound themselves to another . . . any other . . . for eternity.

He watched Julianne, his gaze caressing her lovely, pensive face. A Therian female five years past her maturity had likely made love scores, if not hundreds, of times by now. A woman as beautiful as Julianne would have males lining up, seeking her attention . . . and her bed . . . every night.

Jealousy threatened to choke him. But it was regret that tasted like bile in his mouth.

She'd asked him to be her first. Perhaps he might still have been had he come back when she turned of age. But he hadn't.

Goddess, he was an idiot.

"Those are damned dark thoughts going through your head, Zee."

Zeeland turned as Hawke joined him. The Feral Warrior, one of three who'd joined them tonight, was built much as Zeeland himself, tall and lean, with the sleek muscles of a swimmer or distance runner. The hawk shifter had been his tutor when Zeeland was a kid, before Hawke was marked by the goddess to become a Feral Warrior. He'd known Hawke all his life and counted him among his most trusted friends.

Zeeland fought to smooth the lines of his face. "Just thinking."

Hawke merely lifted a single steeply arched eyebrow in the way he always had when he didn't believe him.

"Does Julianne have a favorite among that lot?" Zeeland knew he was giving away his thoughts, but didn't really care.

Hawke shrugged. "I'm not around here enough to know. She's grown into a beauty, though, hasn't she?"

Acid ate into his bones. How many men had Julianne known?

I could have been her first.

The thought of Julianne in another man's arms, spreading her thighs to cradle another man's body, had his teeth grinding to dust inside his mouth.

Even the other two Ferals watched her, dammit. Kougar and Jag had arrived with Hawke shortly before dinner. While Jag watched Julianne with the eyes of a hunter stalking prey, Kougar's cold gaze followed her every move as if she were a bug under a microscope.

He knew none of the Ferals all that well except for Hawke. Most had been marked centuries before he was born. It used to irk him that he'd never been marked by the spirit of one of the animals to become a Feral Warrior himself, but the animal spirits could only mark the strongest of their own lines. And the only Feral who'd died since Zee's birth had been the fox shifter four years ago, his animal spirit marking the kid, Foxx, in his stead.

The Therians had no way of knowing their own animal heritage except for the stories told by their forebears. And occasionally the dreams.

For all he knew, he was descended from none of the nine remaining lines. So he served his race in another capacity, as a member of the Guard, protecting the enclaves that were too far away to be under the Ferals' protection.

Julianne played for nearly an hour, her audience remaining tight around her the entire time. But as her last song came to an end, and she rose gracefully, she was immediately surrounded by men vying for her attention.

Including the Feral, Jag.

Jag stood out among the other men, a little taller, a little broader through the shoulders and chest, and carrying a hell of a lot more attitude.

He pushed the others aside and slung his arm around Julianne's shoulders. "Nice job, sugar. How about you trail those magic fingers over me?"

"Jag . . ." Hawke groaned beside him.

Julianne attempted, without success, to free herself from Jag's hold. Was the Feral the reason she was playing Beethoven? Had he hurt her?

I'll kill the son of a bitch.

Zeeland didn't think, only acted, pushing his way through the throng to reach Julianne's side.

"Release her, Jag."

The surly Feral's lip curled, and he pulled her closer. "Finders, keepers."

Fury surged. Zeeland balled his hand and swung, planting his fist solidly in the jaguar shifter's jaw. Another man, he might have tackled, but not a Feral. Not if he wanted to live.

As Jag stumbled backward two steps, Zeeland grabbed Julianne's arm, freeing her even as he kept her from falling. As he shoved her behind him, Jag righted himself, violence in his eyes.

The shifter's fingertips erupted with claws. Inch-long fangs dropped from his upper jaw, while the incisors in his lower jaw grew and sharpened. His eyes changed, the irises expanding until no white showed, until his eyes looked like those of a jungle cat.

A very pissed-off jungle cat.

Jag hadn't actually shifted into a jaguar, but only *gone feral*—that in-between place between man and beast, a place of lost tempers that could be fatal to any creature who couldn't draw claws and fangs of his own.

Pulling one of the knives he always carried, Zeeland crouched into a fighting stance and met the angry Feral's gaze. "You really want to do this, cat?"

Jag smiled with that mouth full of fangs, a look in his eyes as sharp as a well-honed blade. And oddly cunning. "Julianne and I are old friends, aren't we, sugar?"

Jealousy roared in his ears, but as he tensed

to spring, Hawke and Kougar pushed between them.

Kougar cuffed Jag hard. "Time to go."

"Like hell," the jaguar shifter growled.

Hawke's hand landed on Zeeland's shoulder. His gaze turned to Jag. "You've already been ordered to stay away from two enclaves. Do you really want to make it three?"

Jag made a sound deep in his throat that sounded exactly like the growl of a jaguar. But his fangs and claws retracted, and he swung away, stalking out of the living room, Kougar close behind him.

Zeeland stared after him, his breathing heavy, his fist clenching tight around his knife. Everything inside him itched for a fight. If he found out that Feral had hurt Julianne, no one and nothing was standing between them next time.

Hawke turned back and met Zeeland's gaze, Hawke's own seeing too much, asking questions Zeeland wasn't prepared to answer.

"I'll be back tomorrow night for the Valentine's party." He lifted one winged brow. "Without Jag."

Hawke released Zeeland's shoulder and thrust out his hand, but when Zeeland would have clasped it, Hawke reached farther, gripping Zeeland just below the elbow in the greeting the Ferals reserved for one another and a select few outside their ranks. Being offered such was a sign of deep respect and friendship, and Zeeland accepted it as such.

Zeeland dipped his head. "It's good to see you, Hawke."

Hawke smiled. "Tomorrow."

As Hawke strode off behind his companions, Zeeland sheathed his knife and turned to find Julianne slipping away behind him. He was in no damned mood for any more games.

He caught up to her in three long strides, his hand clamping around her upper arm.

Her surprised gaze jerked up. For a single moment, fear glittered in her turquoise eyes. Then a curtain fell, a mask of indifference.

"We're going to talk," he told her. "*Now.*"

"I need to help in the kitchen, Zeeland."

"Damn the kitchen."

She tried to pull away, but his fingers tightened. It occurred to him he was treating her little better than Jag had. But where Jag had been looking out for his own needs, Zeeland's sole concern was Julianne.

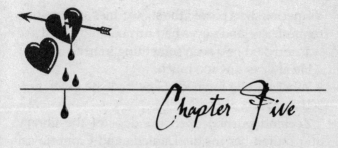

Chapter Five

Julianne clenched her jaw, fighting panic, as Zeeland steered her to the door of the library. She had to get away from him. He couldn't know what was going on.

In some ways he hadn't changed. He was the same take-charge Zeeland he'd always been. As a child, she'd believed in him implicitly, knowing she could depend on him above all others. She'd trusted him to move heaven and earth to keep her safe.

Until the day she'd driven him away, and he'd turned his back on her.

And she'd grown up enough to know no one could keep her safe.

She'd thought Zeeland had forgiven her for ten years ago, but now she wasn't so sure. Shortly after dinner, as she'd played the show tunes at Grayson's request, Zeeland's eyes had turned angry, and she was terrified he'd seen something in her own.

He always saw too much.

What had he learned? How had she given herself away?

Zeeland pushed open the door of the library and pulled her inside. Daniella and Cambria sat on the window seat, their conversation dying.

"Zeeland," Daniella said by way of greeting, her eyes lighting up.

"Ladies. If you'll excuse us, I need a word with Julianne in private."

Cambria and Daniella exchanged amused, interested glances, their encouraging gazes turning to her.

Couldn't they see his anger? They acted like they thought he was interested in her, but there was nothing soft in his touch. They'd like nothing better, she realized, than for Zeeland to develop an interest in her and decide to return to Alexandria for good.

She loved them both, but they didn't have a clue what was going on. As the pair rose, she was infinitely glad she didn't have to have this conversation in front of them.

The door clicked, leaving them alone. Zeeland released her, and she stifled the urge to run, knowing Zeeland too well. He was determined to have it out with her. Whatever *it* was.

Goddess help her, she had to stay in control. And the best way to do that was to go on the offensive.

She swung to face him. "That was rude."

"They'll get over it. You've been avoiding me since I got here, and I've had enough. You're going to tell me why you're playing Beethoven, and you're going to tell me now, Julianne." He crossed his arms over his chest. "Start talking."

Ten years he'd been gone, yet he acted like he hadn't left at all. Like he expected them to simply pick up where they'd left off, with him acting like an overprotective older brother.

The worst of it was that there was nothing she wanted more than to lay her multitude of problems firmly in his lap.

But she couldn't.

She had to convince him he was mistaken. Crossing her arms over her own chest, she managed to give him a long-suffering look even as she felt as if she held herself together by a thread. "What exactly do you want to talk about, Zeeland?"

"Dammit, Julianne." He grabbed her shoulders.

She began to tremble beneath his touch, her longing to step into the circle of his arms almost too much to bear. He couldn't know. She couldn't let him know!

As if he could see right through her, could see her crumbling inside, his grip softened, his hands caressing instead of gripping.

"Sunshine . . ." The name he'd called her since he'd coaxed the first smile out of her all those years ago sounded soft and caring, tearing a strip from her soul. His warm hands slid down her upper arms and back up again, firm, yet infinitely gentle. "Something's wrong, Julianne. I see it in your eyes. I hear it in your music. I feel it. You're *trembling*, sweetheart." His brows pulled down, his mouth hardening. "Is it Jag? Is he the one that hurt you?"

She couldn't hide her surprise, and he seemed to see the truth clearly enough.

His brown eyes lost that razor-hard edge as his gaze searched hers. "Confide in me, Sunshine. You know you can tell me anything."

The velvet-steel promise in his words tore at her resolve. Everything within her begged to believe he could handle her truths and keep them both safe. But she wasn't a child anymore. She knew even childhood heroes could die.

And the only thing she could do for either of them was push him away.

"Zeeland . . . I have nothing to confide. I'm fine."

His grip on her tightened, the plea sharp in his eyes. "Don't lie to me. Please?"

"I'm all grown-up, Zee. I have a job and a life and relationships that have gotten complicated. You've been gone ten years. You don't know me anymore."

"I was told you weren't with anyone in particular. Did they lie to me?"

"No," she said with a sigh. "There's no one in particular." Everyone in the enclave knew it.

He stared at her, searching her face and her eyes, looking too deep. It was all she could do not to turn away, but she *had* to make him believe she was fine.

"Juli." His expression softened, his hands caressed her shoulders. "I'm sorry. I shouldn't have left without telling you I was going. I should have called you."

She stared at him, her brows drawing down with confusion. Had he forgotten that night? Forgotten why he left?

Or was he only pretending, as she was?

She shrugged, pulling that mask of indifference more firmly into place. "You were busy. As was I."

"You're mad at me. I don't blame you."

Mad? "I'm not mad, Zeeland. Please don't take this the wrong way, but I'm not anything with regards to you." She swallowed hard, forcing the lie. "I barely remember you."

His mouth tightened, and he watched her, studying her. A single dark brow rose. "You barely remember the man you offered your virginity to?" he asked softly.

She flinched. Goddess, she couldn't do this. "Let me go, Zeeland. I was young and foolish, and you'd turned my head. I'm not that girl anymore."

His thumbs slid along the fabric covering her collarbones, but she felt the warmth of his flesh right through the dress. "So you feel nothing for me, now?"

"No."

"Not anger?"

"Why would I be angry?"

"Not resentment?"

"Again, why?"

He released one shoulder and lifted his hand to brush his knuckles lightly over her cheek.

Her heart tripped, sensation racing over her skin. Her pulse began to pound as she watched his eyes darken.

"Not desire?" he asked softly.

"*Don't*." Julianne jerked away from his touch, stepping back out of his reach as the old humiliation rose to swamp her. How could he . . . ? He'd acted like she was a slut for offering herself to him ten years ago and now . . . now he was treating her like one?

She whirled away from him, but he caught her before she'd taken a step.

"Juli . . ."

Tears burned her eyes. If they started falling, if he saw them, her humiliation would be complete. "*Let me go, Zeeland.*"

"Dammit, Julianne, *talk to me*. What just happened? I always used to be able to read you, but I'm lost here. I'm sorry for abandoning you ten years ago. It was unforgivable. But I did it for a reason. A reason I always assumed you knew. *Don't you know why I left?"*

He gripped her jaw and lifted her face, forcing her to look at him.

She had to blink back the tears to see him through the moisture. "Don't make me say it, Zee. I know. I saw the look of horror on your face. I heard the anger in your voice when you ordered me to my room. I felt the disgust in your hands when you pushed me away."

She'd been five years too young, but she hadn't wanted to wait. She'd loved him too much. Wanted him too badly.

To her utter humiliation, the tears began to fall. To her mortification, Zee began to smile. It was a sad smile that didn't meet his eyes, but it was a smile all the same.

"You were wrong, sweetheart. On all counts. It wasn't disgust or anger I was feeling. Not with you. I'd been riding a razor-sharp edge of control with you for two years. Wanting you. But you were too young. My control had been thinning by the day because you were starting to feel the same. I could see the desire in your eyes, but you were too young!"

Julianne shook her head. "No." He couldn't just rewrite ten years of her life.

But Zeeland didn't stop. "And when you offered me your virginity that night, it was all I could do not to haul you into my arms and cover your mouth with mine. If I had, I knew deep inside my soul, I wouldn't have been able to pull back. I would have given you exactly what you asked me to, exactly what we both wanted. So I pushed you away with the last ounce of strength I possessed and ordered you out of my reach before I broke the law of our kind. And I left, putting an ocean between us so I couldn't lose my resolve until you were of age."

"Why didn't you tell me?"

"I thought you knew."

"Why didn't you ever call? I thought you forgot about me."

Zeeland groaned. "I couldn't stop thinking about you. If I'd heard your voice . . . I don't think I could have stayed away. Instead, I talked to Serenity and Gray. I asked about you, checked up on you, nearly every day, Sunshine. Nearly every day."

She stared at him with a mixture of disbelief and wonder. "I didn't know. I knew they talked to you, but they never told me you asked about me."

"I asked them not to say anything. I suppose I was afraid you'd try to find me."

"I might have." If she'd known he still cared. If she'd realized she hadn't sent him away in disgust. Her heart tried to lift, tried to shake off ten years of carrying the weight of that night, but something still didn't fit.

"If you stayed away because I wasn't of age,

why didn't you come back when I turned twenty-five?"

He watched her for long minutes, his expression at once thoughtful and pained. "I don't know," he said at last.

But she knew. At some time during those ten years, she'd stopped mattering. Nothing had really changed at all. Maybe he hadn't left for the reason she'd thought, but in the end, it was all the same.

"Zeeland, it happened a long time ago. We're not the same people we were then." He had no idea how true that was in her case. She wasn't what either of them had thought.

Zeeland cupped her face in his hands, his brown eyes warm and soft as he looked down at her. "I stayed away too long, Julianne, but I'm here now." His thumb traced her cheekbone, his touch sending small shivers of delight skating over her skin.

His expression tightened, his eyes turning impossibly darker. "I haven't stopped wanting you."

His words sent a rush of damp heat straight to her core, as her pulse leaped into a fast, erratic pounding.

But with the flood of desire came dismay. This was worse than his probing questions. How could she push him away when all she wanted to do was to lean into his touch?

She steeled herself against the warmth of his fingers and the heat in his eyes. "I'm sorry, Zeeland, but I no longer feel the same way about you." To her relief, her words came out with just the right amount of regret and pity.

But his expression told her he didn't believe her. Not one bit.

Lightly, he brushed the pad of his thumb across her lower lip, startling a soft gasp from her. She told herself to move, to back away, but she couldn't. His touch snared her in a net of sensations. Wonder sang through her heart. He'd never been horrified by her. He'd wanted her all along.

But it was too late.

"You've never been a liar, Julianne," he said softly. "Don't lie to me now."

Her whole life had turned into one huge lie. "Zeeland, let me go."

Instead, he lowered his face as if he meant to kiss her. Panic shot through her. She'd wanted this for too long. Too long. If he kissed her now, she'd be lost.

She turned her head. His lips brushed her cheek, his breath stirring the wisps of hair at her temple.

A shudder went through her. "Don't."

He ignored her whispered plea, trailing kisses along her cheekbone, around the curve of her ear, and down her jaw.

Her body shivered and burned. "Zeeland, *please.*"

He held her prisoner with her own need as his lips trailed lower, to the sensitive skin of her neck. Teasing, licking. How many times had she dreamed of this? Of Zeeland taking her into his arms as a man does a woman? Of Zeeland *wanting* her?

"*Zee.*" On a shuddered sigh, she reached for him, her will crumbling beneath the weight of her longing. Her trembling hands gripped his head where it dipped low against her neck.

He inhaled deeply, as if he would take her inside him and never let her go, then slowly raised his head and met her gaze, probing her secrets.

Fear skittered through her, then vanished at the sight of Zeeland's beloved face, fierce and gentle, and dark with passion. For her.

"You really are attracted to me," she breathed, hardly able to believe. *Ten years* she'd thought him disgusted with her.

He laughed, but the sound was low and strangled. "*Attracted* doesn't begin to describe it, Sunshine." He dipped his face to hers, and this time she didn't turn away.

The first featherlight brush of his mouth against hers exploded her senses, nearly buckling her knees.

How many years had she dreamed of this? Yet the dream was nothing compared to the reality.

His lips moved over hers, soft as silk, yet warm and demanding, the pressure increasing moment by moment, the kiss becoming more insistent, more desperate.

Gripping her head with gentle fingers, he slanted his mouth over hers and parted her lips with a single stroke of his tongue. Julianne gasped, then moaned as he dove inside her mouth, staking his claim.

Her senses spun at the clean, masculine taste of him. Her body shuddered, heat flowing through her limbs, pooling between her legs. She melted against him, her hands sliding up and around his neck as she gave herself up wholly to the kiss. To Zeeland.

His arms tightened around her, pulling her close enough to feel the beat of his heart, to feel the hard, pulsing length of his erection against her stomach.

He swept the inside of her mouth with his tongue, exploring every surface, every indentation as if he were learning the feel of her. She moaned with pleasure as his hand gripped the back of her head, slanting her head one way, then the other as he sought to deepen the kiss.

If he lifted her dress and spread her thighs, would she push him away? No. Heaven help her, but no.

As if reading her mind, his hand slid down the curve of her back, cupping her rear, then began to pull up the hem of her dress.

Her heart skipped a beat.

The sound of male voices broke through the

haze of lust a mere moment before the door opened behind them. Zeeland released her. Julianne whirled away, hiding her mortification as Grayson and two others burst into the room.

"There you are!" Grayson's voice boomed. "We're putting together a poker game. You in, Zee?"

Head down, Julianne made her escape, slipping between the men and out of the room, her cheeks flaming, her body shaking with need.

Her life had shattered. Everything she'd ever wanted was finally in reach of the woman she'd once been. But she was that woman no more.

Zeeland met Grayson's look of expectation with a frustrated sigh, running a hand through his hair, willing his body to cool the heat that still raged through every cell.

"Yeah. Count me in."

Dammit, Julianne. He still didn't know what had put the fear in her eyes. He'd pulled her in here for one reason, to find out what was scaring her. Not to kiss her. Not to force her to admit she wasn't as unaffected by him as she pretended. Though both had been on his mind from the moment he'd returned, from the moment she'd greeted him, not with a smile and a hug, but with the cool, haunted eyes of a stranger.

He'd brought her in here to finally get at the

truth, but the moment he'd had her alone, he'd forgotten everything but the fierce need to touch her, to taste her.

That kiss had been everything he'd known it would be and a hundred things more.

Yet the woman herself had become a mystery to him. A mystery he was determined to solve.

Julianne paced her bedroom, her silky purple nightgown sliding around her legs as her agitated steps carried her from one end of the small space to the other. Though it was well past midnight, the laughter and loud voices still carried up from the floors below. The party remained in full swing.

But it wasn't the noise keeping her awake. With nineteen full-time occupants and a regular contingent of guests, the Therian enclave was rarely a quiet place, even in the dead of night.

No, what kept her awake was Zeeland.

Her unsteady fingers touched her lips as her body burned with unfulfilled desire. Never had she felt so confused. Even after her mother died, she hadn't felt this lost. Because there had always been others around her, watching over her. Protecting her.

There was no one to protect her now. No one to protect any of them.

Yet Zeeland was determined to try. His kiss had stirred up all the old feelings again. She'd feared she'd never stopped loving him. Now she knew it was true.

He'd known she was in trouble the moment he'd learned she was playing Beethoven. Even after all these years, Zeeland understood her.

She needed him so badly. Her friend, her confidant. Those strong arms that had always kept her safe.

How was she supposed to keep pushing him away when he was the only thing in life she wanted?

Maybe, *maybe*, if she could find that damned necklace, Melisande would go away and leave her alone. Then maybe her life would return to normal. Or as normal as it could ever be now that she knew she was part Ilina.

Running her fingers through her hair, she looked at the bed and knew she'd never sleep. She might as well search a bit more. This might be a good time to tackle the kitchen, the one place she'd yet to search adequately since doing so was bound to make noise. Why a necklace might be hiding in the kitchen, she couldn't guess. But with the party in full swing, she could come up with some excuse for rooting in the cupboards, and no one would pay her much attention. Probably.

Unless Zeeland found her.

With a shudder that was as much anticipation as dread, she reached for her sweatpants.

A knock on her door had her dropping the pants back on the chair. She'd taken only a single step when the door swung open, and Zeeland stepped inside.

"Zee?"

"You're not sleeping." He closed the door behind him. "I'm going to stay right here because every time I get too close, I forget what I'm doing. Tell me what's going on, Julianne. You're scared, and I want to know why."

She took a step back to keep from flinging herself into his arms. "You need to leave, Zee."

"No." His jacket was gone, and he crossed his arms over his broad, muscular chest. "You're either going to tell me what's going on, or you're going to make love with me, then tell me. Your choice."

Her body melted at his words, heat erupting in her chest and washing downward until she thought she might turn into a puddle on the floor.

She laughed. There was not a single thing funny about her situation, but his options were so classically Zeeland—no options at all. Yet he said them so seriously. As if she had a choice, as if she weren't wholly overwhelmed by the whole damned thing. Her laughter changed, choking off, as fat tears began to roll down her cheeks.

"Juli . . ."

Her vision swam beneath the weight of her tears. "I've missed you, Zee." Her voice was little more than a whisper, but he heard. She knew he heard because a heartbeat later she felt his strong arms go around her.

As she pressed her tear-streaked face against the buttons of his shirt, his gentle hands stroked her back and her hair, holding her tight, protecting her against the world.

"I'm sorry, Julianne. I'm sorry I wasn't here when you needed me. But I'm here now." He held her close, playing with her hair, letting it slide through his fingers as her tears ran their course, and silence finally cocooned them.

He pulled back and lifted her chin, forcing her to look up at him. His knuckles brushed her cheek. "Tell me what's going on, Juli. What has you afraid, Sunshine?"

She tried to look away from those too-perceptive eyes, but he wouldn't have it.

"Don't, Julianne. I'm not letting you go until you tell me the truth."

She stared into his warm brown eyes and swallowed. The lies wouldn't come. Not anymore. "The truth is, I can't tell you, Zeeland."

"You can, sweetheart. You can tell me anything."

Her mouth twisted with wry frustration as those words echoed from her childhood.

"Quit using that fatherly voice on me, Zee. I'm no longer a child."

His mouth clamped shut, his eyes darkening. "I am all too aware of that." The husky note in his voice slid along her flesh like warm silk.

At the feel of his hands falling away, she thought he'd decided to release her. Until she felt his fingers at her waist. He gripped her tight, his hands shaking ever so slightly as if he were barely in control.

Excitement spiraled through her, need pulsing low and hot.

Zeeland's palms slid down over her hips and back up again with sharp, needy movements.

"Tell me what's the matter, Julianne." His words demanded, but his tone was rough with another emotion. He leaned forward, his lips grazing her temple. "Tell me."

"I can't." Her own voice sounded no steadier than his. She felt drugged by his nearness, and by his rich, masculine scent, swept away on a tide of longing.

His hands slid up, his thumbs brushing the undersides of her breasts through the silky gown. She sucked in a long, slow gasp of a breath, reveling in the intimate touch, trembling with the need for more.

His finger rose to stroke a sensitive nipple. Fire

shot through her, the thin silk doing little to protect her from the heat of his flesh, tearing a moan from her throat. He brushed her nipple again, back and forth with his thumb until her head fell back, her eyes half closed from the pure, intoxicating feel of his touch.

"*Zeeland.*"

She knew the moment his control snapped. His touch changed from slow to frantic, from gentle to greedy. His palm replaced his thumb on her breast, his fingers kneading with fierce tenderness even as his other hand cupped the back of her head to hold her captive. His mouth descended, taking hers in a feverish kiss.

With a single, well-aimed blow to her senses, the sweep of his tongue inside her mouth wreaked havoc on her intentions to send him away. For too long, she'd dreamed of this. Of being in his arms. Of feeling his passion. Yet the reality was far beyond any dream.

She felt as if she were burning up from the inside, blazing with a need as desperate as it was exhilarating.

"Make love to me, Zee," she gasped against his mouth.

At first she wasn't sure he'd heard her, then he pulled back just far enough to see her clearly. His eyes were heavy-lidded and dark with desire, even as they throbbed with tenderness.

"Please, Zee. I've waited for this for so long."

Those heat-filled eyes of his erupted in pure flame, sending her own desire tumbling into the conflagration, filling her with a deep, reckless joy.

His head dipped to her neck, nipping and licking with feverish kisses. "I have to be inside you, Julianne. *Now.*"

Chapter Seven

"Yes, Zee. *Yes*."

Zeeland's control was gone, shattered as if it had never been. Lust rode his skin, sinking into his pores, wrenching him free of himself, of his humanity. The deep animal nature buried inside him rose and took over as need roared through his body, turning him hard and heavy. His limbs quaked with desperation to be inside her.

Years, he'd waited for this. *Years.*

Julianne's surrender sealed both their fates.

He kissed her hard, desperate to be one with her in every way, but kissing her wasn't enough. Wasn't nearly enough. *Goddess, I have to be inside her.* Lifting her into his arms, he deposited her on the bed, then tore off his shirt and unfastened his belt as he joined her there. The wildness raging through him demanded he mount her in the most primal Therian way. Later, he would make love to her, but not now. Not now.

"Julianne . . ." His breaths were coming hard and fast. "Get on your hands and knees for me, Sunshine. I need to take you in the old way, from behind."

She met his gaze, a slow feral smile lifting her mouth. "Like the animals we should have been."

He matched her smile. "Exactly like." Goddess, he was shaking in his need to be one with her.

Without hesitation, she turned for him, arching her back and pushing her sweet buttocks toward him, giving herself to him, telling him in no uncertain terms of her desire for him.

"Now, Zee. I want you now."

He yanked her nightgown up over her hips and tore away the silky scrap of panties covering her precious flesh. The sight of her open flower nearly sent him over the edge. His control was shot. As he freed his erection, he bent and nipped the flesh of her hip, eliciting a gasp and a moan of pure feminine desire, then licked the place where he'd marked her.

He grabbed her hips, desperate to plunge into her, but managed to hold back by the barest thread of self-restraint. He had to know she was ready. His finger probed her opening, finding her wet and open, her lips wide with welcome. With a feral growl of satisfaction, he shoved his finger fully inside her.

And ripped through a barrier he'd never expected to find.

Julianne gasped.

Her hymen.

Zeeland froze, shock rolling through him. *A virgin.*

"No. No!" Julianne wrenched away from him, crawling to the headboard, blood streaking her inner thighs. She whirled to face him. "Go. Get out of here, Zeeland! Go!" Her face had turned white as a sheet. She was quaking.

Zeeland reeled, light-headed from the shock short-circuiting his system. She'd waited for him. *She'd waited for him.* And he'd hurt her. Terrified her.

"*Juli.*" Her name tore up from his heart, slicing his constricted throat into a million pieces. His hands shook from the need to hold her, to comfort her. But it was him she was afraid of. "I didn't know. I would never hurt you."

"*Go!*"

The look in her eyes slew him. A desperation he couldn't fathom. Horror. *Terror.*

Of him.

Zeeland stood on unsteady legs, zipped up his pants, and stumbled from her room, closing the door behind him. He collapsed against the wall outside her room, shaking with a cold that came from deep in his soul. All those years he'd dreamed of being her first. He'd imagined how he'd stroke her and gentle her, preparing her body for that first intimate invasion.

Instead, he'd handled her roughly, hurting her. Terrifying her.

She'd waited for him. Five years past maturity and still a virgin. She'd waited for him and he'd hurt her.

"Ah, goddess. What have I done?" He tipped his head against the wall at his back, digging his hands into his hair and clutching his skull. His body still raged with need, but it was his chest that felt as if it had been stabbed with a dozen knives. It was his heart that felt as if it would crumble.

"What have I done?"

Julianne lay on her bed, curled in on herself shaking with a fire, a need, she barely understood. And a terror she understood all too well.

"Zeeland," she whispered, her heart breaking. *So close.* After all these years of waiting, he'd finally come back. He'd finally been prepared to make love to her.

Now he never would.

She couldn't let him try again. She'd felt a pinch of pain when his finger first breached her, but it had been followed at once by a rush of pleasure so intense, she'd felt her control vaporize. Tiny, warm bubbles had begun to replace the blood in her veins. If she'd let him continue, she'd have turned to mist, just like Melisande.

She'd have given herself away, signing his death warrant and probably her own. And she'd have had to watch as the passion and tenderness in his expression changed to shock and revulsion.

But, sweet heaven, he'd thought he'd hurt her. She'd seen the look on his face, that look of horror, and for a moment she'd feared she'd already lost form. But then she'd realized she was still firmly corporeal and known his horror was all for himself. His words had confirmed it. *I would never hurt you.* Yet he thought he had and hated himself for it.

She knew her Zee.

Julianne rose and went to the door, hesitating as she reached for the handle. What if he was still out there? What would she say to ease his guilt? What could she say without telling him the truth?

Nothing. There was nothing she could tell him.

But maybe there was another way to ease his suffering. She knew the Ilinas were able to do more than turn to mist. There was another ability Ilinas possessed, a trick Melisande had pulled on her more than once.

If she could turn to mist, perhaps she could do this, too.

If it worked, she might be able to make things right with Zeeland, in a way. She might be able to ease his terrible guilt.

Her miserable Ilina blood had to be good for something.

* * *

It was nearly dawn when Zeeland finally let sleep overtake him, simply to escape the self-recrimination for a while. He dreamed, as he often did, that he was a shape-shifter, that he still possessed the ancient power of his race. In the dream, he was on a wide-open plain, standing the height of a man. As he lifted his arms to the heavens, he pulled the energy from deep within himself and felt a rush of power on a sweep of exquisite joy. A flash of sparkling lights, and his vision suddenly shifted until he was looking at the landscape from a lower vantage point.

His eyesight changed, his hearing sharpened. The smells of the land burst, engulfing his senses. On four legs, he took off running across the empty plain, the wind in his face thrilling his whiskers, his powerful legs carrying him with joy and ease.

In his dreams, he always shifted into the same animal, a large cat of some kind, with brown fur. He'd never seen his reflection to know precisely which feline.

He ran, reveling in the freedom, only slowing when a beam of sunlight suddenly appeared before him, deepening and widening until a woman stepped forth from the glow.

Julianne.

She wore the same purple nightgown he'd lifted over her hips as he'd prepared to plunge into her a short while ago. The gown, a sleeveless satin that clung to her body, set off her coloring and her curves to fine advantage, filling his man's brain with admiration and lust.

But as his gaze rose to her face, he saw the tracks of tears and remembered all too well what he'd done to her.

His cat's body pulled up not twenty feet in front of her.

She stared at him, her eyes wide and uncertain. "Zee?"

He spoke to her telepathically. *It's me, Julianne. I won't hurt you.*

"How did you shift? You're not a Feral."

It's a dream. The memory of shifting lives deep within my Therian blood. I often dream I'm an animal. A lot of Therians do. Don't you?

"No." Her eyes filled with sadness. "No. I don't dream as other Therians do."

He feared she'd disappear again or, at the very least, turn and run from him. But she did neither. Instead, she started toward him. Slowly. Carefully.

The unhappiness in her eyes tore him apart. *I'm sorry, Julianne. So very sorry. I never dreamed you'd waited for me. It never even crossed my mind. You're so beautiful. Every man wants you.*

"You're the only one I've ever wanted, Zeeland."

You waited for me. And I hurt you. I'll never forgive myself for hurting you.

She stopped in front of him. "You didn't hurt me, Zee. That's why I'm here. To tell you that."

For a moment, his heart seized on her words,

holding them like a balm to his bleeding soul. But it was only a dream.

You're telling me what I want so desperately to hear, Julianne. If only this were real.

She stepped closer and cautiously reached for him, stroking her hand through his fur. "The way you touched me felt good, Zee. Too good."

You forget, sweetheart. I saw your face. You were horrified, and I can't blame you. I was getting ready to take you like an animal. It's not that you wouldn't have enjoyed it like that. If you'd been experienced. I would never have mounted a virgin in such a way. It never crossed my mind that you'd waited for me. He dropped his head, staring at the ground in shame.

To his surprise, she knelt in front of him and wrapped her arms around his thick neck. "It might not have been the perfect introduction to sex, but your desire was real and fierce. Heady, Zee. You didn't hurt me. You didn't do anything wrong. My reaction wasn't to the lovemaking but to something else. I can't tell you more. I just wanted you to know that. Don't blame yourself, please? But we can't try again. We can never try again."

He heard devastation in her tone and something more. Fear. Raw, ugly fear.

Julianne, tell me what you're afraid of.

She released him and rose. He pulled on the power within him and shifted back into a man in another flash of light.

"What are you afraid of, Sunshine? I won't let anything hurt you." But as he took a step toward her, fear leaped into her eyes.

"Don't, Zee. I shouldn't be here. I shouldn't have come."

And just like that, she was gone.

"Julianne!"

The sound of his voice woke him. Zeeland sat up in his bed with a start, his gaze searching the room. *Goddess, but that dream felt real*—vivid in a way dreams rarely were. He raked his hands through his hair as Julianne's words, at once reassuring and unsettling, replayed in his head. That he hadn't hurt her. That it wasn't him she'd been afraid of.

"It was just a dream," he muttered with disgust. "You created what you wanted to hear." And yet, the fear he'd sensed in her from the moment he'd returned was all too real. He kept getting sidetracked from the very reason he'd come back—to get to the bottom of what was bothering her.

He swung his long legs out of bed and pulled on a pair of jeans and a T-shirt. He had to talk to her, even if he had to wake her to do it. Maybe half-asleep, she'd give him the answers he sought. Later, she'd try to avoid him, he was sure of it.

He *had* to get to the bottom of this. And he needed to hear her forgiveness. If he could even get her to speak to him again.

It was too damned bad it had only been a dream.

He made his way to Julianne's room, but as he reached for the door, voices drifted out. Two voices, both feminine. Julianne's and another he didn't immediately recognize. She must be confiding the night's horrors to a friend.

The thought kicked him in the gut, but didn't deter him from his intent to speak to her. He reached for the door handle.

"I can't find it!"

The agitation in Julianne's tone made him pause. The last thing he wanted to do was get into the middle of an argument.

"Twenty-four hours, little sister," the other woman said, her tone hard. "Find it within twenty-four hours, or I'll drag you before the queen and let you explain your failure to her in person."

The queen? What queen? The Therians had no queen.

"Then I'll return here and find it myself," the woman continued. "And woe be to anyone who sees me."

A muffled cry met his ears, the sound of pain. *Julianne's pain.*

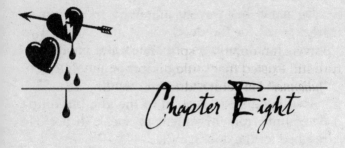

Zeeland burst through the door and rushed into the room to find Julianne kneeling on the floor, her arms around her middle.

His gaze searched for her attacker. But the room was empty, except for Julianne.

What the hell?

"Where is she? Where did she go?"

Julianne's head snapped up, her eyes going wide as her pale, pale face jerked in the direction he was certain the woman had stood a moment ago.

He pressed his palm lightly to the top of her head as he visually searched every corner of the room. "Are you all right?"

"Yes."

He left her to yank open the closet doors, then

bent to look under the bed, but there was no one there.

Shivers ran down his spine. *Impossible.* No creature still existed that could disappear at will.

"Julianne." He returned to her, fighting against the need to sweep her into his arms until he understood what he was up against. What *they* were up against. "Is she gone?"

He felt Julianne freeze, felt the breath catch in her throat. "Who?"

Hell.

"I heard her, Sunshine." His voice turned hard with warning. He'd had all the subterfuge he could take. "I heard her clearly. Don't lie to me." He knelt in front of her, his hands gentle on her shoulders despite the hardness of his tone.

She looked up and met his gaze, her eyes swimming with hopelessness.

"Sweetheart." He stroked her head and cupped her cheek. "Are you injured?" Therians healed almost any injury within minutes, but there was more going on here than he understood.

To his relief, Julianne shook her head, but her chin began to quiver.

He reached for her, needing to comfort her, then stilled, remembering how badly he'd scared her the last time he was in this room.

"Julianne, I'm going to pick you up. I'm going to hold you. Just hold you."

Her nod, though small, was enough. He swept

her into his arms and strode to the large, over-stuffed chair by the window and sat with her on his lap, tucking her head against his shoulder.

"No more lies, Juli. You're in trouble, and I'm going to help you. But first you're going to tell me what's going on. All of it. Most importantly, you're going to tell me what you need me to do to help you."

Zeeland stroked her head, waiting for her to talk to him, but she said nothing.

"Julianne?"

"Just hold me, Zee. Please? I just need you to hold me."

"No, angel. We've been doing this two-step since I got home. You're going to tell me what's going on. Now, love."

"I can't." The bleakness in those two words tore at his heart. And drove his frustration. But instead of demanding, yet again, he tried a different tack.

"Why not?"

"Because if I tell you, you'll die."

Something deep and tight loosened inside his chest. She wasn't pushing him away because she was angry with him, or because she no longer wanted him. She'd been pushing him away because she was mistakenly trying to protect him.

He pressed his lips against the soft crown of her head as tenderness flowed through his heart like a swift-moving stream, stealing the last of his doubts. She still cared.

"She's not going to kill me, Juli. And she's not going to touch you again. I won't allow it." He was a skilled fighter, one of the elite Therian Guard.

But he needed to understand what he was up against. "What is she? She was here, then she was gone."

"I can't tell you."

The misery in her voice made him ache. He kissed her hair. "Then tell me this, at least. What happened when I tried to make love to you? Did I horrify you by my roughness? I need to know that, Juli. I dreamed you told me it wasn't me you were afraid of. I need to know if that's true."

Her soft hand lifted to stroke his cheek. "I'm not afraid of you, Zee. Even when you were a cat, I wasn't afraid of you." She stiffened, her hand freezing on his cheek.

Zeeland jerked back and stared down at her, but Julianne kept her face averted.

"You were in my dream. *You remember.*"

He could feel her heart speed up, beating too fast. Tension turned her stiff and unyielding in his arms. Her muscles bunched, and she tried to push off his lap. He held her fast, turning her until she sat sideways on his lap, but she wouldn't be contained.

She jabbed him hard in the arm with her elbow. "*Let me go.*"

The moment he released her, she jumped off his lap and paced away from him, putting distance between them. The little she'd told him teased his mind. Memories of old stories rose like a horrible specter to the surface of his brain. Tales of a race, long gone, who could appear and disappear at will. Who could enter a man's dreams and drive him mad. Goose bumps raced along the surface of his arms.

He growled low in his throat, his body going tense as a wire. "The Ilinas." He stared at her, but she avoided his gaze. "They're gone. They've been extinct for more than a thousand years!"

Julianne said nothing as she continued to pace, wrapping her arms tight around herself.

"Their extinction was a lie, wasn't it?" He shot to his feet and blocked her path, his hands clamping onto her shoulders. *"Wasn't it, Julianne?"*

She lifted her gaze to his, her eyes sharp with a raw, wild fear.

And he knew he was right. *Goddamn it*, he was right.

She wrenched out of his hold and backed up. "Go away, Zeeland." Her voice was tight, but hard. "Go back to Britain. You know nothing, and we're going to keep it that way." She bared her teeth even as terror swam in her eyes. "Your life depends on it."

He stared at her, the ramifications flying through his mind. The Ilinas lived. Though he hadn't been around a thousand years ago, he'd heard enough stories to know that the once-peaceful, all-female race had turned violent shortly before its demise. Most believed they'd been infected by dark spirit and become evil and corrupt. Many believed they'd destroyed themselves from the inside out, though some held that their queen . . . *their queen* . . . Ariana, had destroyed the race herself rather than see them turn against the creatures of the Earth.

Now . . . *goddess* . . . it appeared they hadn't been destroyed at all.

What did they want with Julianne? *Little sister,* the woman, *the Ilina,* had called her.

Chills raced over his skin as the truth clicked into place. She was one of them. Of course she was. Who else could have entered his dream as she had?

His Julianne.

Holy shit. *An Ilina.*

Powerful. Dangerous.

No. Not Julianne.

"How long have you known you were one of them?" he asked softly.

She blanched and looked away, shaking. Visibly shaking. And his heart broke for her.

"Sunshine," he said softly. "Come here."

She stopped her pacing and met his gaze, as vulnerable as he'd ever seen her. Her head gave a quick shake. "I'm not what you thought I was."

He held out his hand to her. "Come here, Juli. You may not be *what* I thought you were. I suspect you aren't what you thought you were, either.

But the very fact that you're trying to protect me tells me you're *who* you've always been. My sweet, strong Julianne."

For long moments, she didn't move, just watched him, searching his face for a truth he hoped she'd find. Finally, she reached for him, placing her hand and her trust in his and allowing him to pull her into his arms.

As she pressed her cheek to his chest, her arms wrapping tight around his waist, a deep, violent shudder went through her, followed by a sigh of surrender. He held her and promised himself he'd never let her go.

"I've only known for a month," she told him.

"That Ilina came to you? The one who was just here?"

"Yes. Melisande wanted me to find something for her, so she told me what I was—the daughter of an abomination, a half-breed."

"Everyone thinks they're extinct."

"That's what they want the world to think. They'll kill to keep their secret, Zee. Melisande told me they killed my mother when she broke that promise. And my father because she'd told him."

His grip tightened on her, hearing the threat inherent in her words. "She's never going to hurt you." His words came out as a growl, and a promise. "I won't allow it, Julianne." She pressed closer to him, and he cradled her against his heart. "Tell me the rest."

With a shudder, she did. "A long time ago, one of the Ilinas became pregnant by one of the human males she'd forced into sexual slavery. The baby was my mother. Since only true Ilinas can survive for more than a short time in the Crystal Realm, the Ilina took the baby where Therians would find her and raise her as one of their own. Then she watched her carefully from afar to ensure that she developed none of the Ilina's powers or abilities. As long as she didn't, they never had to tell her what she was.

"Her human blood seemed to have counteracted the Ilina blood. All except her immortality. She posed no threat to them." Julianne's body grew tense. "Until I was born. My birth apparently triggered her magic. The Ilinas are connected in some way, and they felt it. My mother was warned never to tell, and she didn't for nine years. Then she told my father the truth. Melisande silenced them both," she said bitterly.

Zeeland tightened his hold on her. "Melisande told you that?"

"Yes." She began to tremble again.

"Dammit, Julianne. That's an act of war."

She pulled back until she stared up at him with haunted turquoise eyes. "They'll kill whoever discovers their existence." Her face tightened. "They'll kill you, now."

"Let them try," he growled. "Why the hell is it so important to them to stay a secret?"

"They have enemies. It's the way they've protected themselves."

"What of all the other half-breeds? Or mixed breeds?"

"There are no others. I'm it." She reached for him, her cold palms pressing against his cheeks, her eyes sharp with pain. "I couldn't bear it if anything were to happen to you. That's why I tried to stay away from you, Zee. I was afraid you'd see what I am."

His arms tightened around her. "What kind of power have you developed that worries you so much?"

She flinched and looked away. "I turned . . . to mist. When I got angry." Her gaze turned back to his. "It almost happened again when we . . . when you . . ."

Suddenly he understood. "When I put my finger inside you?" He finally believed what she'd been telling him all along, that he hadn't hurt her.

Her eyes darkened, desire suffusing her features. "Yes," she said huskily. "If we'd continued, you'd have had a wraith in your arms. Or not in your arms. You wouldn't have been able to touch me at all."

He leaned down and kissed her, a gentle touch on the lips. "Don't run from me again, Julianne. We'll deal with this together. All of it."

"She's going to try to kill you. She'll try to kill us both, now."

His arms tightened around her. "Forewarned is forearmed." But how in the hell did one fight an Ilina? He'd better figure out their weaknesses and their strengths, and do it soon. Without asking anyone else. The last thing he wanted to do was endanger the others. "Tell me everything, Sunshine. You said she wanted you to find something for her?"

Julianne sighed. "She says there's a necklace in this house somewhere, a rare bloodred moonstone. She wants it."

"Did she say why?"

"She needs it to heal her queen."

His brows drew down. "I've seen it."

Julianne started and stared at him in surprise. "*Where*?"

"I don't remember, but I vaguely remember thinking it was an odd place to put a necklace. I wasn't interested enough to ask anyone about it at the time. Let me think. It'll come back to me."

He hooked his arm behind her knees, then lifted her into his arms, cradling her against his heart. "You need sleep, Sunshine. We both do."

Julianne clung to him and placed a sweet kiss on his cheek. "The last thing I ever wanted to do was put you in danger, Zee. You of all people." A shudder went through her body as she pressed her forehead against his neck. "But I've needed you so badly. Thank you for not letting me push you away."

His arms tightened around her with a fierceness that shook him to the depths of his being. She was *his. His.*

"You're not getting rid of me, Julianne." *Ever.* The pledge rang in his head, echoing in his heart. *Ever.*

His mind tried to balk. He wasn't talking about forever. He didn't *do* forever. No one in his right mind promised forever.

But his arms only tightened their grip. *She's mine.*

With a sudden, startling clarity, he knew why he'd stayed away all these years. It was that very fear that she *was* his. That she was destined to be his mate. And he, hers.

He'd avoided the inevitable.

Goddess, what a fool he'd been. If she'd have him . . . *if* she'd have him . . . he was never letting her go again.

But right now, the only thing that mattered was keeping Julianne safe. He set her in the middle of the bed and climbed in after her, fully clothed. Pulling her into his arms, he kissed her forehead.

"Sleep, Sunshine. I'm not going to let anything happen to you. To either of us."

She melted against him, her head on his shoulder. "Zee?" she asked sleepily.

"Hmm?"

"I love you."

His chest tightened, his mind tumbling with

joy, then pulling up abruptly as he remembered how she used to say those precious words to him every night when he tucked her in when she was a child, repeating a nighttime ritual she'd shared with the mother she'd lost.

"I love you, too, Julianne." The same reply he'd given her every night all those years ago.

But the words rang in his heart, so much more than a simple ritualistic reply, or even the terms of deep affection they'd later become.

"I love you," he whispered as she slept. And knew they'd come to mean the most profound feelings a man could have for a woman. For the woman he'd always been destined to mate. He'd known it. Even as he'd fought the knowledge, he'd known for years she was the one.

He'd stayed away, driven by that deep-seated fear of forever, certain that if he stayed away long enough, the need for her would eventually end.

He'd been a fool.

He loved her and would always love her. But would it be enough? He wasn't at all certain she felt the same.

And even if she did, they faced an enemy he knew too little about. A creature of legend said to be able to devour men's souls.

Goddess help them both.

Julianne looked up from the stack of books in her lap, her gaze going to Zeeland as he searched through a pile of his own. They were in the library on the main level of the mansion, searching for a book with a pocket hidden in the cover. Zeeland had finally remembered finding the necklace in such a pocket years ago. But which book was anybody's guess.

As she watched, Zeeland searched the books, one after the other, the strong planes of his face catching the light from the oversized window. She never saw him that her stomach didn't do a little flip, freeing the butterflies to flutter around her insides. He was the most handsome man she'd ever known.

And she loved him.

She remembered telling him so last night. It had slipped out when she was falling asleep, but he'd responded in kind. Just as he always had when she was young. He was watching out for her and protecting her as he'd always done. But she couldn't guess how he felt about her. He desired her, she knew that now. He loved her in his way.

She loved him more. So much more.

Even with her terrible secret out in the open between them, he never flinched. His fierce protectiveness of her never wavered. If it bothered him that she wasn't fully Therian, he hadn't let on.

Instead, he'd held her as she'd slept, watching over her. And she'd slept as she hadn't since Melisande first arrived, secure in the warm safety of his arms.

Through with the books in her lap, she stood and replaced them on the shelf. She glanced back at Zee, pushing an errant lock of dark hair out of her eyes. He was reading.

With a wry look, she planted her hands on her hips. "That doesn't look like searching book covers to me."

He glanced up at her with a faraway look in his eyes. "Just reading something that caught my interest." His eyes seemed to focus on her, a glimmer of humor in their depths. "You're a harsh taskmaster, woman."

She'd been teasing him. Sort of. In truth, she was desperate to find that necklace. It was already midafternoon, and they'd barely searched half the library. The rest of the enclave was busy preparing for the big Valentine's party, and she'd already put off Serenity's and Cambria's requests for help. She was feeling guilty. And desperate.

Zeeland closed the book and set it aside. "Okay, let's find that thing."

A half hour later, Zeeland rose, holding the ancient-looking volume he'd been reading tight against his chest. And a book of fairy tales, one of the books she'd brought with her from New York.

"I found it," he said quietly. "Along with information that might come in useful."

Julianne's eyes went round. Melisande had claimed Julianne had the moonstone. Apparently she had, though she hadn't known it. She'd never known the book had a hidden pocket. She said nothing as he held out his hand to her and helped her up. She replaced her small stack of books on the shelf, then turned to him.

"Let me see."

"In your room."

With a nod, she took his hand, feeling the relief to the soles of her feet. He'd found it. When Melisande returned, she'd give her the necklace and pray that was the end of it. With any luck, Melisande need never know of Zeeland's involvement . . . or knowledge.

And if Melisande figured it out?

She gripped Zeeland's hand tighter, a fierce and furious protectiveness rising inside her.

Neither of them was going down without a fight.

"I'm ready. You can turn around, Zee."

Zeeland rose from the chair in Julianne's room where he'd been reading about what little was known of the Ilinas while Julianne dressed for the Valentine's party that was already in full swing downstairs. He refused to leave her alone, now, even to prepare for the party, but she'd refused to let him watch her get ready.

He turned and stilled as he beheld the vision that was Julianne. She wore a silky red dress with tiny straps over her slender shoulders. The form-fitting dress skimmed her slender curves as it fell to midcalf, setting off her figure to perfection. A pair of sexy, red, high-heeled sandals lengthened and accentuated the fine shape of her legs. She'd swept up her dark hair in a casually elegant knot, a few artful wisps brushing her neck, eliciting a need in him to press his lips just there.

Beautiful. "You steal my breath, Sunshine."

A sweet blush stained her cheeks, but the smile she gave him sent the blood in a wild tumble through his veins.

He closed the distance between them in three long strides, covering her bare shoulders with his hands. Her scent wrapped around him. His grip tightened.

"Forget the party," he said huskily. "We'll have our own party right here."

With a small musical laugh, she twirled out of his grasp. "Not a chance." She came to a stop, meeting his gaze, fire lighting her eyes. "At least not yet." A smile of seductive innocence lifted one corner of her mouth. "I want to dance. And have a glass of champagne. Besides the others would never forgive you if you missed this party."

There was also the small matter of her being untried. And the party he had in mind was far too carnal. Another night, perhaps. Maybe another time.

He reached for her hand, then hesitated. "The moonstone."

Julianne's smile died. "What if Melisande comes for it while we're gone?"

"Unlikely. But I was thinking that someone in the enclave might know what it is. Or what it does. We might get some valuable information if someone recognizes it."

A flash of alarm crossed her features. "If you start asking, it'll raise too many questions."

"I agree. That's why I think you should wear it." He shrugged. "It goes with the dress."

A small smile of understanding lifted her lips. "If anyone asks where I got it, I'll say I found it in the library."

"The absolute truth."

She retrieved the moonstone and handed it to him. He placed it around her neck, letting the small stone, framed by fine silver filigree, settle against the satin perfection of her skin. Unable to resist the temptation, he placed a slow, lush kiss on her shoulder, drinking in the scent and taste of her. Goddess, but he wanted to stay right here and explore every inch of her with his mouth.

"Zeeland."

Reluctantly, he released her and held out his hand. She looked up at him, meeting his gaze with a look of dark passion and deep affection, stealing his heart all over again.

"I should warn you, Sunshine. I'm a jealous man."

She grinned at him. "No, you're not."

He smiled, unable to do otherwise when his heart was near to bursting with pleasure just from the sight of that smile on her face again. "With you, I am. I was about to bust some heads last night even before Jag approached you."

Her brows lifted. "Why?"

"Because they were all looking at you, wanting you as badly as I did. I could see it in their eyes."

"I didn't notice." Her expression turned warm and serious. "You were the only one I was paying any attention to, Zee."

"Good." He kissed her cheek. She was his. Whether she knew it yet, or not. He held out his arm for her and led her down to the main level of the house, then down another open flight of stairs to the basement, which had long ago been finished as an expensively appointed club. Known among the Therians as Club Alex, the room possessed a full mahogany bar, a first-rate sound system and dance floor, two pool tables, and more than a dozen small round tables for the audience to sit and drink and enjoy the entertainment.

Tonight, red and pink hearts hung from the ceiling on accordion streamers that ran from one end of the room to the other. Pop music blasted from the speakers.

And every pair of eyes in the house watched Julianne as she accompanied him down the stairs, every male eye shot through with a mix of raw male appreciation and jealousy.

With a savage smile, he understood. For five years she'd been of age and never once taken any of them to bed. For five years, they'd vied for her attention and failed.

No wonder the sorry suckers were jealous.

His chest swelled with a pride and satisfaction he couldn't contain. She was his, dammit. She'd always been his.

Always.

Hawke broke away from the crowd and was the first to greet them. He met Zeeland's gaze with warm approval before turning to Julianne. He bent to give her a quick peck on the cheek.

"You look lovely, Julianne."

"Thank you, Hawke." She smiled at the Feral, then turned to grin up at Zeeland, letting him and everyone else know that not even a Feral Warrior could steal her attention from the man at her side.

Grayson slapped him on the back, joining them. "About time you two got together. Nice dress, Squirt." He winked, earning a feminine roll of turquoise eyes.

"Thanks, Gray."

At least Grayson didn't seem to be standing in line to attract Julianne's attention. Then again, Grayson and Ryland were the only ones who'd known why he left the enclave ten years ago. Both had known how he felt about her.

Perhaps better than he had himself.

He'd figured it out, finally. He just prayed to the goddess, it wasn't too late.

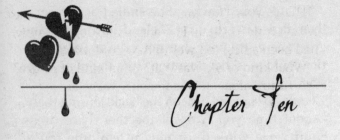

Chapter Ten

Julianne saw Cambria waving her over, Daniella at her side, like a couple of gossiping schoolgirls. She knew what they wanted, of course. To know what was going on with Zeeland and her.

If only she could figure that out herself.

Zee was acting protective and loving, much as he always had. And very, very interested in her sexually, which was entirely new. But he'd said nothing about staying in Alexandria. Nor anything about her going back to Britain with him.

With a sigh, she knew it no longer really mattered. If things were different, if *she* were different, she'd have being hoping and praying he would someday come to love her as she loved him. That he might even, eventually, wish to bind himself to her, taking her for his mate.

But she wasn't who they'd thought she was. She wasn't fully Therian. Her entire life, up until now, had been a lie. And would have to remain a lie.

What kind of life was that? What kind of future?

A future alone. It was the only way.

As long as Melisande never found out that Zeeland knew. If that happened, Julianne wouldn't have any future at all.

The thought brought her mood crashing to the ground, but she struggled to mask her unhappiness with so many eyes on the two of them. She didn't have to make any decisions tonight, but now that she had the necklace, the decisions would have to come soon.

Leaving the enclave and those she loved loomed all too large as the only way to save them.

She looked up at Zeeland, wishing things could have been different. He was breathtakingly handsome tonight, in black pants and a matching black turtleneck sweater. Tall, dark, and sexy as hell.

Zeeland met her gaze, his eyes narrowing with concern. "Are you okay?"

He always read her moods too well. "I'm fine." Now wasn't the time. She wasn't sure she'd ever find the right time to tell him, and maybe that was for the best. She'd slip away and leave him behind, too. Safe from what she was and the danger she brought to them all.

She pulled her hand from his arm. "I'll be right back. The girls want the gossip."

Humor lit his dark eyes, then fled, replaced by a warrior's caution he didn't express out loud. *Don't leave my sight*, his eyes said.

As if she had any desire to face Melisande before she had to.

Julianne patted his arm, letting him know she understood. "Cambria and Daniella are going to burst with questions if I don't give them a moment. I'll be right back."

But as she crossed to where the women waited, the Feral Warrior, Kougar, stepped directly into her path, forcing her to stop abruptly to keep from running into him.

"Kougar," she said, looking up into his hard face. Even if the Feral didn't wear a perpetually glacial look, the combination of mustache, goatee, and pale, pale eyes would have done nothing to dispel his hard, almost sinister air.

His gaze fell to the moonstone resting in the hollow of her throat. "Where did you get that?" Every word was glazed with frost.

Her pulse accelerated, tripping erratically, and she took a step back, unable to stop herself. "I-I found it." Her fingers fluttered to the stone. "Do you know what it is?"

Kougar's gaze snapped to hers. Without a word, he turned and walked away a second before Zeeland reached her side.

Zee's arm slipped around her shoulders as he

steered her toward the wall and a measure of privacy. "What was that all about?"

"I'm not sure. He asked me where I got the moonstone. I told him I found it, and he walked away. But his eyes . . ." She looked to make sure no one was close enough to overhear easily. Unfortunately, Ferals, with the strengths and abilities they gained from their animals, tended to have excellent hearing.

She reached up, gripping Zee's face in both hands and pulled him down to her. But instead of kissing him, she pressed her cheek to his and whispered in his ear.

"I think he recognized it, Zee."

Zeeland's lips grazed her temple, then her cheek. "I'll talk to him. Wait here."

She grabbed his hand as he released her. "I'll be with Daniella and Cam."

He nodded, squeezed her hand, then turned to make his way to the bar, and Kougar, while she went to join her friends.

"Spill," Cambria said the moment she walked up.

"Your guess is as good as mine," Julianne replied truthfully. Her gaze turned back to Zeeland, watching as he spoke to Kougar, as Kougar said something and walked away.

Zeeland turned back, his gaze finding her unerringly.

"He can't take his eyes off you," Daniella said approvingly. "Methinks our errant Zeeland may decide to come back home."

Cambria squeezed Julianne's hand excitedly. "I'd figured he'd be back the moment you turned twenty-five, Jules. Took him long enough."

Julianne barely heard them, her gaze locked on Zeeland's as he crossed the large club to join them. Without acknowledging anyone but her, he took her hand and pulled her onto the dance floor and into his arms.

She could find neither the voice, nor the will, to object.

Zeeland ran his hand over the cool flesh of her bare back, sending heat rippling across her skin as he pressed her closer. The thick ridge of his arousal brushed against her abdomen.

Julianne's breath turned shallow. "What did he say?"

His lips grazed her temple. "He didn't know what I was talking about. Kougar's . . . different. From what Hawke says, not even the other Ferals really know what to make of him. I have a feeling you intercepted what was meant to be a Kougar flirtation. If he does know anything, he wasn't sharing. And I don't dare push."

Zeeland pulled her even closer as the song turned slow and sultry. His body was warm and strong—anything but relaxed. She could feel the vibrations coming off him, almost a fine shaking in his limbs, telling her how much he desired her. His hands were at once gentle, yet firm and insistent, as if they couldn't get enough of her. As if he held on to control by a thread.

His warm, male scent drew her, heating her blood and turning her limbs to soft putty. They danced every dance for an hour, letting the music wrap around them and pound with their racing hearts.

As the music turned to yet another slow song, Zeeland pulled her tight against him and dipped his head, his mouth once more pressed to her temple. "*Goddess*, I want you, Sunshine. I don't know how much more of this I can stand. Holding you in my arms, not being able to touch you where I want. *How* I want."

His husky words made her shiver with a mix of anticipation and trepidation at the thought of doing what he wanted . . . what they both wanted.

But what if they tried and she started to fizz again? What if his touch turned her to mist?

Julianne pulled back far enough to meet his gaze, his eyes hot enough to set her aflame where she stood.

He was so much taller than she was, another factor of her being Ilina, she realized. She lifted her face and pressed her cheek against his jaw, where she could speak without being overheard.

"Zee, I tried to get you to bed me ten years ago,

and I haven't stopped wanting you since. But I'm afraid of what will happen if I lose control."

He stroked her hair and dipped his mouth close to her ear, where not even a Feral would be able to hear over the music. "You don't have to be afraid of that."

"How do you know?"

"Remember the book you caught me reading in the library?"

"Was it about . . . ?" *The Ilinas?* Her heritage.

"Yes."

"But what if I . . . ?" What if she lost her form and turned into a wraith when he was trying to make love to her?

He cupped her cheek in his warm hand. "We'll handle it. One way or another."

"If Melisande returns?"

He pulled back, a battle gleam in his eyes. "We'll handle her, too."

Looking up into those dark, intense eyes so filled with promise, she believed him.

"I'm kind of tired of this party, Zee."

A devil's smile lifted his lips. "Me, too." He took her hand and pulled her through the crowd and toward the stairs.

Twice she heard someone call his name in greeting, but Zeeland ignored them as they made their escape. His need, and his excitement, telegraphed themselves to her through the almost too-tight grip of his hand.

"Do you have a room?" she asked him as they started up the first flight of stairs.

"No. I'm bunking with Grayson. We'll use your room."

Julianne looked up at him. "That's where *she* comes."

Zeeland slowed and met her gaze. "Do you think she'll come tonight? With me there?"

Slowly, Julianne shook her head. "She's never come when there's been anyone else around."

He winked at her. "I think we'll risk it. And if she comes . . . we'll deal with it."

"Okay."

She was out of breath by the time they'd climbed two flights of stairs and made the trek down the long hall to her bedroom, but her breathlessness had little to do with the physical exertion.

Zeeland pushed open the door to her bedroom and led her inside, then kicked the door closed again and pulled her into his arms. His mouth covered hers in a kiss at once tender yet blindingly intense. His need melded with her own, driving her desire until she was trembling from the force of the passion.

His lips caressed and stroked hers, his tongue sliding into the waiting warmth of her mouth, filling her. His hands slid into her hair, freeing the mass to tumble around her shoulders. One hand dug into her hair, his fingers softly caressing her scalp, while his other hand dove down her back, cupping her rear and pulling her against him until she could once more feel the hard evidence of his desire.

Her breath caught in her lungs at the feel of him, then resumed on small, thready gasps.

He smelled like forests and wild winds, and her head spun from the heady assault on her senses, and from the knowledge that Zeeland, her beloved Zeeland, was in her arms at last.

He pulled away from her mouth and kissed her cheek, then dipped to taste her shoulder, sending shivers rippling over her skin.

"I've been wanting to do more of this all night." His lips caressed her as his mouth moved into the curve of her neck, then slowly upward.

She tilted her head, giving him full access, reveling in the tingling sensations running over every inch of her body. Deep inside her, heat bloomed, warming and liquefying, making her legs weak. Making her quake with pleasure.

One of his warm hands moved, sliding over her shoulder, then down to cover her breast. Pleasure arced through her as his hand worked the soft flesh, plucking at her nipple. Every touch sent desire tightening inside her, his fingers playing her like a master musician. With those same deft fingers, he slipped the strap from her shoulder and brushed away the scrap of gown, uncovering her breast.

She watched his eyes darken as his thumb brushed the dusty rose flesh of her nipple, making her gasp for another trembling breath.

The low sound of pleasure deep in Zeeland's throat sang through her veins. His head moved, dropping as if by gravity, diving for her flesh. His mouth closed around her breast, his tongue stroking, his lips suckling.

Julianne dropped her head back at the exquisite pull, cradling his head against her, loving him as he loved her body, bringing her incredible pleasure.

Finally, he pulled away, trailing kisses up her neck until his mouth once more covered hers. He kissed her thoroughly, one hand in her hair, the other covering her damp, tingling breast. Slowly, he pulled back, breathing like he'd run up and down the stairs two dozen times. But as he looked down into her face, a decidedly male smile lifted the corners of his gorgeous mouth.

"You look thoroughly ravished."

She smiled, unable to do otherwise when he made her so happy just by being here, by wanting her the way he did. "*Ravished?*"

He brushed her cheek with his knuckles, a faint tremor in his hand. "An old word, from another time, young'un. But appropriate."

"I'm not too young for you, Zee."

"No, sweetheart. You're not. Not anymore, thank

the goddess. But you're new to this, and I'm going to take it slow if it kills me." He took a shaky breath and grunted. "Which it damn well might."

Julianne pressed her hands to his chest, then slid them down and under his turtleneck, sliding her palms over the bare flesh of his torso.

He sucked in a breath. "*Juli*."

"Don't go slow, Zee. I'm melting inside. On fire for you."

"I won't hurt you again."

"Last time hardly signified. I barely felt it. I was afraid of what was happening to me, of the Ilina power. Not of you. Never of you."

He turned her around and pulled her against him, her back to his chest. "Then we're going to slow down for me. I won't lose control with you this time." He held her to him, his arm around her waist while his other hand covered and kneaded her bare breast.

She dropped her head back and drank in the sweet touch of his hands, and the feel of his hard body at her back.

"While you got ready for the party, I did some more reading, Sunshine."

She stilled. "About the Ilinas?"

"Uh-hmm. An Ilina's natural state is spirit, but she can turn corporeal at will and stay that way for as long as she wants with little effort. Millennia ago, half-breeds and mixed breeds weren't quite so rare. According to the account, few of them could enter the spirit state, but those who could, were almost never able to maintain it for more than short bursts of time."

The arm around her waist loosened, his hand sliding down to her thigh. His fingers tugged and pulled, and she realized he was lifting the hem of her dress.

Her breath caught, her mind trying to remember the question his words had triggered. "So I can't get stuck like that? In the spirit state?"

"No." He kissed her hair. "Even if you turn to mist, you won't stay like that."

"Zee?"

His hand found the edge of her dress and slid beneath it, his palm splaying erotically against the warm flesh of her leg.

She nearly forgot her question. "If all Ilinas are female, how do they reproduce without creating half-breeds?"

His palm rose, his fingers stroking the inside of her thigh, making her pulse race and her body overheat.

"They reproduce as needed through magic. And ritual."

A single finger stroked the damp silk of her panties and the ultrasensitive flesh beneath.

Her legs buckled at the intense shot of pure pleasure.

Zeeland caught her tight against him. "You're soaked."

Her face flamed. "I can't help it. Don't make fun of me, Zee. Not now. Not over this."

He growled low, an intensely satisfied sound. "I wouldn't dream of making fun of you, sweetheart. Ever. Your wetness is what tells me you're ready for me. Or getting there. It's exactly what I'd hoped to find."

"Oh."

He laughed and nipped her ear as he slid his finger back to her thigh, then slid it under the edge of her panties. The touch of his bare finger against her heated flesh made her cry out.

"You're so wet. So perfect." He stroked her flesh, sliding along the inner edge of the folds until she thought she would go insane with wanting . . . *more*.

"Zeeland, please. You're just tormenting me now."

He chuckled low. "Believe me when I say I share your pain, angel. I think we've both waited long enough."

He turned her around to face him, then grabbed the hem of her dress and pulled it up and over her head, dropping it on the floor and leaving her standing in nothing but her panties and heels.

His gaze moved over her slowly, his dark eyes gleaming with appreciation. With a quick move, he swung her into his arms and deposited her in the middle of the four-poster bed. She wasted no time. While he stripped off his sweater, she sat up and removed her strappy red sandals, one after the other. Her gaze drank in the play of muscles across Zee's chest as he unfastened his belt and shucked off his pants.

As he came to her, naked and fully aroused, she was certain he must be the most beautiful man who'd ever lived. He looked at her, meeting her gaze, soft adoration in his eyes.

Her heart contracted. "Zeeland. If I turn into a ghost . . ." She swallowed the lump of dread wedging itself in her throat. "Don't freak out. Please?"

He stretched out beside her pulling her down until she lay lengthwise on top of him, looking down into his face. His erection lay between them, their bodies separated only by the tiny scrap of lace of her panties.

He reached up and stroked the hair back from her face. "We'll handle it, Juli."

She tried to be reassured, but now that they were naked, were so close to finally *doing it*, her fear began to get the better of her. "I don't know if I can go through with this, Zee."

He cupped her cheek. "It'll be okay."

"Once you see the real me, you may not want anything to do with me."

His dark eyes softened. "I've already seen the real you, sweetheart. Inside and out. If you have a few extra *gifts*, I can deal with that."

"You've run from me once."

"That was different. You scared the crap out of me."

She laughed, a sharp sound of playful outrage, but the words pinched. "Thanks a lot."

He cupped her face in his hands, his expression utterly serious. "You still scare me, Julianne. Not what you are or might do when I make love to you. But the way I feel about you. How badly I need you."

She stared into his eyes, longing to ask *how* he felt about her. But his hands slid down her bare back, burrowing inside her panties to cup her rear, and her thoughts fled on a moan.

"Sweet goddess, Julianne, *I need you now.*"

He rolled her beneath him and pulled off her panties with a single quick tug that told her he was on the very edge of control. The realization filled her with hot excitement.

In a frantic storm of pent-up passion, his hands touched her *everywhere,* his mouth kissed every inch of her flesh until she was feverish with need for release from the torment of desire that raged within her.

"Zeeland, come inside me. *Please.*"

His finger touched her as it had before, sliding along the inside edge of her folds. But this time it pressed deeper, and deeper still, until it could go no farther.

"Is that okay?" he asked, his voice tight as a bowstring.

"Don't tease me, Zeeland," she gasped. "It's not enough."

His chuckle was hoarse. "Not enough. It's a damned good thing."

With his knee, he spread her thighs, then positioned himself over her, his weight on his forearms, his gaze glued to hers.

"If I hurt you, tell me, Juli. I'll stop."

Her hands lifted to grip his back. "Do it, Zee."

She felt the touch of him against her slick opening, then the press of flesh as he sought entrance. He was too big. For a brief moment, she panicked. He'd never fit inside her!

"Juli, kiss me." He bent his head and took her mouth, sweeping his tongue inside. Pleasure rushed through her, stealing her fear and opening her body. And suddenly he was in, sliding freely without causing her any pain, only a thick, welcome pressure.

"Okay?" he gasped.

"Yes. Oh, yes."

He began to move, pulling back, then pressing forward again, slowly at first, then more quickly as her body softened and opened farther. Her own passion lifted, urging her to drive her hips against him, to seek more. Closer. Faster. Harder.

She gripped his shoulders, holding on as he plunged into her body over and over. Passion swept her up, spinning her in a tighter and tighter arc like a cyclone gaining strength and speed.

She was gasping, meeting him thrust for thrust,

the climax nearly upon her when her blood began to fizz like champagne.

"Zee!" But it was too late. The storm broke over her, broke over them both. As Zeeland shouted, his voice low and triumphant, she cried out her own release, a brilliant, exquisite orgasm that ripped her from herself and sent her spinning into a million pieces.

Literally.

She could feel her body turning to mist.

Chapter Eleven

Zeeland felt the moment Julianne began to change. The shift wasn't immediate. The body beneath him began to turn soft, began to shimmer. He felt himself sinking. Into her. *Into her.*

A frisson of panic bolted through him. His instincts told him to vault off the bed, away from her. But within her shimmering eyes he read the fear that he would do just that. He fought the instinct, his body still pulsing from the most incredible release he'd ever had.

Amazingly, instead of dimming, that incredible pleasure only seemed to grow as he slowly sank into the shimmering, insubstantial form of the woman he loved. He felt as if, in merging with her, she wrapped him in the very essence of her warmth and beauty. And love.

"Am I hurting you?" he gasped. He could be crushing her. *Destroying her.*

"No." Her voice was filled with the wonder rushing through him. "It feels . . . wonderful. As good as the sex, but in an entirely different way."

He kept his head lifted, peering down into her shimmering, beautiful face and saw the tears in her eyes.

She laughed softly, and he felt the ripples of pleasure caress him inside and out. "I've heard the term *becoming one*, but I think we've taken this to a whole new level."

He grinned at her, then sobered. "Just don't go solid with me inside you or we'll *be one* in a way we never intended."

Julianne's eyes went wide as saucers. "Maybe we'd better not press our luck."

"I agree." Zeeland pushed himself up and off her, feeling the loss, then turned and sat facing her as she rose to sit beside him.

He looked at her, really looked at her. Her body, so petite, so beautifully ripe, yet perfectly proportioned, shimmered like an angel's come to Earth. But he was ready for her to reclaim her corporeal form. He didn't like that he couldn't touch her.

How could he protect her if he couldn't touch her?

In her eyes, he saw glimmers of the same worry. He'd promised her she wouldn't stay this way, but neither of them had ever experienced anything like this before. Neither of them knew anything for certain.

Zeeland rose and pulled on his pants. Maybe the book . . .

An odd breeze blew through the room, scented with pine.

Julianne gasped, her insubstantial face whitening as her gaze stabbed the space behind him.

He whirled. Behind him, near the end of Julianne's bed, floated a petite, blond woman, her misty body outlined in a red glow. Anger blazed from eyes the color of sapphires. An Ilina's eyes.

"You'll come with me. *Now,*" the small blonde snapped. "Both of you."

"Like hell." Zeeland strode to the bed to stand beside Julianne, putting his arm out to protect her, accidentally passing it right through her shoulder. *Hell.*

He faced the Ilina. "We're not going anywhere with you. None but a true Ilina can survive in the Crystal Realm, and we know it as well as you."

Melisande's face darkened with anger. "How dare you reveal yourself to him!" She lifted a hand and pointed two fingers at Julianne. To his horror, Julianne gasped, doubling over with pain.

"I didn't mean to," Julianne cried, her voice little more than a whisper.

"Leave her alone!" How in the hell was he supposed to protect her when he couldn't touch her? When he couldn't touch either of them?

Still bent double, Julianne began to rise off the bed. He watched in disbelief as she slowly moved toward the Ilina's outstretched hand.

She was calling her. *Taking* her.

"*No.*" Zeeland lunged for Julianne, but his hands went right through her. "Juli! She's pulling you to her. Stop her! If she takes you into the Crystal Realm, you'll die."

He swung to the Ilina, fury and desperation rippling through his muscles. "*You can't have her. She's mine.*"

Melisande's lip curled. "You can't stop me, Therian."

Zeeland's fingers curled into his palms. Maybe he could and maybe he couldn't. But he sure as hell wasn't going to stand here and do nothing.

Running on pure instinct, he launched himself at Melisande, diving into the heart of her essence and blasting her with his will and his hatred, anything to break her hold on Julianne.

Melisande turned his fury back on him tenfold, lighting every nerve ending in his body, setting them on fire until he was in so much pain he had to fight just to remain standing, to remain conscious. He felt as if his flesh were being scorched from his bones, as if his blood had turned to acid.

But through his own pain, he could sense the Ilina's, and he held on with everything he had.

Little by little, he felt her hold on Julianne weaken. He knew the moment it was gone.

His spirit sang with relief . . . until he tried to free himself, and couldn't. With bone-deep dismay, he realized he was trapped fast. He'd held on so tightly, he'd become one with his enemy.

The cool wind blew across his face, the scent of pine trees heavy in the air—air that shimmered and sparkled like refracted crystals.

The Crystal Realm. She was pulling him out of the bedroom, out of his world, and into that place he would never survive.

"Zeeland!" Julianne cried behind him.

He felt her rushing up beside him.

"No, Juli. Go!"

But she ignored him. And he felt the sweet, intense *rightness* of her body beginning to merge with his once more.

The terrible pain began to ease.

"She'll kill you." Julianne's strong voice sounded in his head and his ears as if she spoke both within him as much as without. "We'll fight her together."

"Juli, no. My hatred hurts her. I won't . . . hurt you, too."

"Your hatred can't touch me, Zeeland. It's not for me."

As she merged with him fully, strength poured into him, warm and pure. With his heart, he held tight to Julianne. With his mind, he flayed the Ilina, pushing her away.

They broke free with a hard shove of pine-scented power. Zeeland fell back against the bed, Julianne floating a foot away, naked at his side.

The Ilina collapsed as if half-conscious, to float inches above the floor, her glow a pulsing yellow.

His gaze flew to Julianne as he righted himself. "Are you okay?"

"Yes."

The door burst open and Kougar strode inside, kicking the door closed behind him. The Feral's cold gaze moved from the Ilina to Julianne and back again. If he was surprised to find two ghost-like women floating in the room, his expression didn't show it.

"Melisande," Kougar said coldly.

Zeeland's gaze jerked toward him in surprise.

"Kougar," Melisande replied as coldly, struggling to her feet. "This is none of your concern."

Holy shit. They knew one another.

Kougar's gaze returned to Julianne. Zeeland's jealousy began to rise as the Feral stared at the naked woman, but the Feral's pale eyes held no carnal interest.

"Hold the moonstone in your palm and make yourself whole," Kougar told her matter-of-factly.

Julianne's head cocked with surprise and she reached for the now mistlike stone. Her hand clamped around it. Seconds later, she began to regain form as she floated down to settle on the floor.

Zeeland snagged Julianne around the waist and

hauled her against his left side, his body singing with relief that he could touch her again. That he could physically protect her.

"I must have the moonstone," Melisande cried angrily. "Queen Ariana suffers without it."

With his foot, Zeeland scooped Julianne's dress off the floor and slid it over her head.

"Ariana is a bitch and a parasite," Kougar snarled. "She deserves to suffer."

"You don't understand."

"I understand better than you think." The Feral turned to Julianne. "Don't ever remove the stone. The longer you wear it, the less chance you'll accidentally turn to mist. If you do feel yourself starting to turn, hold the stone as you did just now until you're back in control."

Julianne stared at him. "How do you know . . . ?"

"The Therian must come with me." Melisande snapped. "He knows the truth."

Kougar shook his head dismissively. "He's practically bound. I can feel the mating bond that all but links them. Once the ritual is complete, the bond will be unbreakable, and he'll be unable to betray her. Your secret will remain safe."

"How dare you interfere! They must die."

"No."

Melisande's expression turned to fury. "I must at least return with the moonstone!"

"The moonstone will ensure that Julianne doesn't turn to mist and give you away. Your bitch of a queen can do without it." Kougar took a threatening step toward the far smaller woman. "Go, Melisande. The threat to your race has been nullified. Your job here is done."

Melisande turned to Julianne, shooting her a killing look. "If you ever betray us . . ."

Zeeland tightened his hold on Julianne even as he turned, putting himself between them. "Get the hell out of here."

With a shout of pure fury, Melisande threw her hands outward, rattling the furniture in a fine show of temper, then disappeared in a rush of cool, pine-scented air.

For several moments no one else moved. Finally, Zeeland relaxed his hold on Julianne, but his gaze remained fixed on the spot where Melisande had stood, not trusting she wouldn't reappear.

Julianne stepped in front of him where she could see his face. "Are you okay?" The softness in her eyes filled his heart, and he pulled her into his arms and held her tight.

Julianne pulled back enough to turn to Kougar. "She killed my parents."

Kougar met Julianne's gaze with cold, expressionless eyes. But his voice was not unkind when he answered. "Your parents were unmated. Unbound." His gaze flicked to Zeeland's. "You must bind yourselves to one another immediately. Your knowledge is a threat they will not allow."

As Kougar turned toward the door, Zeeland released Julianne and followed.

"Kougar. You've known the Ilinas still existed all along."

Kougar didn't turn around. "Yes."

"Why do they let you live?"

The Feral glanced over his shoulder, meeting his gaze with cold eyes, then turned and left without replying.

Zeeland stared after him, then shook his head and turned back to Julianne.

She watched him with pensive, uncertain eyes.

His heart expanded until it ached in his chest. She was so beautiful. So precious to him.

He went to her and pulled her into his arms, cradling her against his chest. "You're sure you're all right?"

Her arms slipped around him, and she clung to him. "Yes."

"Me, too, though I'll be better once we're mated."

She pulled back to look up at him, an aching sadness in her eyes.

"Zee . . . I hate that you're being forced to take me as your mate."

"I'm being forced into nothing."

"You never intended to bind yourself to me."

He smiled. "Not true. I think I knew from the start you were going to be mine someday. I tried to fight my fate, probably because I'd spent a century believing I never wanted to be bound to another. But I was wrong, Sunshine. I spent a century alone and lonely. This past decade without you, I've been miserable. Only with you have I ever been happy. Have I truly felt alive."

Tears gathered in her eyes. "I love you, Zeeland. With all my heart, I love you."

He took her face in his hands and kissed her, tasting her tears. And her joy. And feeling his heart burst in his chest, overflowing with a love that would not be contained.

"I love you, Julianne. Be my mate and my companion for all eternity."

"Yes, Zee. A thousand times yes."

He pulled back and grabbed her hand. "Come on. We'll go downstairs and do it right now, in the middle of the party." A grin spread over his face. "That should get the festivities popping."

Julianne laughed, a sweet, musical sound that sang through his veins and made him feel like he was the one floating this time.

"Are we really going to marry on Valentine's Day?"

He stroked her cheek and smiled with all the love in his heart. "Can you think of a better time?"

"No. It's perfect. You're perfect."

He kissed her again. "As are you, my beautiful Julianne. *Perfect*."

When **PAMELA PALMER**'s initial career goal of captaining starships didn't pan out, she turned to engineering, satisfying her desire for adventure with books and daydreams until finally succumbing to the need to write stories of her own. Pamela lives and writes in the suburbs of Washington, D.C. Please visit her on the web at *www.pamelapalmer.net*.

Kiss and Kill Cupid

JAIME RUSH

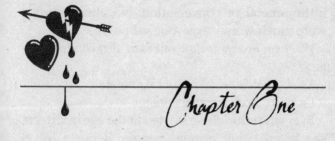

Chapter One

Anyone who hyped Valentine's Day should be locked in a cold theater and made to watch sappy movies for an entire month. While eating nothing but chocolates. No sleeping allowed.

Kristy walked into Casey's Coffee Shop and snarled at the pink and red hearts dangling from the ceiling like an obstacle course. *Five days to go. Let's not forget this mushy stuff has been in my face for three weeks now.* She got into the line and cranked up her iPod to drown out the noise. She bobbed to the funky-alternative-rock band, Does It Offend You, Yeah, as she moved ahead in line. To say that the MP3 player had saved her sanity was not overstating a fact. Reluctantly, she paused "Dawn of the Dead" and pulled out the earbuds as she stepped up to the counter.

"Mondo white chocolate mocha, please."

She readied herself for the noise. Not steam-hitting-metal or conversation. No, these sounds were much worse: everyone's thoughts.

What am I going to do about Stan, that cheating bastard?

Kewl. That hot chick's checking me out.

Crap, my stock just took a dump.

Ever since this curse started at the age of fifteen, she hated being around people. Being a travel writer was much preferable to having to work in an office or in retail. It was also why having a relationship—heck, even having sex—was a nightmare. Hearing the guy's every thought, not so good. For example:

"John, does this skirt make my butt look big?"

"No, not at all, honey." *Only as big as a freakin' mountain.*

Even worse was when they lied about where they had been and with whom.

Being able to pop those earbuds in and hear her fave tunes instead of everyone's thoughts was a godsend. If only she could learn to resist moving her body to the music.

She wasn't just here to grab a coffee, though. She had an important meeting. The magazine she'd been doing freelance assignments for was closing. She needed to line up a new gig. This opportunity had come out of nowhere, a real coup. She was early enough to snag a java and get her bearings before the people she was meeting arrived.

She was going to have to watch *her* thoughts. If everything worked out, Adrian Kruger might be her new boss. From everything she'd read and seen about him online, he was funny, down-to-earth, and mouthwateringly gorgeous. *Bad idea, Kristy, and a good way to lose an assignment.*

The place was a cacophony of voices, audio, and thought, and she tried to tune them out. One thought, though, stood out because it was more menacing than the jumble of other thoughts:

Oh, yes, there she is. That face would look lovely on the news as Kiss and Kill Cupid's next victim.

She turned around, feeling as though she'd been dunked in a vat of ice water. Kiss and Kill Cupid. He'd been menacing New York City for five years, killing a woman on Valentine's Day. The most disturbing aspect was his signature: he left a lipstick kiss along with the words "Kiss and Kill, Cupid" across the dead woman's stomach. The media, of course, had been playing that up as well as the romantic aspects of the holiday.

Had she heard the words correctly? Maybe it was a mix of two people's thoughts that only sounded like . . . all right, she couldn't kid herself. The killer was in here, and he'd found his next victim.

Then her body went even colder. Had he meant *her*? A few men were looking her way though none with an evil gleam in his eyes.

And that long blond hair, I'll bet it's as silky as, well, silk. Maybe I could use it to strangle her with.

She involuntarily clamped her hand over her hair, her heart hammering in her chest.

"Kristy Morgan?"

She jumped at the voice coming from right beside her.

The man standing next to her looked like the pictures in the write-ups, only he was bigger than she'd imagined. And even more gorgeous. He had to be six and a half feet tall, with broad shoulders and straight brown hair that fell to his shoulders. In a cable sweater and jeans, he looked every bit the part of the outdoorsy adventurer.

He smiled. "Sorry, didn't mean to startle you. Are you Kristy?"

Take a breath. "Yes." She held out her hand, jabbing it toward him, feeling flustered and taken off guard in more ways than one. "You must be Adrian Kruger."

He nodded to another man sitting at a table. "My business partner, Owen, and I are sitting over there."

When the barista told her the amount due, Adrian put his hand on hers. "Allow me."

"That's not nec . . ."

He'd already paid the young man, and another barista called out her order. She looked around the café again, fear tightening her throat. *Why is this happening during what might be the most important meeting of my life?*

She took her cup, feeling the warmth seeping into her cold fingers. "I, uh . . . thank you."

He led her toward their table, but her thoughts were a scramble. Owen stood and extended his hand. He wasn't nearly as tall or as built as Adrian. His smile was bland, his gray eyes blank behind his square, black-rimmed glasses. The shaggy blond hair and wrinkled, linen shirt gave him the look of someone confused about what style he was going for: business, college student, or surfer.

She shrugged out of her coat, and Adrian took it from her and draped it over the empty chair. He held out her chair for her. She tried not to seem surprised at the act of chivalry as she thanked him.

She was faced away from most of the café and had to fight not to turn around and keep studying the crowd. Okay, just a glance. Still, no one obvious. The thoughts she heard weren't the killer's:

I've got to get this formula memorized before the exam tomorrow.

When is she going to get here?

Her elbow tipped over her coffee. She caught it before it hit the table even as Adrian tried to grab it, too. Their hands collided, but she kept a hold on her cup. She smiled and tried her best to compose herself. It didn't help that through her earbuds, which were hanging around her neck, Katy Perry was singing about kissing a girl. Kristy yanked down the wires and set them in her lap.

She focused on the two men sitting across from her, her forced smile still in place. "It's so nice to meet you both."

Adrian and Owen had gotten publicity by being twenty-year-olds who'd started a successful outdoor adventure magazine three years ago. They were hailed as "Beauty and the Brain" by one snarky magazine because someone had found a modeling shoot Adrian had done to earn money while he, as he'd put it, worked and lived his way across the country.

She knew she'd like him when he commented in a later article that he was glad he hadn't done the nude layout he'd been offered. That would have given the name of his magazine a whole new meaning.

She tried to push aside the creepy sensation of being watched and focus on the interview. "I love *Get Out!* It's fresh, fun, a bit irreverent, and pushes the boundaries. Maybe I shouldn't say this at the outset, but I'd really like to write for you."

Adrian's perfect smile and white teeth made her heart flutter. "I feel the same about your writing." For such a masculine man, he was surprisingly soft-spoken. "Most of our articles are in-your-face, out-there, rugged adventures. When I read your article about finding inner peace while sitting on a rock in a rushing creek in Helen, Georgia, I forgot about the five meetings I had scheduled that day, forgot about the pile of phone messages sitting on my computer, forgot about the looming deadline. I was there on that rock. I want to share that experience with my readership. I'm thinking a monthly column of about six thousand words to start."

Oddly enough, she had also done some modeling, nudged by her mother, and when she found herself in exotic locales, she became lost in the moment, journaling about how the place made her feel . . . much to the annoyance of the photographer who was waiting on her. She quit modeling and pursued a freelance writing career, covering far-flung (and thus not-so-populated) places.

Owen spoke his first words so far. "As soon as he read your piece, he was determined to bring you on board."

Adrian gave her a pointed look that demonstrated his determination. "You're good. I want you."

Those words shimmered through her. *Want you.* Her writing, of course. With all the other thoughts flying around, she couldn't quite pick up theirs.

Owen's voice was as deadpan as his expression. "As the sales manager, I need to make sure your kind of column would integrate well with the rest of the magazine. And with advertisers. We'd like to see some sample pieces, with *Get Out!* and its high-octane readership in mind." He pulled out three issues of the magazine from a leather satchel and handed them to her.

She nodded as she fought to filter out random thoughts, including one she knew was about her: *That girl's wearing socks with her high heels?*

She involuntarily crossed her ankles beneath her chair, then uncrossed them and even extended her left leg. Yes, pink socks with the periwinkle blue heels that matched her dress. A pink silk scarf around her neck matched her socks.

"I can write up a couple of pieces over the next few days." She brushed a lock of hair from her forehead, taking the opportunity to glance back in hopes of catching someone leering at her with menace in his eyes. No such luck.

She turned back to the two men at her table. Could it be one of them? The thought startled her. *Get hold of yourself, girlie. You're good at masking your reactions. Put on that perky smile, no matter what the other person is thinking.*

'Course, she'd never heard someone plotting her murder before.

Adrian's blue eyes were filled with concern. "Are you all right?"

She took a sip of her coffee, taking a moment to compose. "I'm fine. I'd better get going, though, get to work." She tapped the magazines Owen had given her. She'd read the current issue before the meeting.

She stood, scanning the café. The line of people down the middle blocked her view of the far side of the room.

Oh, yeah, she's perfect. I could have fun with that pink scarf, too.

She grabbed at her scarf as she got to her feet, stumbling as she spun around too fast. Adrian's hand clamped onto her shoulder to steady her.

She laughed in such a god-awful phony way, he couldn't have missed it. "My heel caught on the chair leg."

He turned to Owen. "I'm going to walk her out."

"It's okay. I promise, I'm not a klutz."

His laugh was soft. "Walking a lady out is just something I do."

Really? Is this guy for real? Or is he a murderer?

Damn. All she'd wanted was a freelance job.

"Thanks," she managed, as he held her coat for her.

She slid into it, belting it at the waist and searching the crowd for the face that went with those horrible thoughts. It was her. The killer had definitely targeted her. There wasn't another woman wearing a pink scarf in the whole place. The blood fled her face as she stepped out into the cold.

Maybe Adrian's walking her out was a good thing. She could read his thoughts once they were out of the din of the café.

"I'm taking the subway," she said, nodding toward the entrance from where she'd come.

"I'll walk you. It'll give us a chance to talk more."

She took one last look inside the café. Owen was watching them, that flat look on his face.

"Your business partner is your childhood friend, right?" she asked.

Out in the sun, she could see faint freckles across Adrian's nose and cheeks. It was somehow endearing on such a rugged guy.

"Since third grade."

She wanted to know more about why he'd been so determined to bring her on board. Not to hear accolades about her writing. In the small magazine she'd been published in recently, they always ran her picture. She didn't want to think Adrian had fixated on her, really didn't want to consider that he might be Kiss and Kill Cupid.

"It's hard to imagine. You and he are so different."

She tried to tune in to his thoughts between their banter. Nothing.

"I guess that's what makes our friendship and the magazine work. He's the analytical, business type. I'm the adventurer."

She gave him a lopsided grin. "Beauty and the Brain."

He rolled his eyes. "The write-up I'll never live down."

She found herself laughing at his chagrined expression. "But great publicity, you have to admit." Of course, it would help if she wasn't wishing he'd gone ahead and done that nude layout.

She took a deep breath, inhaling the scents of the city: a hot dog vendor on the corner, spicy Indian food wafting from a restaurant, and cologne that smelled familiar. She picked up the random thoughts of passersby: to-do lists, the kind of mundane stuff she was surprised to find muddled most people's minds a lot of the time.

Except . . . nothing from Adrian.

She paused as she reached the entrance and turned to him. "Thanks for accompanying me." *Thank goodness, not a trip or stumble.*

"My pleasure. Call me when you've got the articles ready." He held out his hand, and when she shook it, hers became lost in that gentle grip. She imagined herself enfolded in his strong arms, her body against his, feeling completely protected, safe, and . . . she pushed away her own intrusive thoughts and focused on his.

But no. Absolutely nothing coming from him. She realized she was still shaking his hand and let go. "Thank you. I'll be in touch soon."

"The sooner, the better." At her surprised look, he added, "I'd like to start working together for the next issue."

She nodded, still stunned she could hear nothing from him. Was it a fluke? Or was he the only person whose thoughts she couldn't hear? She needed more time with him to be sure.

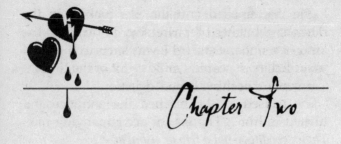

Once Kristy got on the subway, her mind started racing. She'd put in her earbuds and cranked the tunes. She had enough to deal with, like her own whirlwind of thoughts. The man sitting across from her with a wide berth around him talking to himself . . . she did *not* want to hear what was going on in his head.

She'd spent one scary week with people like that. Just before the whole thought-hearing thing started, Kristy had been trying to prove to her younger brother that she wasn't afraid to climb the big oak tree at the park. When she'd reached the top and raised her arms in triumph, she lost her balance and fell. She wasn't hurt, but they had a mother who ran her two children to the doctor at the slightest sniffle.

The doctor confirmed that her brain was fine. Then she'd started hearing voices. After seeing numerous doctors, she'd been taken to a psychiatric facility. It scared her to think she was going crazy. She'd been evaluated, questioned, and while she'd waited in that terrible place, she'd heard real craziness. The patients lived in a haze of paranoia and nonsense. Then she could hear the doctors' thoughts about the patients. That was when she'd realized she was hearing their thoughts.

She sat on the hard plastic bench on the train and thought about what to do. At least she knew what was going to happen. She could prepare for it, protect herself. Not like those other women she remembered seeing in the news. Not like her friend Patsy in college. If he couldn't get to her, though, would he abort his plan for the year? No, he would find another victim. No way could she let that happen. She had to go to the police and convince them she wasn't nuts. Yeah, that was going to be easy.

Do it for Patsy.

She got off at the next subway stop and got back on to return to the stop close to the coffee shop. She found the nearest police station and asked to see an officer. Detective Jake Voigt came out to fetch her. He was good-looking, with short, brown hair, probably in his early thirties. Though he was clean-shaven, his weary eyes and crooked tie made him look as though he had been working twenty-four hours straight.

"You're working the Kiss and Kill Cupid case?" she asked, just to make sure.

"One of a few. You have information?"

She nodded. "I'm going to be the next victim."

He blinked at that. "You'd better come on back."

She followed him into a large area filled with desks and people and thoughts. Her chest got tighter with each step. She'd envisioned talking to the detective in an office or interview room, but he led her to one of those desks and nodded for her to take the plastic chair beside it.

He sat down. "What makes you think you're going to be the next victim, Ms. . . . ?"

"Morgan. Kristy Morgan." She looked up, a slight grimace on her face. "You're going to find this a bit, uh, hard to believe. And I don't blame you, but please hear me out. I can hear people's thoughts."

It was hard to hear any particular thought, but she was pretty sure she heard one of his: *Oh, brother. Another loony.*

"I am *not* a loony." She softened her tone with a smile. Hotly denying it wasn't going to help make her case. She was still sensitive about it, even after all these years. It didn't help that her parents treated her with kid gloves even though she'd long ago lied and told them she didn't hear voices anymore. "See, I knew you thought I was a loony."

He raised one eyebrow. "That's not a stretch."

"I can prove it. Think of something."

I don't have time for this.

She gave him a shocked look. "You don't have time to catch the killer?"

His eyes widened, but he didn't look convinced. "I don't have time for this weird stuff. Do you know how many psychics have come in to give me *clues*?" He did finger quotes on that last word.

"A lot?" she guessed. "But I'm not a psychic. I'm a target, and you can use me to catch him."

He released a soft breath. "Tell me what you came here to say."

"I was at a coffee shop four blocks from here and heard someone thinking I would make a great next victim. He commented on my hair and on my scarf." She fingered her scarf but quickly released it.

"So I suppose you want us to put you under protective custody." He didn't look like he was going to do that anytime soon.

"No. I can take care of myself, lock myself in my apartment with my finger on the 9 on the phone and a kitchen knife in my other hand. What I'm concerned about is the next victim. And the next. I had a friend who was murdered. Raped. Left naked and bloody in her dorm room. The murderer was never found." She swallowed the hitch she felt in her throat. "I want you to use me as a decoy, put me under surveillance, and catch this guy."

He leaned forward. "What am I thinking now?"

She tried to focus in on just one thought, but there were so many. "That you don't believe me."

"Wow, you *can* read minds." He feigned surprise and wonder. "Look, we can't assign men to watch your place because you . . . heard the killer's thoughts." He shook his head. "Yeah, I can see the captain going for that."

"If you have a chance to get this guy, keep him from killing someone else . . . please, you have to."

"We are doing everything we can, ma'am. We've got leads, normal, sane, logical leads—"

"You have leads?"

A man about her age interjected himself into their conversation. He had a shock of blondish brown hair that fell into his eyes and a face that reminded her of a petulant five-year-old.

Voigt rolled his eyes with a loud exhale. "No comment."

"Look, if you've got a suspect, people have a right to know." He flung his hand out, indicating the world at large and nearly smacking Kristy in the face. "They're scared out there. There are only three days until Valentine's Day, and they know he's planning his next murder."

"They're scared because you're stirring them up." Voigt stared at the man, whose fierce passion didn't waver in that withering look. "I have nothing to say to you. What are you doing here, anyway?"

"I came to talk to Detective Frank, and he didn't

say a word about having any leads. Imagine that."

"I'd better not read a damned thing about us having a suspect in that rag of yours."

The man perked up. "I'm honored you read my articles."

"Now go away." Voigt pointed, and the man walked away, glancing back every few seconds. He turned back to her. "I'm sorry, ma'am, but we can't help you. If you hear voices, there are people who *can* help."

She pushed to her feet and turned on her blue heel, muttering, "You knew it would be this way. You shouldn't be surprised." But she'd had to take the chance she would get, perhaps, someone enlightened or open-minded. She looked around. Maybe one of these men would help. No, not a one of them looked any more open-minded than Voigt.

The young man who'd butted in was still in the lobby. He eyed her as soon as she entered and opened the door for her. As it turned out, it wasn't for any chivalrous reason.

"The detective said something about them not being able to watch your place, that you heard the killer."

She eyed him warily. How much had he heard? She paused outside the lights of the police station, not wanting to continue the conversation while walking farther away from safety. "Who are you?"

He held out his hand. "Dale Soza. Maybe you've heard of me?" He looked like he really, really wanted her to have heard of him.

"Sorry, no." She couldn't ignore his outstretched hand and gave in by shaking it halfheartedly. Not her style, but she wasn't sure what this guy was about.

"I write for the *New York News.* It's going to be as big as the *New York Times* someday. I've covered the Kiss and Kill Cupid story since the first murder. He obviously didn't believe you. If you know something that can help this case, try me."

Oh, great. If she told him anything—if he'd overheard more than he was letting on—she was going to be in the paper as a freak. There would go her career. And her potential new assignment. The thought of not working with Adrian made it all the worse, despite her conflicts.

Dale handed her a business card. "I'm legit, if that's what you're worried about. Look me up online. You'll see all my bylines."

"No, it's just that . . . I don't really know anything. I thought I overheard something, but I was probably wrong. Excuse me, I have to get going."

He grabbed at her arm as she began to pull away. "Sorry," he said, pulling back just as quickly. He walked closer, looking at her, standing too close for comfort. "I know you think I want information because I want to break the big story. And I do, of course. But I want this guy put away."

He fisted his hand. "I want to bring him down. I've talked to the victims' families. I've seen their tears. Felt their pain. I'm supposed to be unbiased, uninvolved. But I can't detach like that. So if you know anything, anything at all that will help, tell me. I'll believe you."

"I don't. Really, I don't."

She tuned into his thoughts, wondering if she could believe his earnestness.

I know she knows something. If only I could get her to trust me. I could crack this case. I wonder if she knows she has lipstick on her front teeth.

She couldn't help herself. She rubbed at her teeth as she said, "I've got to get going." She walked away, relieved he hadn't followed. For the first time since she'd moved to the city, she felt afraid. Paranoid. She watched all around her. Of course, she knew always to be aware of her surroundings. As a city girl, she'd learned to walk confidently and not look afraid while using her instincts and common sense.

Her instincts told her someone was watching her. So did the churn of her stomach and the prickle of ice across her skin. She turned, knowing she was giving away her fear. People walked by, minding their business as usual. One was rarely alone in the city, but just then she felt very alone.

Adrian came to mind. Big, muscular Adrian.

"Who might be the killer."

She doubted that, but she wasn't sure why she

doubted it. Maybe because she didn't want him to be, which wasn't a good reason. She breathed a sigh of relief when she walked into the apartment she shared with another woman, who, thankfully, worked nights. She closed her eyes and breathed in the silence for a moment.

Between Kristy's travel and Berta's work schedule and boyfriend, the two rarely saw each other. What Kristy wanted was a place of her own, and with a regular and lucrative assignment, she could swing that.

"If you don't mess it up by getting involved with your potential boss."

She dropped down on the couch but sprang up a minute later. No way could she relax. She got onto her laptop and pulled up Dale's articles on Kiss and Kill Cupid. She read in horrifying detail about the murdered women. Cupid had strangled the last one while her boyfriend slept right next to her. Fear mounted inside Kristy with each gory detail. The killer was cunning and bold and, as the article quoted the police as saying, escalating. He never raped his victims, but there was evidence he tortured them sexually. He strangled them and left his creepy message across their bodies.

She shuddered.

The articles where Dale had interviewed the families were heart-wrenching. She knew how devastated her friend's family had been, how torn up they all were. Tears sprang to her eyes as she stared at the photo lineup of the victims, all women in their early-to-mid twenties like her, smiling, living their lives without a care.

"Well, I'm not letting you get me, you sick son of a bitch. But how am I going to stop you from continuing to wreck people's lives?"

She hadn't been able to take note of all the men in the coffee shop when she'd heard the thoughts. Damn timing. She had three days to figure out who Kiss and Kill Cupid was.

The face that sprang to mind was Owen's, speaking of creepy. Didn't serial killers have flat eyes? Little emotion? Owen was a viable suspect. Her only suspect. What made it tricky was that he was Adrian's best friend.

Or maybe that would help. Who knew Owen better than Adrian? First, she was going to find out everything she could about serial killers. Then she was going to come up with some sample articles to take to the magazine's offices the next day. She would try to hear Owen's thoughts without all the noise. Then she would pick Adrian's brain on Owen's past, his behavior.

She read article after grueling article until her eyes were gritty and her head hurt. All she could think about was how her family would feel if Dale Soza was interviewing them.

She stripped out of her clothes and put on some

flannel pajamas. Tomorrow, she would get some answers that might lead her closer to the truth. And she'd get to see Adrian again.

Adrian watched Kristy disappear into the depths of the subway entrance. Everything about her was gorgeous and intriguing and sweet. Heck, she even dressed like a confection.

He turned and started walking back to the coffee shop. People, all wrapped in coats and scarves, flowed around him. He hardly saw them. All he could see was Kristy's face, a smile breaking out when he'd praised her writing. Vivid pink lipstick, glossy over delicious lips. Dimples at her cheeks.

Liking her, especially being so attracted to her, was going to make this even harder. How was he going to convince her to write for his magazine, talk with her, maybe even flirt a little, knowing she was going to be Kiss and Kill Cupid's next intended victim?

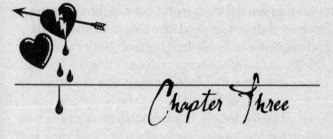

Chapter Three

The next day, Kristy bounced along to a Ting Tings'
song as she walked toward the building that contained *Get Out!*'s offices. Bundled in a dark pink
wool coat with buttons as big as the palm of her
hand, she couldn't get warm. Her thoughts were
chilling her from the inside. She paused her player
after every song and tuned into the thoughts
around her, a total change from what she usually
did.

   She stopped again outside the glass doors at the
entrance and tuned in. The wind blew her hair
into her face as she scanned the sidewalk. She
could almost convince herself she'd imagined
the whole thing. Almost. Truth was, she couldn't
afford to do that. She might end up dead.

   I could be one of those pictures in the paper.

She opened the door and went inside, cringing a minute later at her reflection in the brass walls of the elevator. She combed her hair with her fingers as the door opened. Anticipation tingled through her. The potential job. Finding out if Adrian or Owen was a killer.

A brushed-steel snowboarder catching air adorned the door. She pushed it open and was surprised to find classical music wafting through the air. The walls of the small lobby were covered in dramatic prints of both men and women doing daring things, like skydiving and mountain climbing. The young woman at the curved reception desk was on the phone, so Kristy stepped over to the skydiving picture. The man in the jumpsuit was obviously being photographed by another skydiver. His hair was flying everywhere from beneath his helmet, but his smile was as bright as the sun.

"That's Adrian Kruger," a woman's voice said.

Kristy spun around to find the receptionist smiling at her. "Oh. Cool."

"That's him over there, too." She pointed to one of a man catching a major wave.

Kristy could actually sense the excitement he must have been feeling at that moment. His muscular body, poised on a surfboard, showed perfect form. She turned to the receptionist. "I'm here to see Owen and Adrian. I'm Kristy Morgan."

She'd spent the morning going through some of

her previous articles and reworking the best ones to present. But her mind wasn't on the job. Finding Kiss and Kill Cupid came first.

She planned to meet with both men, hopefully in a nice, quiet conference room. Owen came around the corner and started at the sight of her.

She gave him a wave. "Hi, Owen. I brought those articles you asked for. I thought I'd deliver them personally."

He glanced up and beyond her. "I'll let Adrian handle it. I've got a conference call . . ." He gestured behind him and turned to leave. Odd. Was he avoiding her?

"Well, hey there, Kristy."

She turned at the deep, smooth voice she knew was Adrian's and gave him the I'm-not-a-soft-girl-but-a-businesswoman handshake. "Good to see you." She waved a bright green folder. "I brought the sample articles."

That little pause as he took her in before he said anything . . . she felt it in her gut. He smiled, warmth lighting his eyes. "Excellent. I'm glad you dropped them off in person. I was just heading out to lunch. Join me."

Bad idea, one part of her brain said.

Wouldn't that give me another chance to see if I can read his thoughts? another part of her brain chimed in. "Sure, I'd love to." She glanced down the hall where Owen had disappeared. "Should we wait for Owen?"

"Only if you're dead set on him joining us."

"Oh. I suppose that's fine."

"Be back in an hour, Kyle." He handed the receptionist the folder. "Put this in my office, please."

He held the door for Kristy, and when she passed him, she inhaled his scent. As soon as he closed the door, she turned. "Are you wearing Intuition?"

He had intriguing eyes, made more so by thick eyebrows that perfectly balanced his narrowed eyes. He raised one of those brows. "Oh, you mean my cologne? Yes, Intuition."

"I recognized it because I wear the women's version. Wow, isn't that . . . wild?"

They wore the same brand of cologne. How synced was that?

All of her thoughts ceased when he leaned close and breathed her in. "You're right. I thought you smelled great yesterday, but I didn't realize it was the same. Yeah, wild."

He pressed the CALL button. "Do you like Italian? There's a great café down the block."

"Uh, sure."

She waited in silence. *Silence.* No thoughts. Could it be that he just wasn't having any? No, impossible. She could only still her thoughts for a few seconds at a time.

And if she couldn't read his thoughts—which was amazingly exciting in itself—then he wasn't the one she'd heard at the coffee shop. She couldn't help the cat-ate-the-canary grin on her face and so as not to have to explain it, she kept her head down. *You're feeling way beyond relief. Remember, potential boss. And his best friend, your other potential boss, might be a killer with his eye on you.*

The elevator came, and they stepped inside.

He really made her smile when he said, "I know I'm going to love the articles. Your writing is amazing."

She had to keep from rolling her eyes in ecstasy. Even more than hearing she was pretty, hearing that about her writing made her swoon. "Thanks."

"I've already got an assignment in mind for you."

"Don't the rest of the folks at the magazine have to read the articles and give the okay?"

He gave her a boyish smile that transformed his oh-so-masculine face. "Sure. But Owen and I are the bosses. We get to say who plays."

Focus on Owen. "So I have to win him over. I could swear he was trying to avoid me at the office just now."

"Don't let that worry you. Beautiful women throw him off. He'll get over it."

She could hardly murmur a thank-you at the compliment. Most serial killers had trouble maintaining relationships with women: check.

"He seems pretty serious."

"Always has been. He used to chide me about climbing mountains and jumping out of perfectly good airplanes. I used to chide him about spending all his free time in his room reading."

Serial killers were often antisocial: check.

The elevator doors slid open at the lobby level, and he gestured for her to walk ahead of him. They stepped into a rhythm, walking side by side.

They ended up at a cozy café with the ubiquitous wine bottles in baskets on the tables. The maitre d' led them to a table near the window. Adrian took her coat and gave her outfit both a questioning and appraising look.

"I know, I'm in denial." Her sleeveless yellow dress flared midthigh. White knit tights hugged her legs, and her chunky shoes matched her dress. "February is when I start hating winter, so I put myself in a spring state of mind."

"Aren't you cold?"

"I'm hot-blooded. My body temperature runs a degree warmer than most people's." She shrugged. "My doctor said it's not anything weird."

"Bet you're nice to cuddle up with on a cold night."

She was about to sit in a most dainty way. Those words made her drop the last few inches onto her chair and nearly tip it over. "Well, I wouldn't . . . know. I've never cuddled with myself."

She was so not good at this flirting stuff. All those years of avoiding it had left her way out of practice. Like, she wasn't even sure if he *was* flirting.

She broke off a piece of crusty bread and dipped

it into the herbed oil the waiter had poured into a dish. "One of the articles I read about you said you and Owen are like brothers."

He nodded. "He had a rough childhood. His dad took off, and his mom . . . well, let's just say she wasn't the most nurturing soul. Owen spent a lot of time at our house. We had a warm, loving home, with my stepdad and half brother and half sister. All the neighbor kids hung out there, Owen more than any of them. My mom treated him like another son. I'm seven and nine years older than my half siblings, so I've never been close to them. Owen was like a brother to me, then and now."

Broken home: check. Uncaring mother: check. Oh, no. Owen's background and temperament were sounding more and more like a textbook serial killer. Could she ask, without sounding morbid, if animals had died in heinous ways or disappeared? If Owen had wet his bed or started any fires?

Mm, probably not.

She shifted her foot and felt his shoe next to hers. Their eyes met over the contact. "I'm not playing footsies with you," she said, then stuffed a piece of bread into her mouth before she said anything else dumb.

His mouth tilted up in a half smile, one eyebrow arched. "It's okay if you do."

Whoa. He'd laid that right out there. Of course, a gorgeous guy like him probably had no trouble flirting and lots of experience. Why did he have to be so perfect and so complicated at once?

She didn't remove her foot. Neither did she move it. She glanced away, composing herself. "Your mom sounds like a great person."

He nodded, a soft smile on his face. "She taught me what it was to be tough, to stand strong and take what life gives you. She gave me the love for classical music. I think she had dreams of me becoming a musician. I took cello lessons and played in an orchestra in high school. That was the most mundane thing I ever did. I liked it, but I didn't love it. She was cool about my quitting music, though she didn't like my adventures. Mostly I didn't tell her what I did or the risks. It was better that way."

A man who loved his mother. Could she just die right there? Except dying euphemisms were not particularly good right now.

"It's hard to imagine you playing cello in an orchestra." She leaned back in her chair, her fingers on her chin. "No, wait. I *can* see you. It's an interesting dichotomy, rugged, outdoorsy guy among the classical instruments." She grinned. "I like it."

She liked him. Oh, more than liked. It was as though the energy from where their shoes touched radiated up her leg and into the rest of her body. He was the only person whose thoughts she couldn't hear. That would be wildly appealing even if he wasn't the kind of guy who climbed mountains and dove off cliffs and embraced life. And, most importantly, he wasn't Kiss and Kill Cupid. Her foot shifted ever so slightly against his. *But he might, very likely, probably, will be your boss.*

She pulled her lower lip between her teeth. "So, what's this assignment you've already thought of?"

His eyebrow lifted the tiniest bit at her move beneath the table. "I've read a few of your articles, and a couple focused on areas with energy vortexes, ley lines, things I don't profess to understand but find . . . fascinating." His mouth quirked as he watched her worry her lower lip. "I've been to a town I think has that kind of weird energy: Wimberly, Texas. A bit off the beaten path and involves a little hiking. You'll like it, as long as you're not claustrophobic. You go down into a cave. Not far. It feels as though you're in a cathedral. There's a pool of water, and all around are stalactites and stalagmites. Go early in the day; you'll want to spend a couple of hours there."

She had propped her chin on her hands, elbows on the table. "Mm, sounds almost spiritual. You've been there, I take it."

"It's on a friend's property. I've been meaning to go back for years." He looked wistful. "When I was in high school, I wanted to travel and experience life. After I graduated, I took odd jobs as I traveled, just enough to pay my expenses. That's how I ended up doing that modeling gig, climbing a wall in an indoor entertainment place. Then I had this dream of starting the magazine. The ironic thing is I publish an adventure magazine but don't have time to have adventures anymore."

She frowned. "That's very sad. And wrong. Sounds like you have to make time."

The food arrived, and she dug into her fettuccini Alfredo. Twirling the strands around her fork was a challenge. *Way to go, pick a sloppy meal, Kristy.* When she looked up at him, he was watching her. Not in an amused or *God, what was I thinking taking this woman out to eat?* way but like he was a million miles away worrying about someone he cared about.

"Is everything all right?" she asked.

He blinked, as though rousing himself from a shadowy thought. "Fine." He picked at his chicken Parmesan. He did not look like the type of guy who picked at his food. "I'm going to ask the staff to give your samples a read tonight and give me their thoughts tomorrow. What's your schedule look like in the next few days?"

Hm, learning about serial killers. Worrying about being the next victim. Trying not to get killed. She gave him a perky smile. "I'm mostly free."

"Great. I want to get together and go over the particulars of the assignment I mentioned."

"You're pretty optimistic that Owen's going to like my stuff."

He gave her a heart-stopping smile. "I usually get my way."

Uh-huh, she bet he did. They passed on dessert once the waiter had cleared the table. When he brought the check, Adrian reached for it. So did she.

She tugged it out of his hand. "My treat. This is a business lunch." Even though, for a few moments there, it had felt suspiciously like a date. She slapped her credit card on the little tray and handed it to the waiter. Her smile was as coy as the one Adrian had given her. "I'm good at getting my way, too."

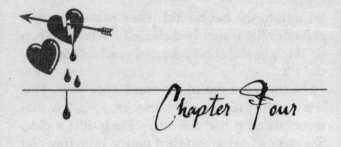

After lunch, Adrian helped Kristy into her coat, his big hands resting on her shoulders for a second. She felt the tips of his fingers at her back as they wound their way around the tables to the entrance. He grabbed a couple of mints from the glass bowl and handed one to her. She slipped it into her mouth and crunched it as he held the door for her. She stepped out into the windy afternoon, he right behind her. Dark clouds scudded across the sky. Her hair whipped around her face, and she twisted it into a ponytail and held it in one hand.

"Are you taking the subway?" he asked. "I'll walk you to the entrance."

"Thanks."

As they started walking down the sidewalk, a

whirlwind of dirt and garbage swirled around them, making her cover her eyes.

"Let's duck in here." He took her arm and pulled her into an alcove of a store that had closed. "That cold front is moving in. I'm going to call my car service. You don't want to be walking in this. It's only going to get worse." Before she could say *That's not necessary*, he was on his cell phone. He must have had the number in his speed dial. He gave someone an address and hung up. "They'll send a car in fifteen minutes."

"Thank you."

Wind and dirt blinded the people they saw braving the gusts, but they were protected in the alcove.

"You should start writing again," she said. "I read some of your earlier pieces on your Web site."

"I'd love to, but there's too much managing to do."

"I love what I'm doing. I can't imagine giving that up for anything."

"The last time I left for a week, Owen nearly ran off half the staff. I know it's hard to believe," he added with a wry smile, "but he's not very personable." Cold mist hung on his words.

How unsocial was he? There were so many questions she wanted to ask but couldn't without sounding hinky. "Is he just not good with people?"

"He's more of a loner personality." Adrian was

being diplomatic. A good friend for Owen, not helpful for her investigation.

He reached toward her neck with one hand. She thought he might cup her cheek, which was icy cold. He held up one of her earbuds, and she heard the tinny sound of music floating out.

"What are you listening to?"

"I forgot to put them away." She gave him a sheepish smile. "I usually tuck them out of sight." She was so used to hearing it, she hadn't even noticed.

"I saw you coming down the sidewalk earlier, bouncing away."

She rolled her eyes. "I can't not move. I must look like a dweeb."

"You looked charming, actually." He tucked one of the buds into his ear. She took the other and put it in hers to see what was playing.

"Puscifer," she said in answer to his earlier question. "I've gotten hooked on what I call punky alternative rock." She gave him a serious look. "I don't think they use cellos."

"I doubt it."

The song was "The Mission," from last year and still one of her faves. She thought he might turn his nose up at her music, but he was smiling and even . . . yes, bobbing his head a bit.

And he was very close, his nose nearly brushing hers, his mouth only a couple of inches away. *I'm too close to landing this gig to mess it up right now by kissing him, but oh my Lord, do I want to.*

His gaze slipped down to her mouth but lifted back to her eyes. "I have a personal rule about getting involved with people I work with," he said, though he hadn't moved away.

"That's probably a good idea." Her breathy voice didn't sound exactly convincing.

"I've worked with attractive women before. It's never been a problem." He lowered his head. "I've never wanted to break my rule before . . . until now. I've never met someone who mesmerized and enchanted me as completely as you have."

She felt her heart hitch, but words weren't even thinking of coming out.

"I want you to write for my magazine."

She met his eyes, hers feeling heavy at their closeness. "I want to write for your magazine, too."

"I want you."

He leaned close and kissed her. First a gentle, soft kiss. He was looking at her, gauging her reaction. *Okay, forget all that safe thinking, forget the ramifications.* She kissed him back, closing her eyes and sinking into it. And she couldn't hear his thoughts. No running commentary, no critiques, just her thoughts and the feeling of his mouth sliding against hers, taking his time, toying with her.

Sinking? No, she was falling. She parted her lips, and he took the invitation and dipped into her mouth with his tongue. Her heart was beating at a pulse point at her throat, and she felt a delicious thrum throughout her body. She put her hands on his shoulders and pulled him closer. She had to lean her head back to kiss him, which reminded her how tall he was, how big and strong, and what a turn-on that was.

He slid his hand behind her neck, rubbing it in slow, languid movements. His mouth tasted fresh and minty. He must have crunched his mint, too, because she didn't feel it as her tongue explored him. His kiss was deep and slow and playful, and she couldn't help but think he probably made love the same way.

Groan.

The ache for a sensual touch washed over her. To be held, to feel his hands on her body, everywhere, his naked body against hers, to feel every inch of him . . .

Groooaaannn.

All those long-neglected parts of her body weren't actually dead to the world like she'd thought. They sprang to life with painful heat. Would she seem slutty if she suggested they go back to his place right this second?

Yes, yes, yes . . . uh, what was the question?

Just as she was drowning, a picture in her mind jarred her completely out of the moment. Like the flash of a scene from a movie, she saw a woman lying naked on the floor. A dark ring of bruising around her neck. Her eyes lifeless. A lipstick kiss on the creamy white skin of her stomach. Those horrid words written in bloodred.

Oh, God. Me.

She pushed back with a gasp.

"What's wrong?" he asked. "Did I hurt you?" But he looked startled, too, as though she'd just up and smacked him in the face with her purse.

"I . . . saw something." She rubbed her mouth, stunned by the image now seared into her brain. She couldn't hear Adrian's thoughts . . . but she'd just *seen* them. That was the only explanation. With wide eyes she backed away from him. "You're him. Kiss and Kill Cupid. I saw . . . I have to go."

He pulled her back, pinning her against the glass door. "What did you see, Kristy? You have to tell me, because I saw something, too, when we were kissing."

The fear in his eyes was nearly as intense as what she was feeling. "I saw myself dead. The lipstick message on my body."

He nodded. "That's what I saw. I'm not the killer, Kristy. But you're his next victim." He released her and took a step back. "This is going to sound crazy. Bear with me. Sometimes I see things. Images, visions. The first time it knocked me sideways. I was fifteen. I shook hands with this man, a friend of my parents, and *saw* him in a hospital with tubes and wires coming out of him. He looked healthy in person. I thought, *Man, did someone slip something into my drink at that party last night?*

"A couple of days later I heard my parents talking about the man, saying he was in the hospital, and my mom was upset after they'd gone to visit him. You guessed it: he was hooked up to machines. He suffered another heart attack a day later and died. I was freaked out. And I couldn't tell anyone about it. My parents, they're open-minded, but not *that* open-minded. It's happened a few times in the last eight years. Sometimes I see the person dead, no clue as to how it happened. That's the most frustrating." He saw the shocked expression on her face. "I know, you think I'm nuts, and you want to hightail it out of here. But for the sake of your life, you have to take me seriously."

She couldn't believe what she was hearing. No, she could believe it. He'd started getting these visions at around the same age as she started hearing thoughts. That was way more coincidental than their wearing the same fragrance. "I don't want to hightail it out of here."

That seemed to surprise him. "Really?"

"Really. I'm just trying to get my head around it. You saw my death when we met at the coffee shop?"

"No, that was the weirdest part. I saw it after I read your article. One second I was thinking I liked your writing and maybe your style would work for the magazine, then I saw your picture and thought, *Damn, and she's beautiful, too*, and then I saw you . . . dead." His face paled at that. "I saw the lipstick kiss and, with all the publicity recently, I remembered how Kiss and Kill Cupid leaves that and his signature on his victims' bodies. I had to do something. I had intended to contact you anyway, but this made it urgent. I figured I'd either send you out on assignment on Valentine's Day or ask you out so I could protect you."

What he'd told her hit her in several ways. He'd liked her writing *before* he'd seen her picture. That was good. His wanting to protect her was nice, too. "So the kiss . . . that was all part of your plan?"

He shook his head and rubbed the back of his neck. "That wasn't planned at all. I never dreamed the moment I laid eyes on you I'd be knocked flat. I've never felt like this with anyone. And now you think I'm nuts, and I don't blame you if you never want to see me again, but you've got to let me be your bodyguard on Valentine's Day."

She tilted her head, still taking in everything he'd said. "I believe you. And I don't think you're crazy." Something bright and shiny was growing inside her. He possessed the same kind of ability she did. She had met the only person whom she could tell the truth and not risk being called crazy. The only person who could understand.

He stared at her, dumbstruck. "Seriously? Just like that?"

She smiled. "Seriously. I know Kiss and Kill

Cupid has targeted me." And she told him about her own strange ability and what had happened at the coffee shop.

"No shi—sorry. This is incredible that we both have some kind of psychic ability. Maybe that's why I feel so connected to you."

She smiled. "I feel that, too."

Now it looked as though he were trying to wrap *his* mind around it all. "So you can . . . read my thoughts?"

"Not yours. For some reason, you're exempt."

A car horn honked. Adrian looked over at the black Lincoln parked at the curb. "That's the car I called for you. I want to talk more about this. I want to see you tonight."

I want you. His earlier words still tingled through her.

"I can't. I've got a family obligation: dinner at my parents'. Kiss and Kill Cupid only strikes on Valentine's Day. I'm safe until then. I'll see you tomorrow at the office. You can tell me what the others thought of my articles. And we can talk more."

She felt the urge to kiss him good-bye and pushed past it. They weren't there yet. They had a lot of things to sort out. But one thing she knew for sure: she *would* kiss him again.

Kristy didn't return to her apartment until eleven that night. Surprisingly, her roommate was home, shut in her bedroom with the television blaring.

The place smelled like tofu and curry. Kristy wrinkled her nose. The kitchen was sparkling clean, and Berta had left a sticky note for her:

Found coffee grounds on the counter! Clean, clean, clean!

Berta described herself as "lovably chunky." In her early twenties, she had pretty brown eyes nearly hidden by a fringe of black bangs and thick eyebrows. She'd taken one look at Kristy and proclaimed that she didn't want a buddy, especially not a skinny blonde one—just a roommate. And that had been that. Whenever they did cross paths, Berta would invariably look her up and down and sniff. Whatever that meant. Her only clue was that once Berta had rolled her eyes, and uttered, "*Pink.*" This from a woman who wore black all the time.

Kristy wasn't particularly fond of Berta, but the apartment was nice, close to the subway, a small park, and the best sushi restaurant in the city, at least in her opinion. She poured herself a half glass of white wine and closed herself in her room.

Immediately her body stiffened. The bed was mussed. Now, she wasn't a make-the-bed-so-a-quarter-can-bounce-on-it kind of person. But her small room was neat, all her clothes hung up and organized by color, shoes in racks beneath them. She'd made her bed that morning, pulling the vibrant blue comforter covered with pink flowers over her pillows and tossing the shams over them.

Both shams were askew, and there was a big wrinkle at the foot of her bed. Fortifying herself with a sip of wine, she walked over to the second bedroom door and knocked. She could hear laughter and a comedienne, Margaret Cho, she thought, talking about a disastrous date.

Berta yanked open the door. "Yeah?"

"I was just wondering if you'd had some reason to go into my room today. Not that I'm accusing, mind you. In fact, I hope you did go in there."

"I don't have no business in your bedroom. I told you that from the outset, you don't go in my room, I don't go in yours. For no reason."

"Okay, just checking. Good—"

The door had already closed.

I really need to find a new place. She went back to her room, looking around. Nothing was missing as far as she could tell. Most of her jewelry was costume, only valuable to her. Her clothes weren't valuable to anyone but a clotheshorse who wore a size seven. That definitely excluded Berta.

She closed the curtain on her one window and got undressed. She wore frilly panties and a matching bra. Not for anyone but her. Until that day, she hadn't thought anyone else would ever see her underthings.

She tossed her panties in a special basket for her lingerie and slid into silky pajamas. Dinner at her parents was nice, as always. She'd given them an extralong hug before she'd left. Not that she was worried.

Okay, she was a little worried. But with Adrian promising to watch over her, she could breathe a little sigh of relief. The hard part, though, was still to come.

He laid the pink, lacy thong underwear on his dresser, like a gift to the god of death. Next to that was Kristy's picture, smiling, so beautiful. After her death, he would burn it and anything else he'd taken from her apartment. He knew the errors other serial killers had made. He wouldn't make those dumb mistakes.

It had started when he was twelve, this desire to create a sensation by murder. He'd been walking home from school and seen a group of people gathered in front of an empty lot. Sirens wailed in the distance. He'd run over, nudging his way to the front of the crowd.

One woman had tried to stop him. "Oh, honey, you're too young to see such a terrible thing."

Of course, that had made him more determined. When he finally pushed through, he'd seen the most amazing sight: a woman's body, sprawled naked on the weed-grown lot, her skin gray, her legs spread apart. Someone had done that to her, and he'd left her in a grotesque position to garner the most reaction.

He'd followed the news. It was all everyone talked about, every tidbit, every clue, who the woman was, her last day alive, even her last meal. Then, two months later, another woman turned up dead in the same way. People were whispering about a serial killer. He didn't even know what that was, but he looked it up: someone who got off by killing people. He'd become fascinated by serial killers. Kill a couple of people, especially decent, beautiful women, and you were a freaking star. People were scared of you. They talked about you. The news reported on you, gave you a cool nickname. Sometimes they showed sketches. He devoured books and articles on Son of Sam, the Zodiac killer, and Danny Rollins.

When a third woman showed up dead, the town went crazy. Women walked in groups, never alone. The sales of alarms and dead bolts skyrocketed. Fear escalated. All because of this one man. The thought of it was intoxicating. From that moment on, he knew what he wanted to be when he grew up: a serial killer.

The killer who inspired him got caught eventually. He made a stupid mistake, got too eager, let his passion overcome his good sense. Escalated. That was what the police called it.

He stroked the edge of Kristy's picture. That wasn't going to happen to him. One kill a year was enough, would have to be. He wasn't driven by madness, wasn't after the control or even the sexual aspect. Controlling one woman, big deal. Controlling an entire city, now *that* was cool. He wanted the fame, the glory, the fear. He didn't rape the women because of the possibility of leaving DNA. No, what he loved was the game. The anticipation. Finding his next victim. Getting to know her. Seeing the horror on her lovely face, watching her fear as he stripped her naked, bound her arms and legs, and toyed with her. The power of taking her life, his gloved hands circling her throat, pressing hard, hearing her last gasps. All heavenly.

Last year he'd forgone that to throw the police a curve by changing his victim type. But always, he left his signature and the kiss, so the police would know exactly who was responsible. He put lipstick on wax lips and pressed them to her stomach, taking no chance that a flake of his skin would be left behind in the lipstick.

Mostly, though, he hungered for the first news report: television footage of the victim's body being carted out of her apartment; the crime-scene tape; the flashing lights and the crowd pushing as close as they could get to catch a glimpse of something gruesome to tell their friends about. That's what got him off.

He smiled. Kristy was only a bit player. He would be the star. He kissed Kristy's picture. "Soon, my dear, the show will be on."

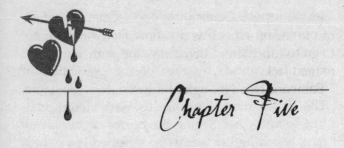

Chapter Five

The next day Kristy strode into the offices of *Get Out!*, anticipation buzzing through her. Her gaze went right to the skydiving picture, though, with the classical music playing, she imagined Adrian playing a cello. She couldn't help the smile that broke out on her face. She aimed that smile at Kyle, the receptionist with long, curly hair.

"Kristy Morgan, here to see Adrian."

"I'll ring him."

Kristy was a jumble of nerves. Excited about the job prospect. More excited about the prospect of Adrian being someone in her life. Scared about Kiss and Kill Cupid.

It figured . . . find the man of her dreams and become the target of a killer at the same time.

She hung up her coat on the rack. Kyle's thoughts ran to the mundane, as most people's did. Where to go to lunch, her upcoming date with someone named Jack.

Someone else's thought, though, jarred her.

Mm, I can see her tied spread-eagled to the bedposts while I torture her.

She spun around, catching Owen walking into the lobby. The blood fled her face. He was the only man in the vicinity. It had to be his thought. More disturbingly, his expression remained passive, giving away not a hint of his dark musing.

She pushed away her fear. She had to engage him, see what other thoughts came out. "Owen, good to see you again." She forced herself to reach her hand out to him.

He reluctantly took her hand, and she cringed at the dampness of his palm. He wasn't meeting her gaze now, though, shifting his light gray eyes away to Kyle. "I've got to run out for a few minutes." He glanced her way. "Uh, see you later."

He sprinted out the door.

"That's odd," Kyle said with a shrug. "I've never seen him move so fast."

He was acting odd.

Couldn't meet her gaze.

Nervous.

Check, check, check! She had definitely found the Kiss and Kill Cupid—and he was Adrian's best friend and business partner.

"Hello, there." Adrian's voice, even low and soothing as it was, couldn't calm her jangled nerves.

Kristy managed a smile anyway. Just the feel of his hand enveloping hers injected a sense of protection, like a warm, pulsing energy flowing through her.

His dark blue knit shirt set off his eyes, and the warmth of his smile, which reached those eyes, tempered the cold inside her. He gestured down the hall. "Come on back to my office." To Kyle, he said, "Hold my calls."

Your friend . . . your business partner . . . the words wanted to burst out. *Stay calm. You can't throw something like that out there. You have to ease into it.*

He allowed her to precede him into the first office on the left, then closed the door behind him. He leaned against the front edge of his desk, and that angle put them more face-to-face. She realized he was doing it for that reason.

"The staff loved your writing."

And he didn't even make her ask or wait through small talk. Lord, she could love this man. She wanted to hug him, but that seemed inappropriate here and now.

She clasped her hands together. "That's great. Awesome. Amazing."

"I'm going to have my secretary book you a flight to Texas first thing tomorrow. You'll come back on Monday, the fifteenth."

Her smile faded. "You're trying to send me away over Valentine's Day."

"You bet. He can't try to kill you if you're not in town."

She rubbed her hand down her arms. "He'll find someone else, then."

His determined expression faltered. "I didn't think about that. All I was thinking was getting you out of harm's way."

"I couldn't live with myself if I came back and saw the woman who was supposed to be me, her face in the paper, those memorials people do . . . she'll be this wonderful, nice, sweet woman who volunteered at the children's hospital." She pushed forward, stopping only a few inches from him. And a few inches below him, of course. "We have a chance to actually catch this guy. We know I'm his target. We can stop him."

She saw a mix of disbelief and awe on his expression. "You're serious?"

"You bet," she said, using his earlier words.

"And you have a plan, I suppose?"

"Well . . . no. Not yet. It's not something you can just look up on the Internet. We'll come up with something."

"I know one thing: I'm not leaving your side on Valentine's Day."

She shook her head. "As appealing as that idea is, that'll scare the guy away. He'll find some other gal who's not lucky enough to have a big, bad dude watching over her."

"I'll stay out of sight, but not far away. Not for a second."

"That could work." His protectiveness warmed her down to her toes. "I've been reading up on Kiss and Kill Cupid. Typically he's broken into a single woman's apartment while she slept or sometime that evening. Last year he deviated from his M.O. and broke into a couple's apartment."

"And strangled her right next to her boyfriend whom he chloroformed." His expression was sour. "I've been reading, too."

"He's getting more daring. Which means we have to be more careful."

He touched her chin, tilting her face up to his. "I don't like this."

"I agree. But I can't live with hiding out and letting this monster get someone else. And I don't think you could, either. We just have to play this smart."

"When you heard his thoughts at the coffee shop, did you get a good look around?" His eyes widened. "That's why you looked so distracted."

"I'm only a klutz when I've heard someone plotting my demise. I did check for men who were looking at me in menacing ways but didn't see anyone obvious. But there were people I couldn't see on the other side of the line. I'm not sure I'd recognize anyone there if I saw him again." She decided to broach the subject. "Except for you and Owen, and I know it's not you."

"If this guy's been watching you, and he probably has, then he knows that you and I have had lunch. He doesn't have to know it's business. We're in the beginning phase of dating. So we go out on Valentine's Day. But we kiss good-bye at the door—a really good kiss—and I leave. Or so it appears."

"And sneak around the back of the building, where I let you in. He's outside . . . watching me." She scrubbed her hands down her arms at the thought. "He thinks I'm alone. I've got a roommate, but I overheard her making Valentine's Day plans with her boyfriend. I'll make sure to walk in front of the windows a few times, so he knows I'm alone. Then I'll close the curtains and tuck in for the night."

"Is there a fire escape or any exterior way for him to get in?"

"I'm on the second floor. The stairs to the fire escape don't look as though they would work. It can be climbed, I suppose, if someone was good at that kind of thing." She gave him a mock-suspicious look. "Like you are."

"As soon as he's in, I flatten him." He flexed a fist big enough to flatten about anybody.

She ran her fingers over his hand, looking up at him through her eyelashes. "My, sir, what a big fist you have."

"All the better to save your pretty little ass, my dear."

She giggled despite the circumstances. "Kiss me. Now that we have a plan, let's see if your vision changes."

He rolled his eyes. "The things I have to do for you." He kissed her.

One of the songs on her iPod was "Electric Feel," by MGMT, and they sang about being shocked by an electric eel. That was how she felt, an electric shock buzzing through her, from where their tongues danced right down to her toes.

No ugly-death vision yet. This was good. She slid her hands around his neck. Oh, yes, this was very good. His hair was silky soft, and she loved the way it felt sliding through her fingers. His hands were splayed across her back, holding her close against his hard body and one hard part in particular.

Just as she was revving up, the gruesome image of her dead body flashed into her brain, knocking her back.

"I guess she accepted the assignment," a voice said from the door—the open door where Owen had been watching them for who knows how long. He didn't look pleased, or embarrassed, or much of anything. The guy creeped her out, especially after what she'd heard him thinking about her. Which made her realize that the man Adrian would have to flatten might be his best friend.

Adrian gave him a smile without a hint of chagrin at being caught necking in his office. "It's our lucky day."

It's his lucky day, Owen thought, walking in. "I did knock, but obviously you were too preoccupied to hear it." He handed Adrian a blue folder. "Here is the advertising summary for the March issue." He gave her a dark look before turning. "I'll leave you two alone." He pulled the door shut with a loud click.

She stared at the closed door for a second, her arms crossed over her chest. "He's not happy about my coming on board."

"It's the mixing of business-pleasure thing."

She turned to him and lowered her voice. "I hate to say this, I really do. There was one person who came off as a bit strange at the coffee shop: Owen."

"No way." He shook his head, not a doubt on his face.

"You're a bit biased, don't you think?"

"I've known him almost all my life."

"Yeah, but do we really know the people in our lives? People who knew Ted Bundy never suspected his terrible hobby. Owen is odd, you have to admit that."

"Absolutely. He's always been that way. But I've never seen him so much as lift his hand in anger. Or muse about killing someone. To be honest, I'm not even sure he likes women. He doesn't seem to date, or if he does, he doesn't talk about it to me."

"Another commonality of serial killers: social impairment with the opposite sex. And he does like women. When I came in today, he had a thought about . . . me: *Mm, I can see her tied spread-eagled to the bedposts while I torture her.* Torture!"

"He could have meant in a good way." He looked her up and down. "I could imagine you tied up while I torture you, bringing you to the brink, backing off." He cleared his throat. "For example. Not that I'm thrilled he's having those kinds of thought about you."

"I couldn't hear anything else; he nearly tripped over himself to get away from me. You didn't tell him I could hear people's thoughts, did you?"

"No. He doesn't even know about my visions. He's a see-it-to-believe-it kind of guy. Doesn't believe in ghosts or psychics or anything like that. So I never told him." He walked over to the window, looking down at the sidewalk. "I won't even go there. It's not Owen."

She couldn't blame him, but *she* wasn't going to accept his belief in Owen. "Okay, we won't go there. But what if, and just humor my wild imagination here, it is Owen who climbs into my window? What would you do?"

"I suppose I would flatten him, as planned. But it's not him."

She walked up beside him. "Come over for dinner tonight. I'll cook."

That got a smile out of him. "I'd love to. Then we can go over the plan, where I'll hide, all that."

"And we can kiss. I kind of liked that."

She gave him a quick kiss good-bye and walked out, hoping to get another chance at Owen's thoughts. No such luck. She pulled on her coat, and with another glance at the picture of Adrian skydiving, left the office.

Adrian wasn't going to help her pin down the idiosyncrasies that might indicate Owen's murderous tendency. As defensive as he'd gotten, he would never look at Owen objectively.

She stepped into the elevator and dug in her purse for her lip balm. Her fingers bent a business card: Dale Soza's card. He was as eager as she was to catch Kiss and Kill Cupid, though for other reasons. Still, as a reporter, he would be objective. Could she trust him?

She stepped out of the elevator and called him. "Dale, my name is Kristy. We met at the police station two days ago."

"Long, blond hair?"

"Yep, that's me."

"You had information on Kiss and Kill Cupid."

"Not information, per se. But I have someone I'd like you to check out, if I can trust you to be discreet and not to print his name or mine."

"You can't get to my level of success by not being trustworthy. Where are you? I can meet you right now."

She gave him her location. "There's a Starbucks on the corner."

"I'll catch a cab and be there in about fifteen, twenty minutes."

"See you then."

She walked inside, inhaling the rich scent of coffee. After ordering, she stuck in her earbuds and found an empty table. The only thought she could hear was her own: *I sure hope I haven't made a huge mistake.*

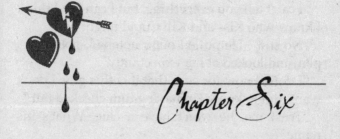

Dale burst in sixteen minutes later, scanning the crowd for her as he untangled his earbuds. He wore a backpack and looked like a college student taking a break from mad-crazy finals. He held up a finger to indicate she wait for a second while he ordered an espresso. From his rapid movements, she suspected he'd already had at least four. His hair was again in disarray, and his cheeks were flushed from the cold.

He dumped five packs of raw sugar into his cup, jabbed the stir stick in circles, and set the cup on the table before dropping down into the seat next to her. "What do you have for me?"

No wonder he had so much energy. He was hyped on caffeine and sugar.

"I can't tell you everything, but I can say I think I know who Kiss and Kill Cupid might be."

"No shit." He pulled out a notepad, poised his pen, and looked at her expectantly.

"I don't know for sure that it is this guy. I don't want him to know I'm having him checked out."

"Trust me, he won't have a clue. What's his name?"

"Owen Bushnell. He co-owns *Get Out!* magazine here in New York."

He was writing furiously in a kind of shorthand. "Never heard of him or the mag. Is it a gay rag?"

"No, outdoor adventure."

He nodded. "Okay, and why do you think he's the killer?"

"That's the part I can't tell you. You have to trust *me* on that."

"Fair enough." He gave her a serious look. "I have a bad feeling about this. About you, in particular. Do you believe in that kind of thing?"

"Sort of."

She tuned into his thoughts among the murmur of everyone else's. *What does she know? What is she holding back? If only she'd tell me everything.*

She took a sip of her coffee. "I know serial killers have certain tendencies. Owen fits some. Socially uncomfortable. Broken home. Loner. Maybe you can find out if he fits the profile. I figured from your articles you know Kiss and Kill Cupid pretty well."

"Unfortunately, that I do. What I really want to write is an article about how they caught the guy." He jabbed his thumb at his chest. "And how I helped." He tapped the notepad. "Has this guy been bothering you?"

"Not bothering, per se." She shook her head. "Sorry, I can't get into it."

"Tell me this: has he just appeared in your life in the past few days? The police think that's what Kiss and Kill Cupid does, targets his victim and gets to know her in the days leading up to Valentine's Day."

Well, that fit Adrian more than Owen. "His friend approached me about a business opportunity."

"His friend." Dale poised his pencil over his notepad. "What's his name?"

"No, it's not him."

"Can you be sure about that?" He studied her. "What, you're into him, aren't you? Can't imagine a nice guy could be a killer? Think again. Ted Bundy was the nicest guy around. He even helped at a suicide hotline. Can you believe that? He helped people to not take their lives, then went out and killed." He shook his head, but his gaze narrowed in on her. "It's not worth your life to trust anyone."

She felt a tightness in her chest. "Just check out Owen."

Dale whipped out his BlackBerry from his backpack. "Owen Bushnell," he muttered as his thumbs danced over the tiny keys. Bart Simpson peered at her from the skin on the back, asking, *Do I know you?* Dale scanned the results. "A few articles connected to the mag. I'll see what I can dig up about his past."

"That would be great."

He tapped his BlackBerry. "I've got your number. I'll let you know if I find anything suspicious. In the meantime, do you have any protection? Gun, pepper spray?"

She patted her purse. "The standard pepper spray." Which she could use to disable the guy so Adrian could whack him.

He shoved his BlackBerry into a pouch in his cargo backpack. "Be careful. And remember what I said: don't trust anyone."

Kristy had run errands the rest of the afternoon. Her cell phone rang with the latest Offspring song while she was checking out at the grocery mart. Her heart jumped. It was Adrian.

"Hey, there," he said. "Where are you?"

"Don't you want to know what I'm wearing?" She couldn't help the grin breaking out on her face.

"I'll find that out later. I'm sure it'll be something bright enough to cheer up this dreary day."

"Actually, I haven't been home yet. I'm getting the fixings for dinner right now."

"Are you close to my office?"

"Not very far."

"Why don't you come here? I'm running a little late. I've got a conference call in three minutes. You can park the perishables in the fridge here. I'll call the travel agent we use to make your travel plans."

"For after Valentine's Day."

"After Valentine's Day," he confirmed, a bit begrudgingly. "Later in the week, just in case this all goes down and we need to stay around and answer questions. After we get your flights hammered out, we can head to your place together."

"Are you trying to protect me?" It was getting dark already.

"Maybe I want to spend more time with you. Then I can help you with dinner."

"Deal. Be there in a few mins."

She arrived at the office shortly after. The door was still unlocked, but it looked as though everyone had gone home. She peered in Adrian's office. He was on the phone, but he gestured around the corner, and she found the break room. She put her bag in the fridge, content to wander the hallways, until she realized Owen might not be in his office.

"Can I use a computer?" she whispered.

He nodded and she took off, looking for an office that might be Owen's. Ah, God bless the nameplate. She found it on the next door and slipped in. The lights were off, and only the watery, gray light outside washed in through the window. She settled into his leather chair and turned on the PC. He had no pictures of friends or family on his desk or credenza. Nothing much of a personal nature. A few seconds later she opened his Internet Explorer page and dropped down the History list for that day.

She scanned the list. Nothing about how to murder a woman, of course, but a couple of newspaper sites. She opened the sublist on one of those. *Bingo.* He'd been reading about Kiss and Kill Cupid. Other news items, too, but those could be a cover. She went to the other newspaper site and found the same thing. That one was Dale's story. She'd made the right decision.

"What are you doing?"

She swiveled to find Adrian—thank goodness it wasn't Owen—standing behind her looking at the screen. "He's been reading up on Kiss and Kill Cupid."

"Who hasn't? It's in the news. People are morbidly fascinated by it."

He had a point. She closed down the computer. "I'm leaving the possibility open that he could be the one. And I respect that you don't see it that way. Let's just leave it at that, 'kay? I don't want this evening to be about all this, other than making our plan."

"Deal," he said, though his expression was a bit darker. "Ready to go?"

"Sure am."

He was quiet as they waited for the car he'd called. She caught herself wanting to make it right, to make her case, anything to smooth things out. Damn, this was when she wished she could hear his thoughts.

No, scratch that.

Forty-five minutes later, they were making dinner together, the tension of earlier finally dissipating. She pulled the sauté pan off the flame and used tongs to set the strips of seasoned chicken on the platter. It sizzled, just like it did at her fave Mexican restaurant.

Adrian arranged the platter with tortillas, shredded cheddar, and salsa, then set it on the small dining table. "Most women wouldn't dare eat something messy like this, much less make it."

She set the chicken on the table. "It's fun food." She nodded to the platter of sautéed vegetables. "And colorful."

"Like you."

She arched one of her eyebrows. "Are you comparing me to fajitas?"

He laughed. "I guess I am."

She plopped down on the chair. "I guess that's better than being compared to, say, tofu or pickles."

He laughed. "Definitely."

They enjoyed the dinner, along with a Riesling

he'd brought, and fun, light conversation that expressly avoided talk of Kiss and Kill Cupid or Owen.

Afterward, she began to take the dishes into the kitchen. To her delight, he helped. One guy she'd had over for dinner actually flopped down on the couch and turned on the television while she cleaned up. And asked her to bring him a beer! She'd nearly lobbed it at his head.

Her cell phone rang. She glanced at the number on the screen: Dale Soza. No way could she take that call.

"Unfortunately, I have to get this cleaned up before my roommate gets in, which will be late tonight. She has fits, even though I always clean up my messes. One time I left it until morning, and she'd put sticky notes on the stove and the table, everywhere where there was a dish."

He ran the water and started rinsing the dishes. "She sounds like fun."

She rolled her eyes. "Loads. She gets on my case about the pan handles sticking out over the edge of the stove. And yes, it makes sense because they can be bumped accidentally, but she's freaky about it. She walks in, and screeches, 'Pan handles!' The only reason I've stayed is I hardly ever see her. I'm hoping to get my own place soon."

Honest to Pete, there wasn't anything much sexier than a man doing dishes. Through Adrian's tight knit shirt, she could see his muscles working. He was wide at the shoulders, tapering to a narrow waist and hips, and in tailored dress pants, she could see one of the finest derrieres she'd ever laid eyes on. The song "I Like the Way You Move" from Outkast played in her mind.

What she wanted to do was slide up behind him. *Calm yourself, girl. Don't be slutty. You're not there yet.* She took a deep breath and walked up beside him, taking the soapy plate he was holding and rinsing it.

She tucked it in the dish rack. "And no dishwasher, can you believe it?"

He gave her a grin. "Well, you've got one tonight."

"If this place came with you, I'd stay here forever." She put a soapy hand to her mouth. "Did I actually say that aloud?"

"Unless I'm starting to hear *your* thoughts." He gave her a playful smile.

She reached for the platter he was holding, and their fingers slid against each other's. Even covered in soap suds, his hands were great, strong, with long fingers, and she imagined them sliding across her skin. The image of that made her face flush with heat. She set down the platter in the sink. He was looking at her, not the next dirty dish. She slid her fingers between his in slow strokes, her gaze never leaving his.

He kissed her, his soapy hand going to the back of her neck, cradling her. She blindly slapped her hand down on the faucet handle to turn off the water and slid her arms up around his neck. His soft hair brushed the backs of her hands. He kissed across her cheek to the sensitive skin beneath her ear. She tilted her head back, lost in the chills sweeping down her body. His arms went down to her waist, pulling her body against his. His arousal, pressing into her stomach, sent a pulsing heat through her. She slid her hands down his back, then over the tight butt she'd just been admiring. He moaned softly, pulling her closer.

He ran his hands over her shoulders, then up and down her sides. Knowing he was a gentleman, she decided to make it perfectly clear that it was okay to touch her. She moved into his touch, her breast filling his hand. He squeezed her gently, sending a cascade of pleasure through her. She let out a soft moan of her own. How long had it been since she'd been touched?

Way too long.

He pushed aside the dishes they hadn't gotten to yet and hoisted her up to the counter. That put her at his level, face-to-face. She kissed him, almost breathless, and then he moved his way down her body.

He unbuttoned her blouse, kissing the center of her chest, the swell of her breasts, and after he removed her bra, her nipples. He touched her, caressed, his movements becoming more fevered, as though he couldn't get enough of her. She'd never felt this way about a guy. This was hot, mindless, wild stuff.

She pulled his shirt up and over his head and kissed over the curves of his chest, her mouth and fingers drinking in the exquisite softness of his skin, the firmness of his body.

She wrapped her legs around his waist, and whispered next to his ear, "My bedroom's the door on the left."

Wearing a skirt, she could feel him pressing right up against her femininity, only the silk of her thong and the fabric of his pants between them.

That was going to change fast.

He wrapped his arms around her and lifted her off the counter. With his hands on her derriere, he held her as he walked to the bedroom. She pushed the door closed in case her roomie came home unexpectedly. He leaned down on the bed, and she let go of him long enough to push her skirt and panties down.

He hungrily took her in, his hand skimming her body and over her pubic hair. His thumb nudged between her folds, and her breath hitched audibly. She reached down to his belt and unhooked it, then unzipped his pants. He stood to get out of them, and her breath hitched again at the beauty of his body.

She wanted him, and not because he was gorgeous or even because she couldn't hear his thoughts. She was sprawled back on the bed, feeling hunger sweeping through her, physical and emotional.

"I want you," she said, her voice husky.

He stroked her inner thigh. "I was going to—"

"I want you now."

He merely arched an eyebrow, but his smile told her he had no problem with her demand. He reached down and pulled out his wallet, extracting a condom. That did it. She really did love him, or was in love with him, because she was so wild with all of her emotions she hadn't thought about that.

She took the foil pack and tore it open. Coming to her knees, she took the length of him in her hand, making him suck in a breath. Damn, she'd never been with a man so big before. She slid the condom down over him, trying not to rush even though she wanted him inside her *now*.

She wrapped her hands over his shoulders and pulled him down. She loved missionary style. It left them face-to-face and body to body. He slid into her slowly, though she could see the urgency in his face, too. He was trying to ease in so he didn't hurt her.

To hell with that. She pulled him down, and when he filled her, the sensation swept through her entire body. He filled her, body and soul. She wrapped her legs around his waist again, pulling her hips even closer to his. They moved together, in perfect rhythm, hitting both her internal and external hot buttons.

He stroked her cheek with his thumb, looking into her eyes as though she were the most precious thing on earth. Making love with Adrian felt like making love for the first time. She couldn't remember being with anyone else, only this man.

Their bodies became slick with sweat, even in the cool room.

"You *are* hot-blooded," he said.

She nodded, giving him a coy smile, then she lost herself in the sensations building inside her. If he could hold on for a few more strokes . . .

She felt the explosion send sparks through her. And still he moved, bringing her to another orgasm.

"Oh . . . my . . . gosh," she uttered on a breathless whisper, her body going completely limp.

She squeezed her vaginal muscles as she moved, and his breath hitched. He came with a long groan, pulsing inside her. He kissed her with the fierceness of his orgasm, fast and deep, plunging in and running his tongue along her teeth, then her lips. He was breathless, too, his blue eyes hazy with senselessness, his face flushed. His body heat enveloped her.

He rolled over so she was on top, their bodies still connected. "That was amazing." He pulled her close and kissed her again. "You were amazing."

"Ditto." And he was still hard.

He didn't get up right away. He stroked her backside with his fingertips, so soft it almost tickled. She laid her cheek on his chest, running her finger lazily around his nipple.

"Stay the night with me." She lifted her face to look at him. "Not because I'm scared of Kiss and Kill Cupid. He won't be a threat until day after tomorrow."

"I'd love to."

"I'll get the wine. We can finish the bottle in bed." She got up. "The bathroom's around the corner. My roommate usually stays with her boyfriend on the weekends, but I'll make sure the coast is clear first."

He walked into the bathroom and a minute later came out to the kitchen, where she was trying to get her hands around two half-full glasses and the bottle. Damn, he was *still* hard. What was he, miracle man or something?

"Here, let me help." He took the glasses and scanned the dirty dishes. "What about the kitchen? We got a bit distracted."

She waved it away. "I'm not in the mood. Let her write her sticky notes in all caps if she comes home early." The phone rang. "Maybe that's her now, and somehow she knows I'm leaving the kitchen in a mess." She laughed. "I'm not getting it."

They were walking back to her bedroom when her roommate's deadpan voice announced, "We're not here, leave a message."

"Kristy, it's Dale Soza. You must have a reporter's instincts; you're onto something with this Owen guy. He's a murderer! Call me right away."

She met Adrian's gaze, now filled with disbelief. "Who's Dale Soza?"

"He's a reporter. I asked him to poke around a bit."

"You had a *reporter* check into Owen's background?"

She set the wine bottle on the table next to the answering machine. "Just to make sure. And I made Dale promise he wouldn't publish anything about Owen." She was wilting under his cold stare.

"You don't think a reporter is going to keep a secret about someone who's had media attention before?"

"I do. Look, I had to find out about Owen's past. You weren't going to tell me. I figured, Dale's a reporter, so he has to be good at finding out stuff. But they protect their sources, too. There was a reporter who went to jail because he wouldn't reveal his sources."

His voice was dangerously low when he said, "Did you tell him about my visions?"

"No, God, no. Nor about my hearing the killer's thoughts."

Then it hit her, what Dale had said. "Adrian, he said Owen killed someone. Is that true?"

He walked into the bedroom and started putting on his pants. She ran in after him, snatching up her pink silk robe. The room felt cold now, stippling her skin. "Adrian, don't go. My feelings were right about him. He did kill someone."

He looked at her as he pulled on his shirt. "You don't know what you've done. You've probably ruined him, both professionally and personally. And maybe the magazine, too. Who knows the fallout once this goes public?"

She followed him to the door, touching his shoulder. "Tell me what he did."

He brushed off her touch. "Yes, he did kill someone. When he was seven, his stepfather beat the heck out of his mother again. Once he was done with her, he usually turned on Owen. That time was the worst. The man had a knife and threatened to cut off her finger. Owen grabbed the man's gun, the one he would probably have used on them eventually. It was the only way he could think of to stop him. He'd tried to do it once before, but the guy threw him against the wall and broke two of his ribs. His mother was too scared to get them out of there. So Owen fixed it, as a kid thinks he can, because that's how it works on television and in video games. He shot the man."

Her hand went to her mouth. "That's terrible."

"There was an investigation, but he was never charged with murder. How that jerk found out about it I'll never know. I've got to warn Owen. I don't want him finding out by surprise. Or worse, having someone else tell him."

He left, slamming the door shut. "Lock it," he barked.

Even mad at her, he was concerned about her safety. That made it even worse. She might have destroyed his friend's life if he wasn't Kiss and Kill Cupid. Now she was going to pay the price by losing the best man she'd ever found.

Kristy called Dale once the shock had worn off. "What did you find out?"

He told her basically what Adrian had told her. "So if he's killed once, he could kill again."

"Dale, you promised you'd keep his name out of the paper."

"Unless he's Kiss and Kill Cupid."

"Right, unless. But otherwise—"

"It's hot news, Kristy. But I did tell you reporters had to have integrity."

She wasn't exactly comfortable with that answer. "Yes, you did." But had he actually promised not to print anything about Owen, in those exact words?

"I think we're onto something here. The tool I saw you with today, is that Adrian Kruger? Owen Bushnell's business partner?"

"Tool?" Before she could get annoyed about his calling Adrian that, she frowned. "When did you see us together?"

"I saw you coming out of his office building. You two look pretty cozy."

Well, they used to. "Never mind him. What do we do about Owen?"

"I'll follow him on Valentine's Day. I've got his home address. But . . . what if he's not the killer? What about you? Are you going to be with the tool?"

"I'll be fine." Would she? No, she knew Adrian well enough to know he wouldn't abandon her. "I'll talk to you later. Oh, and he's not a tool!"

As she hung up, her roommate came in. Her gaze went right to the kitchen. "Oh, great. A mess. And pot handles sticking out!" She trudged to her room and shut the door with a bit too much force.

Kristy turned around and did the same thing. Let her get a good look at the mess in the morning. Kristy just didn't care.

The next day, Kristy held off for as long as she could before calling Adrian: eleven o'clock in the morning. She was relieved when he answered. "Hi. Look, I just wanted to know—"

"I'll be there tomorrow. And yes, you're still hired, and you're still going to Wimberly."

She breathed out in relief. He'd taken the onus off her to ask, which made him all the more wonderful and made it all the worse that she'd probably blown it as far as a relationship went. "Thank you. I spoke with Dale Soza, and he promised not to run the story. How did Owen take the news?"

"Not well. He doesn't believe in our abilities, so he doesn't know what to make of it. What's your schedule like today? I want to come over and go over our plan, since we got waylaid last night."

He sounded cool, businesslike. She smacked her forehead with the heel of her hand. She'd really screwed up. Unless Owen turned out to be Kiss and Kill Cupid, and maybe not even then. "I'm picking up an arrangement of flowers for my mom and going to take them to her. Other than that, I'm free."

"How about four o'clock?"

Too late for lunch, too early for dinner. "Sounds fine."

She hung up and slung her purse over her shoulder. The kitchen was spotless, cleaned through the power of nervous energy. She tied a dark pink scarf around her neck and headed out into a sunny but chilly day.

She returned by four and found Adrian arriving. Damn, why did he look even more gorgeous now that she'd probably lost him?

She gave him a soft smile as he held the door open for her. They ascended the stairs to the second floor, and she unlocked the door. After a quick glance around, she said, "Good, looks like my roommate's already gone." She turned to him. "Come, follow me." She walked into her bedroom, turning to see him standing in the living area looking dubious. "To go over the plan."

She was going to have to act just as businesslike as he was and pretend her heart wasn't breaking. She stepped over to the window. "So I was thinking, he's probably going to come in here."

She looked out at the fire escape and got a shiver. "The fire escape runs almost to the living-room window. If I hang around the living room, he could come into my bedroom so I don't see him."

She walked over to her dresser and handed him a piece of paper that was lying next to her perfume bottles. "This is a rough map of the building. You can come around the back from the side street, here. I scoped out a good place to park and the best way to approach the rear entrance." She pointed to the area she'd marked. "He might be hiding back along here, so you should disguise yourself in case he's seen us together."

"He's always struck in the evening, but I'm not taking a chance he won't break with his tradition like he did last year." He folded the map and put it in his pocket. "If he's seen us together, he'll probably think we're dating."

She bit her lower lip. *Think* they're dating. Not *know.*

"It'll seem strange if we're not together on Valentine's Day, at least for a while," he continued. "I'll pick you up in the morning. We can go to breakfast, walk around, have lunch and catch a movie. Then I'll drop you off here, leave, and come around the way you described. You need to keep those curtains closed until I'm in, then you can open them for a bit. I'm going to be waiting in your closet."

He had it all figured out. "Should we have a

signal? Like, if I say 'bullocks,' that means I've heard something suspicious."

His expression darkened. "I still don't like this."

Well, at least he was worried about her. That was a good thing, right? "I'll be fine. You'll have the phone ready to call 911."

"I've already got it programmed in as a speed dial. And I'm bringing my haul ropes, what I use for climbing. As soon as he comes in through the window and starts to sneak into the living area, I'll grab him from behind and tie him up. I've got my wall hammer if I need it."

"What if he's got a weapon?"

"I've got the element of surprise. And strength." He looked at her. "And determination." For a second, she saw that glimmer of protectiveness in his eyes.

"Thank you. And I'm sorry if I complicated things. I just wanted to cover all my bases."

He looked away from her. "Call if you need me."

"I can . . . make dinner if you're not doing anything."

"I'm having dinner with Owen. He's kind of freaked-out. All this is bringing up some bad memories."

She winced. "All right. I'll see you tomorrow."

After he left, she leaned against the door with a sigh. "I do need you."

She pushed away from the door, the energy drained right out of her. She'd never let herself fall in love before. Maybe a fun infatuation, but not love. The thoughts always got in the way. Nobody told her how hard it would be to lose a real lover.

"At least I had it once."

She trudged into her bedroom and stopped. Her comforter was wrinkled. She hadn't noticed when they'd been in there earlier. Adrian hadn't touched her bed. She walked over to her window and looked out. It wasn't the near darkness or the cold seeping through the glass that sent a bone-deep chill through her. Was her imagination running overtime? Surely she had reason to be paranoid. She could feel someone watching her out there. She turned to her bed. It felt like someone had been in the room, too. Lying on her bed. Going through her things.

That thought was terrible enough. But . . . what if he was still there?

She grabbed her pepper spray from her purse and stalked over to her closet door. Her heart was pounding in her throat. She reached out, wrapped her fingers around the doorknob . . . and yanked it open. Something moved, and she screamed. One of her padded hangers was swinging from the movement of the door opening.

She pushed aside her clothing and searched the dark shadows of the closet. Thankfully, no one lurked there. She walked out into the living area and checked the closet by the door, too. And then, just to be sure, she went into Berta's room. Apparently her cleanliness only applied to public spaces. Her bed wasn't made and unmatched shoes were here and there on the floor. Same went for her closet: clothing was piled on the floor, and what was hung up wasn't done properly. On the upside, no one was hiding in there. Deep in the bowels of her closet she heard the front door open. Had she locked it after Adrian left? She lurched out of the closet and was staring at the door, wide-eyed, when Berta walked in.

She came to an abrupt halt. "What are you doing in here? You're looking through my clothes?"

"Uh, no. *No.*"

"I told you before, we don't intrude into each other's space. And I don't do that borrowing-clothing thing." She pulled at the striped knit shirt that hung down to her knees. "Go get your own clothes."

"I thought I heard a sound in here. Have you noticed anything odd lately, like your bed"—Kristy looked at the rumpled sheets—"anything odd at all?"

Berta's thick, dark eyebrow arched. "Only you in my room."

"I'm leaving." Kristy scooted past her. She really had to get her own place. Living with a stranger wasn't cutting it.

She closed her door and sank onto her bed. One

more night. She wasn't sure she could handle the waiting.

"That was close."

He'd been in her bedroom when she'd come home. Lying on her bed, breathing in her scent on the pillow. Fortunately, he was always on alert. He climbed out the window just in time. He watched the building until she was alone again. A perfect opportunity to go in now and have his fun with her. But not the right time. He hadn't gotten away with four murders by acting on impulse. And he wouldn't be Kiss and Kill Cupid if he struck one day early, would he?

No, he wouldn't.

The roommate trudged up the front steps and went into the building. Hopefully she wouldn't be around tomorrow. No matter who was there, he would handle it. He had an idea. A brilliant idea. He smiled, feeling the hunger flowing into his veins like a drug. Kristy would be his loveliest prize yet. If things worked out right, he would have plenty of time to play with her before he wrapped his hands around that beautiful neck of hers.

Kristy woke early on Valentine's Day. Not that she'd really had much sleep. Between thinking about the day and Adrian and even Owen, who

could sleep? She ran out to get the paper Dale
Soza wrote for. Even with her breath hanging like
icicles in the air, she walked slowly and paged
through it, looking for anything about Owen.

Her last icy breath before she walked into her
building was one of relief. Nothing. Yet. If Owen
wasn't the killer, and Dale ever broke that story,
she knew Adrian wouldn't be as forgiving where
it came to her assignment with the magazine. If
there was a magazine.

She rubbed at the moisture in her eyes. Not from
the cold.

I might have really screwed up.

"Nothing in there yet."

She knew his voice even without seeing him. It
sent a bittersweet flood of emotion through her,
and she took a second to compose herself before
turning to find him at the bottom of the steps. And
he had to go and look really good, too, in a black
wool coat and tight blue jeans. His hair looked
playfully mussed by the breeze, and she wanted
to smooth it out as a way to get close to him, to
breathe him in. He smelled like soap and clean
male, but not of Intuition. He'd probably tossed
the bottle.

She could only shake her head in answer, her
throat too tight to release any words.

"It's only a matter of time," he continued, his expression dark. "I don't know what it's going to do
to him."

Dale would be following him today. Hoping for the big break, *hoping* it was Owen. What a coup that would be, and that he'd killed his stepfather when he was seven would be the icing on the sordid story. It would ruin the magazine, which would then be associated with a serial killer and not bracing adventures. Adrian would lose his dream, and by default, he would be covered in media soot, too. Then it would be "Beauty and the Beast."

Even if Owen wasn't Kiss and Kill Cupid, his unthinkable childhood and crime could be enough to do them in.

"I'm sorry," she said, her voice sounding very small.

"Let's go."

"I'll be right back. I need to get my purse."

He accompanied her, though she was sure it was more out of his protective instinct than any desire to be with her. He remained near the front door while she walked into her bedroom. She reached for her purse strap and heard a noise coming from the closet. The door was ajar. Had she left it that way?

Another sound. Definitely coming from her closet.

Oh, God, he was striking early! She had to get Adrian. Swallowing hard, she took a step toward the door. Another one.

The closet door swung open. She lunged forward, but her heel caught on a loop in the carpet and sent her flying to the floor. Footsteps came up behind her. Kristy let out a cry of fear as she pulled her shoe free and spun around to face him.

Or . . . *her*?

Berta looked at her, her hands on her hips. "I'm missing my black-and-red skull shirt. I thought you might have taken it, seeing as you were rummaging around in my closet the other day. Lucky for you, I didn't see it."

She walked out, leaving Kristy to scramble up from the floor, her heart pounding. Adrian walked toward her, a mixture of confusion and worry on his face.

"What happened?"

She waved it away, just wanting to get out of there. On the stairway she told him what had happened. "It was dumb." But her quivering voice gave away how frightening it had been when she thought the killer was looming over her.

"Kristy, admit it; you're freaked-out. You don't have to do this. We can try the police again."

"No. Been there, done that, got the T-shirt."

She walked beside him to the waiting car. They went to a diner that served old-fashioned breakfast fare: grits and sausage and buttery eggs. Neither ate very much.

"I was thinking," he said, and he sure hadn't said much, "that if we stage an argument, that will make him feel more confident about approaching you later. And it would make more sense as to why we spent the day together but not the evening."

That wouldn't be hard to do in his state of mind. "You could act as though I'd done some horrible thing when all I really wanted to do was put this guy who's been killing women behind bars."

He looked at her—he hadn't done a lot of that, either. "Right now, Kristy, I can't think about why you did what you did. I know you didn't set out to ruin Owen's life. You thought you were doing the right thing. But I thought we were in this together, then you went behind my back and opened a can of worms. Is Dale Soza out there watching you, hoping to catch the big bad killer in action for the morning edition?"

"No. I told him I would be fine on my own. That I was safe. And I tried to talk to you about my suspicions, but you wouldn't hear of it." She set her fork on her plate, giving up on the idea of eating. "I thought about my brother, and what if someone told me they thought he was a killer. I'd be incensed and hurt and probably blind to the signs. I wouldn't be very happy with the person who was telling me. So I wasn't going to push you on it. Maybe I made a mistake in going to Soza. If I'm wrong, hopefully he'll keep his word."

Adrian looked skeptical. "Forgive me if I don't

have a lot of faith in reporters." He pointed to himself. "Remember, 'Beauty and the Brain.'"

"Point taken."

He leaned back in his chair. "I've postponed the trip to Wimberly, at least until we see what happens."

Her heart dropped another notch. He was easing her out, of his magazine and life. She could only nod, her mouth stretching into a frown.

They walked around the city as planned, and the murmur of everyone's thoughts crowded into her head. Again, she found herself wishing she could read Adrian's thoughts. She knew she was in a bad state of mind when even the spring fashions in the windows and SALE signs didn't perk her up. They wandered over to the theater and looked at the movie posters.

"Something light and fun," she said. "I need that."

He eyed the one she was looking at. "No romantic comedies. I'm not in the mood for anything romantic."

They settled on a foreign film, one they'd never heard of. It sounded neutral enough: the story of a widow trying to recover from her husband's sudden death, set in France. Angst would be a good distracter. Having to read subtitles would distract her even more. He bought a tub of popcorn, and they settled into their seats. Every time they reached into the tub at the same time, and their fingers brushed, she felt that jolt. This might be the last day she'd see him. So she waited until she saw him reaching into the tub from the corner of her eye and reached, too.

Save up those jolts, girl. You'll probably never get to feel this again.

Kristy was touched by Adele's deeply moving journey from pain to power. She had gone from overprotected housewife to career woman, proving herself to her brooding boss, Benoit. In French, even when they discussed the consistency of cheese, it sounded sensuous. They were arguing over which angle to use for an ad campaign for cheese when Benoit grabbed Adele and started kissing her. A warm flush washed over Kristy. Now they weren't arguing over anything. No subtitles to distract.

Benoit swept everything off his desk with his arm and laid her on top of it, their mouths sealed together in desperate kisses. His hand ran down her now-bared leg, pushing up her skirt even more.

Kristy squirmed in her seat, resisting the urge to cover her eyes.

Benoit's other hand tore at Adele's dress. Buttons flew. He bared her breast and sucked it like a man starved.

Kristy squirmed again, feeling heat crawling through her body like a thousand ants. She saw Adrian shift, too. It took everything inside her not to look at him, but she was pretty sure he was watching it in the same riveted way she was.

The two actors groaned and breathed heavily, and he trailed kisses down her stomach the way Adrian had done to her only two days ago. That hot, tingling sensation marched right down between her legs. The actor was kissing her thighs, pushing them apart. She realized her own legs were moving apart, too, and she felt exactly what that woman was feeling. She saw not the two actors but her and Adrian, their bodies moving together, felt him filling her, and when she could hardly breathe, she reached over to grab a handful of popcorn to shove into her mouth.

Only she didn't get a handful of popcorn. The bucket wasn't where it had been. But Adrian's very hard penis was, and that's what she got a handful of. He jerked, and she jerked, and the bucket spilled, sending popcorn flying everywhere.

"Sorry! I was grabbing popcorn!"

He swore under his breath and stood. "I need some fresh air."

She followed him, and he stopped near the doorway but still inside the darkened theater, where the heavy breathing continued.

He leaned down, and whispered, "Are you *trying* to drive me crazy?"

"I didn't know it was that kind of movie!"

"I'm not talking about the movie."

"I didn't mean to grab you. You moved the popcorn bucket, and I wasn't looking where I was putting my hand, and—"

He kissed her, just as fierce and passionately as Benoit had kissed Adele. She bumped against the carpeted wall with the force of it, and he crushed her mouth beneath his. His hands were on her arms, then her breasts. She ran her hands down his back and over his buttocks, dying in pleasure with the realization that he hadn't completely shut her out.

He groaned in her mouth, more of a growl, really, pushing his body against hers. She ground her stomach against him, feeling the pressure of his maleness against her pubic area. Would anyone notice them if they made love right there?

No, no, no, uh, what was the question?

She tilted her head back, losing herself in the feel of his mouth sliding down her throat and the hollow where he dipped his tongue and made her think of other places his tongue could dip, and oh . . .

"Oh, hell," he said, and stalked out of the door.

She spun with dizziness at the abrupt change but followed him out to where he walked to the alcove of another movie's entrance. It was quiet, other than one employee who was vacuuming the hallway.

He spun on her, his hand to his forehead. "You have officially driven me crazy. I have never lost it like that in a public place. Especially with a woman who may have screwed up my best friend's life and potentially my career. Right now I'm angry at you, and I'm even angrier at myself. I haven't made it to where I am, haven't survived extreme skiing and mountain climbing, by getting swept beyond my control. There's something about you that does that to me. Your crazy colors and adorable smile and your dimples, the way you walk to the music even if you're not listening to music—" He shook his head. "Right now I don't want you doing that to me. We're getting out of here."

"I . . . can't help it."

"I know. That's the problem. And I can't help it, either."

He started walking toward the theater's entrance. "Wait. Our coats," she called out.

He threw his head back in frustration. She made him crazy, made him lose control. Normally that would be a good thing. At least she thought it was a good thing. But not now. He turned around, and they walked back into the darkened theater.

Benoit and Adele were sitting in his chair, she on his lap, obviously postcoital. He was telling her he loved her, that he couldn't live without her. He would do anything to win her heart forever.

Adrian grabbed their coats and the empty container of popcorn. He tossed it in the garbage as they headed toward the entrance. He hadn't looked at her since he'd last spoken to her. He was going to shut her out. That would be his solution, and she wouldn't ever see him again. The thought of that shattered her heart.

One employee was jogging to the girl who was working the ticket booth. He opened the door, and said, "Oh my God, did you hear? Kiss and Kill Cupid just struck again!"

Kristy and Adrian ran down the sidewalk until they found a bar with televisions mounted to the walls. Normally, she considered them intrusive and distracting, but now she was grateful for them.

They stood as close as they could get to the television that was broadcasting news. The headline at the bottom: HAS KISS AND KILL CUPID STRUCK AGAIN? Everyone in the vicinity was also watching.

The reporter, a woman standing outside an apartment building swarming with policemen, was saying, "Details are sketchy right now, but we know a woman was found strangled to death in this apartment. One officer confirmed the lipstick message was found on her body, but we haven't been officially notified of this yet. Kiss and Kill

Cupid usually strikes at night, though his pattern changed somewhat last year when he entered the apartment of Marcy Sturgiss while her boyfriend was sleeping over. The killer has become more daring."

The camera turned to a woman who was standing outside the yellow crime ribbons, her arms wrapped tightly around herself. "It's kind of a relief, you know. Now we don't have to worry about him for another year."

Kristy thought she saw Dale Soza in the background talking to one of the police officers, but the camera panned away before she could tell for sure.

"We'll have more details as soon as they're released. Stay tuned."

All around her, thoughts zinged about the killer. She, however, was stunned. She turned to Adrian, who looked as confused as she felt.

"I don't understand," she said. "Unless, because of you being in my life, he picked another victim. Maybe you did scare him away."

He released a long breath. "Are you relieved or disappointed?"

"Both, but mostly disappointed. I wanted to stop him. I didn't want to see this newscast. This was our only chance to help catch him."

"Let the professionals figure it out. That's what they do."

She glanced up at the television again, though

they'd moved on to some other story. "But only if they have enough clues." She looked at him. "You're relieved."

"You're not in danger." And he could abandon his bodyguard duty. "Take the car back to your place. I'm going to check on Owen. I'm worried about his state of mind."

She nodded. "When we kissed back there . . . you didn't see the vision, did you?"

He seemed to just realize that. "No. It's over, Kristy." He left, and she watched him walk over to the black car and instruct him to take her home. Then he walked down the sidewalk.

It's over. He meant it. Them. Probably her writing assignment. And worse, maybe Owen's peace of mind.

The only thing that kept her from collapsing into a ball of frenzied tears and screaming was finding out what was going on. She called Dale.

"Did you see the news?" he answered, obviously recognizing her number. Excitement permeated his voice.

"A few minutes ago. Did you . . . follow Owen this morning?"

"Yeah, he went down to Dirty Harry's bar for breakfast and spent the morning nursing a whiskey on the rocks. Then I got the call. I'm here at the scene now. The crime unit is still in there doing its thing. What we know is that it happened this morning, though they haven't pinned it down any closer than that."

Soon, though, all the details would be splayed across the news with those adjectives about the crime—gruesome—and the victim—sweet, such a nice girl, what a shame.

Dale's chirpy voice broke her out of her grim thoughts. "So it wasn't you he was targeting. That must be a relief."

"Yeah." She wasn't going to get into how she really felt. "But I feel terrible for that woman."

"They haven't released her name. One of the neighbors said she was nice, volunteered at the hospital and dressed up as an elf at Christmas."

"Of course!" she blurted out. He was killing her. "I've got to go. I'll talk to you later." Before she hung up, though, she added, "You won't need to print anything about Owen then. Now that we know he's not the killer."

"Don't worry. I won't print your name at all."

"What do you mean, 'your name'? You're not supposed to print any names or any story about him."

"No, I'm pretty sure I only promised to keep your name out of it. His sordid past, too juicy to pass up. The 'Brain,' a killer. People eat that stuff up. Gotta go. They're bringing the body out. Photo ops."

She stood holding the phone for several more minutes, grappling with the cold truth. She was responsible for ruining someone's life. The news turned back to the crime scene, showing what Dale had described: a covered body being carted out to a waiting ambulance. The lights weren't on.

She took the car home, brewed up some chamomile tea, changed into a velour jumpsuit, and called Adrian. This was the hardest call she was going to have to make.

He didn't answer, so she left a message. That was easier, but not the way she'd wanted to do it. "Adrian, it's me, Kristy. I just spoke to Dale Soza, and I think he's going to print the story about Owen. I'm sorry, so sorry. Please come over so we can discuss how we can do damage control. If there's anything I can do, I'll do it. I'm going to keep working on Dale, too, to change his mind. He's busy with the Kiss and Kill Cupid story right now, so we've probably got a few days. Please, don't ignore me. I know you're angry, and you can fire me and write nasty comments about my online articles and whatever you need to do to feel better. But come over tonight so we can work on this together. If Owen wants to come, I'll apologize to him in person. I owe him that. Okay?" She released a breath. "Right, you can't answer because this is a message. Okay. Bye."

She trudged into the kitchen to make five-cheese macaroni and cheese. Comfort food. Because that was the only comfort she was getting today.

* * *

Adrian sat next to Owen at the seediest bar he'd seen in a while. He didn't know what to say once he'd relayed Kristy's message to him. Owen had ordered another whiskey and chugged it. His chin was so low it nearly touched the rim of his glass.

The televisions were going, both channels featuring the Kiss and Kill Cupid story. Owen looked up at the screen, his eyes narrowed. "I could kill her."

"You don't mean that. She made a mistake, but I could hear it in her voice. She feels terrible."

"Not as terrible as I feel. I have to go."

Adrian stood the moment Owen did. "Where are you going?"

"Home."

"I'll come with you."

"Don't worry. I'm not going to do myself in or anything. I just need to be alone."

Adrian watched him wave down a cab, his gait unsteady. He had to let him go for now. Owen needed his stew time. But Adrian would be there for him later.

He thought of Kristy. He couldn't be there for her. How could he forgive her for this? The cab pulled away, and an uneasy feeling settled into his stomach. Something wasn't right.

The apartment filled with the scent of baking cheese and chocolate. Not together, of course. There was no chocolate ice cream in the house and, with

Kristy's reddened eyes and tear-streaked face, no way was she going out to get some. She found a bag of chocolate chips in the cabinet and pulled out her double boiler to melt them. No strawberries, alas, but she would make do with one banana and a box of Ritz crackers. If she got desperate, there was half a jar of sweet baby gherkins in the fridge. She was going to eat dessert first because the mac-and-cheese was taking too long.

She put her hand to her mouth. "Oh my gosh! I left the handle sticking out. Berta, do you see this? Call the pot-handle police!"

Berta wasn't there, thank goodness. Kristy was about to push the handle back over the stove but felt cranky enough to leave it as it was. "Here's to you, Berta, wherever you are." She sent her a raspberry.

The phone never left her side, and every five minutes she picked it up and had to restrain herself from calling Adrian again. He didn't want to talk to her. She'd done enough, and what could she really do to help the situation now, except grovel? She would, but only in person.

She'd also left a message for Dale, this time begging him, tears in her voice and all, not to print the story. He hadn't called back, either.

The knock at her door propelled her off the couch. Adrian had come! She and Berta rarely got visitors, so it had to be him. She yanked open the door and blinked in shock at the sight of Owen standing there.

He walked right in, nudging her out of the way. Her throat tightened in fear. She remained near the door. Would anyone come or call the police if she screamed? Probably not.

He spun around, his mouth in a hard line, his gray eyes finally filled with something other than that blankness.

I could kill her . . . squeeze that pretty throat of hers.

Her eyes widened, and her heart leapt at that thought. "Owen, I'm sorry about what happened, truly I am. I never meant—"

He advanced on her. "You thought I was Kiss and Kill Cupid!"

"I . . . I wasn't sure, but yes, you were a suspect."

"A suspect. So, how many suspects did you have?"

"Just . . . you," she squeaked out. "I got a weird feeling about you, and you kind of fit the profile, and I was like a bulldog, wanting to find the bone. I wanted to fit you into that profile. Adrian wouldn't hear of it, you should know that. He didn't believe it for a minute. And that's why I went to Dale Soza. I figured he could find out more about you, about your past, since he's got research resources."

His face contorted into a snarl. "And he did, didn't he?"

"Adrian told you everything, right? About why I suspected you?"

"Yeah. You're both freaks. Supposedly you can hear thoughts."

"Yes, you just thought you could squeeze my pretty throat."

His mouth dropped open. "What the—?"

"I'm hoping you meant that in a nonliteral sense. You did, didn't you?"

He didn't answer and, as usual, his expression gave away nothing.

Her cell phone rang. "Hold on." She was relieved to have a distraction and to be able to tell someone Owen was there. Dale's number filled the screen.

"Dale, tell me you've changed your mind about printing that story," she said without preamble. "Owen is here now, and he's pretty upset."

"Owen is there? Kristy, you've got to get out of there. The police just pinned down time of death. It happened very early this morning. *Before I started watching Owen.* That's why I'm calling. He could still be the killer."

She felt the blood leave her face. "O-o-okay, so you won't print the story," she said, as though confirming.

"Get out of there. I'm on my way over."

Chapter Nine

After Dale disconnected, Kristy turned to find Owen standing way too close. "Is that what he said, that he wouldn't print my story?"

Had he heard Dale's frantic voice? "Yes." She cleared her throat. "Yes, he promised not to print it."

She smelled liquor on his breath. "I have to get going now. I've got an appointment . . . down-town."

"What about your dinner? I can smell it cooking."

No, he could smell her fear. And he was keeping his thoughts silent, now. She took a step back, and he stepped forward.

"I watched my stepfather beat the hell out of my mother almost every night. She cowered like a beaten dog, begging him to stop. But he wouldn't stop." His voice was low and menacing. "And when he was finished with her, he turned his rage on me. I didn't understand he was a coward who only felt powerful when he could beat up those smaller and weaker than himself. I only knew I couldn't do a thing to stop him from hurting me and my mother. And that no one would protect us. And that he would keep beating us until he killed us one day. Do you know what it's like to live in that kind of fear every damned day of your life?"

She shook her head, though she had lived in fear the last few days, and it was excruciating.

"And when I took that gun from his hiding place in their closet, for the first time I felt like I could finally stop the terror. Nothing prepared me for what it felt like to pull that trigger, to see his blood splatter on my mother and the walls and furniture." He gripped her shoulders so hard it hurt. "Do you know what I felt? Satisfied? Triumphant?"

"I . . . don't know." Her body trembled, and her voice had come out a whisper.

His chin quivered. "I felt shame. Guilt. Horror. Because I had become just like him. I had used violence for my own purposes. I was no better than that monster I had killed. I've lived with that demon on my shoulder ever since. And I will for the rest of my life. It whispers in my ear."

"W-what does it say?" *Kill women?*

"It tells me what a horrible person I am. And then to have you come along and accuse me of being a serial killer, of taking lives for the sheer pleasure of it . . ." His voice broke, though he still kept his hands clamped on her shoulders. "To have you look at me like I'm a killer, coming in and ripping away the only friendship I have, exposing my secret to the world . . ." He dropped down to his knees in front of her, his shoulders heaving with his sobs.

Her knees felt wobbly, but she knelt next to him and tentatively touched his shaking back. "Look, I got a little . . . crazy with my suspicions." *Crazy* was her dark word from her past, the demon that whispered in her ear sometimes. "But I can see I was wrong about you." Her legs gave out, and she sat down. "Owen, we are not what we've done. We are only defined but what we are now. And if Dale Soza does print that story, it will give you the chance to exorcize your demon once and for all. Instead of hiding from the truth, face it. Face the world with it, forgive that little boy, and set him free. Forgive your stepfather, too. Not for him, but for you. Release all the anger and shame that's clogging up your soul and find yourself."

He looked up at her, removing his glasses and wiping his eyes. "I . . . I don't know if I can do that."

"I've lived with my dirty little secret, too, trying to be normal when I'm anything but. My parents thought I was crazy, probably still do. I thought I was crazy. Then, when I realized it was some gift or curse or whatever, I hated it. I fought it. But finally I had to accept and work around it. Adrian was the first person I told about it, and he accepted me. He was the only one I was able to open myself up to. He taught me I could love fully and be open with another person. He accepts you, too, just as you are, and that is the most wonderful gift you will ever receive. He's a good friend. I've lost him"—her voice cracked—"but you haven't. Don't push him away and think you're better off alone. You're not." She wiped her eyes.

"She's right."

They both jerked their gazes toward the door where Adrian stood. She hadn't closed it fully.

"How much of that did you hear?" she said, coming to her feet.

"Enough." He looked at her, then at Owen, who also stood. "No matter what, I'm here for you. We've been friends since we were kids, through all of that garbage you went through. That's not going to change now. If the story breaks, we'll face it together."

Owen hugged Adrian, not in the guy pat-your-back way but a full-out hug. Her heart filled for them. She'd never had a true friend, someone who would stand by her no matter what. She and Adrian didn't have the history these two had. It would be easy for him to walk away from her.

The two men stepped apart. Owen wiped at his nose, and she handed him a tissue. "She's great," he said to Adrian.

She shrugged. "It was only a tissue."

"No, I mean . . . everything you said." He blew his nose and stuffed the tissue into his pocket. "I'm going to buy myself a box of chocolates and rent a sappy movie."

Adrian put his hand on Owen's shoulder. "Want some company?"

"I'm good. No matter what happens, I'll be okay. See you tomorrow at the office." Once Owen left, Adrian looked at her. "What you said to him . . . that was nice."

"I meant every word."

"I know you did."

He stepped closer, and her heart started beating a little faster. He gave away nothing in his expression. "He was all kinds of mad at you when I found him at a bar. When he stalked off, I had a bad feeling. I knew he had access to your address."

"I have to admit, I was scared for a few minutes." She scrubbed her hands down her arms at the memory. "I think he'll be all right." *But what about us?*

Is there an us? She looked at him questioningly.

"I could almost forgive you," he said.

Her heart fell. Almost. But not completely. "But you can't."

He shook his head. "I can't forgive you for being so smart and noble and determined and so intrinsically *you* that I can't get you out of my mind even when I want to. That I can't control myself when I'm around you. That I can't stop being in love with you, and what I really can't understand or believe is that you've done that in only five days."

In love? She pulled her lower lip between her teeth, her smile growing. "Maybe I can make it up to you." She stepped closer, sliding her hands around his neck. "If I work really, really hard at it."

He tilted his head, and only then did he give away the smile he'd been hiding. "I suppose it's possible. We can discuss the terms."

She leaned up and gave him a kiss. "We can start with a kiss. Maybe a nibble on the neck." She scraped her teeth across his skin, breathing in the scent of him. "Then I could move down . . ."

He caught her face in his hands and kissed her. She felt that jolt through her body. Now they could kiss without his worrying about seeing the awful vision. She leaned into him, rubbing her hands over his chest, soaking in the feel of him.

With a gasp, he stepped back. "No, can't be." His face was white with fear and confusion.

"You saw . . . the vision again?"

"Yes." He rubbed his temples. "Maybe it's stuck in my head."

"But you don't really think so."

"No. The murder this morning could be a copy-cat. I'm not taking any chances. I'm going out to the car to get the rope and hammer. I told the driver to wait for me. I'll be right back." He took the stairs as though he were flying down them. "Close the door!"

A few minutes later she heard a knock on the door. She opened it but stopped short. Dale stood there, breathing heavily.

"Oh, I forgot you were coming. Look, it's okay. Owen isn't Kiss and Kill Cupid."

"I know." He shoved his way in and locked the door, dropping his backpack on the floor. He pulled his BlackBerry out of his pocket and punched in some numbers. "I want to report an attempted murder. It's Kiss and Kill Cupid . . ." He gave her address. "Yes, I'll stand by until the police arrive."

"What are you talking about?"

"He's out in the hall. I saw him coming up the stairs with a hammer and rope."

She let out a hysterical laugh. "That was Adrian. He's not the killer."

Dale leaned into her face. "Yes, he is."

"He was bringing up those items to keep me safe from the killer."

"No, he was coming to kill you. I've been watching him, too, though I didn't want to alarm you until I had something concrete. You were so convinced he couldn't be the killer. All day I've worked on matching up his locations with the crimes in the last few years. I talked to his driver. Adrian was in the vicinity of the crime this morning. He had the driver drop him off two blocks away, and the driver saw him go not into the building he was supposed to be going into but around the corner."

"That's . . . no, that's just wrong." She knew absolutely it was wrong. "Where's Adrian? You said you saw him on the stairs. Why isn't he here?"

"I took care of him."

"Took . . . care?"

She started to run to the door, but he grabbed her by the shoulder and swung her around. She nearly careened into him, and the BlackBerry dropped to the floor. His hair was stiff with the hairspray he smelled strongly of.

"You can't go out there. It's dangerous. Wait until the police get here."

"He's not a killer. He's . . ." She looked down at the phone. The line wasn't open as he'd told the operator he was going to do.

Oh, my God. It's Dale. He's Kiss and Kill Cupid. She'd never given him her address. She had to keep her cool, even though her heart was about to shoot out of her chest.

He put his arm around her shoulder. "I know it's a shock. These guys can be cunning, seductive. But the important thing is, you're safe."

"Th-thank you. I can't believe it. What did you do to him?"

"I tripped him on the stairs, then grabbed the hammer he was about to use on you and hit him with it. Then I tied him up with the rope he was going to tie you up with. There's a storage room off the lobby. I pulled him in there so no one would freak out if they came in and saw him. He won't be going anywhere anytime soon."

Her throat tightened in fear. What had Dale done to him? And what would he do to her?

"That was very brave of you," she said, hoping she sounded convincing. "Where did you hit him?"

"In the head. It's going to be a hell of a story." He gave her a wide grin, which disappeared when his nose twitched. "Hey, smells like something's burning."

The aroma of burnt cheese filled the room.

"Maybe we should go down there, make sure he doesn't get away." She started to head to the door again, but he pulled her back. Her voice sounded tight when she said, "He's tied up, right? So he can't do anything to us. We really should—"

"It's messy. You don't want to go down there."

Messy. Oh, God. "But I do." Then she could run outside and scream for help. She walked calmly to the door. Reached for the knob.

An arm came around her neck from behind. "I'm afraid I can't let you do that."

His voice was so calm. She took a breath to scream, but he slapped his hand over her mouth. "Can't have that, either." He pulled her backward, leaning down to his backpack. It wasn't zipped closed, and he dug around and pulled out a wad of cloth.

He was going to gag her! She tried to wriggle free, and he threw her on the couch, coming down on top of her and sending her breath right out of her. He got to his knees, straddling her and pinning down her arms with his legs. He shoved the cloth into her mouth and tied the gag around her head. She struggled, but she could hardly move.

Using all of her strength, she thrust her hips up, sending him off-balance. She shoved him the rest of the way, and he fell toward the coffee table. A basket of dried flowers scattered across the throw rug. She scrambled to the door, but he grabbed her ankle and sent her to her knees.

She tried screaming, but only muffled yelps escaped. She swiped at the gag, but he grabbed her arms and pushed her facedown to the floor. He leaned close beside her.

"You didn't see me in the coffee shop that day. But I saw you. And when I picked you for my next victim, I couldn't believe it when you turned around like I'd said it aloud. Then you touched your hair when I thought about your hair. And your scarf. You looked spooked the rest of the time you were there. I left but watched you through the front window. I couldn't figure it out.

"Then I followed you to the police station. I've got contacts there, so I used the Kiss and Kill Cupid case as an excuse to go in and listen to what you were telling the detective. He didn't believe you, but I did. Yeah, it sounded crazy, but it made sense, too. Then I gave you a final test. I thought about you having lipstick on your teeth, and you rubbed your teeth. You can freaking read thoughts."

What am I thinking now, Kristy? That I'm going to strip you naked and touch that gorgeous body of yours anywhere I please? And that afterward I'm going to kill you?

Her body tensed. Through the gag she asked, "Why did you kill that other woman this morning?"

"To throw you off. You weren't expecting me to come calling, were you?"

He'd killed a woman because of her. And he'd probably killed Adrian because of her. The thought turned her stomach and tightened her throat.

He grabbed something else out of his backpack. Rope. *No, don't do this!*

"And you were so focused on those serial-killer characteristics." He pulled her arms behind her and tied them at the wrists. "Guess what? I had a nice, normal childhood. I didn't kill animals or set fires or wet my bed." He rolled her over, leaning down into her face. "I do it for the story. I *make* the news. Do you know how powerful that is? To make people talk about you, fear you?"

She was trying not to show her fear. Not easy, considering her pulse was throbbing in her throat and her eyes were as big as eggs.

He pulled her to her feet. "Why don't we go into your bedroom? I like it. The blue comforter and those frilly pillows."

He'd been in her room! Those times the comforter was wrinkled, that was him. The thought sickened her, one more violation on top of everything else.

He grabbed his backpack and hauled her to her room. She kicked at him, sending him falling forward. He regained his footing quickly, grabbing her before she could dart to the door.

"You're feisty. I like that." But she could see anger burning in his eyes.

He shoved her into her room, where she lost her balance and fell onto the bed. She tried to crawl off the other side, feeling like a caterpillar with her arms tied behind her back. He grabbed her by the shirt and pulled her back up. He turned her around so that she was lying on her back facing him, her arms under her. He smiled as he climbed onto the bed. With a vicious kick, she sent him stumbling backward. He bumped into her dresser, and several bottles of perfume crashed to the floor, filling the room with the scent of . . . Intuition.

I have to do this for Adrian. I've got to get out of this and get to him.

She scrambled off the bed as he regained his balance. She aimed a kick right at his crotch. He doubled over with a groan. She darted past him, struggling to free her hands.

"Get back here, bitch!" he growled.

She felt the rope around one hand loosen. He raced out of the bedroom and blocked the front door. She ran to the kitchen, eyeing the butcher block knife set in the back corner. He came up behind her fast, shoving her hard. She lost her footing, falling forward. She landed on the floor with a thud, her forehead banging against the tile. A white flash exploded before her eyes.

Stay with it. Don't lose it now.

He turned her over. The world came back into focus. His face flushed with rage. Behind him . . . the pot handle hanging over the edge of the stove.

"All right," she managed in a muffled voice. "Just don't hurt me."

"Like I think you're going to play nice now." He yanked her to her feet.

The ropes were just loose enough so she could turn and grab the pot handle. She flicked her wrist and sent hot, melted chocolate spewing across his face. Boiling water from the pot beneath it scalded his arms. He screamed and wiped at his eyes.

She turned her body to pull open the oven door.

He blindly reached for her. She ran. He stumbled over the door and fell onto it, and his garbled scream was even louder this time. With the gag she couldn't yell loud enough to alert the neighbors, but he was making plenty of noise.

She ran to the front door and turned her body around to fumble with the lock. Facing the kitchen, she saw him writhing in pain. He rubbed the backs of his hands over his eyes to clear away the chocolate. His arms and palms were red and blistered. He looked at her with a kind of hatred she had never seen before. "I'm going to kill you, bitch!" He came at her.

She turned the dead bolt and twisted the doorknob. Pulled the door open. And screamed at the sight of a bloody man reaching for her.

"Adrian!"

A gash on his head was bleeding down into his eyes and over his face. He was weaving back and forth. "Are you all right?"

One of the neighbors opened her door, then a second door opened. An older woman gasped.

Adrian grabbed her and pulled her to the right. She turned to see Dale, blistered and covered in chocolate, grabbing for her.

The neighbor woman said, "See, Frank, I told you this neighborhood was going down the tubes."

"Hold it!"

Two police officers ran up the stairs, guns

pointed. One of them took in the scene, and said, "What the hell?"

She pointed to Dale. "He's Kiss and Kill Cupid! He tried to kill me."

Though both cops pointed their guns at him, the expressions on their faces were confused and wary.

"I'm Adrian Kruger. I called you."

"You're under arrest," one officer said. When he reached over to cuff Dale, he screamed in pain.

"She's the one who tried to kill *me*!"

The officer cuffed him anyway, careful of the burns. "We'll get it all sorted out at the station."

The other officer radioed a coded message to someone, then looked at Adrian. "The medics are coming in now." He looked at her. "Are you all right, ma'am?"

She nodded but was more worried about Adrian. His heart was pounding fast. Too fast. She pulled away to look at him. His face was the color of white chocolate.

He touched her mouth, her cheeks, wonder on his face. "You're all right. You're alive."

She nodded, her eyes tearing up. "So are you." But she wasn't so sure of that, not yet.

The medics came running up the stairs. Adrian said, "Check her first."

"No, I'm fine. He needs attention now."

One checked his pulse and blood pressure, and

the other checked the gash on his head. "We'd better take you in."

"I'm fine—"

She squeezed his arm. "Go. I'll take the car and meet you there."

That he didn't argue spoke volumes about his condition. The two medics helped him down the stairs.

One of them turned to her once Adrian was inside the ambulance. "You have a head injury, too."

She touched her forehead and winced in pain. "Just a knot."

"We'll take her to the hospital," one of the officers said. "Another unit is on the way."

She watched the ambulance take Adrian away, her heart both heavy and light. He was alive. But she so wanted to be with him.

Another police car arrived, and the female officer introduced herself and escorted Kristy to the car. She felt light-headed, either from her forehead whack or the adrenaline draining out of her body. By the time she reached the hospital, she was chilled and trembling.

There would be questions. The officer had said something about each of them being interviewed separately. She and Adrian would have to tell the police everything, including his visions and her ability to hear people's thoughts. It would all have to come out. But if Adrian was all right, she could handle everything else.

Kristy snuggled with Adrian on his leather couch. Since he'd been released from the hospital the day before, she'd been taking care of him.

"I could get used to this," she said.

"What, living here?"

"Taking care of you."

"Mm." He stroked her hair, brushing it back from her face. "Me, too. I could get used to you living here, too."

"Are you asking me to be your roommate?"

"Would I sound crazy if I asked you to be my wife?"

She sat up to look at him. He was serious. Her heart tripped. "My definition of crazy has changed since I met you." She arched an eyebrow. "*Are* you asking me to be your wife?"

He sat up, too, the bandage still on his head. "I hadn't actually planned to ask like this. But yes, I am. I don't want you to leave."

"Are you sure it's not your head injury talking?" She leaned forward and kissed him. "Just so I know it's not, wait and ask me again when you're feeling better. Until then, I'm here, and the answer will be yes, absolutely, you bet. By the way, you know that trip to Wimberly you're sending me on? You're coming, too."

"I am?"

"Owen helped me make the arrangements. After all, you're not supposed to go back to work for another few days. So why not make those days in that sacred cave you told me about?"

He grinned. "Why not, indeed."

Owen had decided to come out, as it were. Unsure what Dale Soza might do while he awaited trial, the three had come up with an offense: integrate Owen's story with the one Adrian and Kristy were writing about the Kiss and Kill Cupid incident. They were going to leave out some details, such as the psychic abilities and the fact that Kristy had suspected Owen of being the killer. The experience had helped Owen to come to terms with his past, and he was working through it with the help of a good therapist.

Kristy cuddled against Adrian again. The trip out of town would do them both good. The reporters were still hanging around trying to get their story. Dale, of course, had become the story he'd wanted to be, though not quite in the way he'd imagined. One of the neighbors had taken a picture with his cell phone and sent it to CNN, so a chocolate-covered screaming Dale was all over the news and Internet. Though the police hadn't yet been able to tie him to the previous Kiss and Kill Cupid murders, they'd found an eyewitness who put him at the scene of the murder on Valentine's Day morning, *before* the murder. They were building their case, and Kristy was their star witness. The district attorney was trying to keep her ability to hear people's thoughts out of the whole thing. Luckily, Adrian's ability was kept out of the reports altogether.

Adrian took her hand and slid his fingers between hers. "When do we leave?"

"Tomorrow afternoon. Your friend Lance is looking forward to seeing you. He's made the cave into a kind of spiritual attraction, now, letting various groups use it for healing circles and meditation." But she'd asked if she and Adrian could have the cave all to themselves.

Three days later, she and Adrian walked up the stone pathway, past a labyrinth, to the entrance of the cave. The moon was nearly full, hanging bright and bold in the sky. She held his hand as they ducked beneath the low entrance and stepped into the belly of the cave. Dim, colored lights did give the place a cathedral feel, as though a light was shining through a piece of stained glass.

They walked down an incline, and she readied herself to feel the chill she'd expect in a cave. Instead, warm, moist heat enveloped her. She looked at Adrian, who had a mischievous gleam in his eyes. "I didn't tell you the water flowing into this cave comes from a hot spring?"

"No, you didn't."

They stepped up to the pool, and she sucked in a breath at the beauty of it. Lights strategically hidden among the stalactites and stalagmites washed a splash of colors over the cave walls and the spiky formations growing down from the ceiling and up from the floor. The water was moving slightly, casting undulating reflections across the cave walls.

"Wow, this place is amazing," she whispered.

"Yes, amazing." He was looking at her.

He stepped up to her and unbuttoned her coat, lifting it off her. Then he ran his fingers along the bottom hem of her sweater and pulled that up and over her head. All the while he looked at her face, and what she saw took her breath away as much as the cave had: love. He reached around and unclasped her bra.

He hadn't worn a coat, obviously knowing how warm the cave would be. She pulled at his sweater, tugging it off him. He unbuttoned her pants, unzipped them, and pushed them down, where he knelt at her feet. He placed one of her hands on his back and lifted her foot, pulling off her boot. He did the same for the other boot, then pulled her pants all the way off, folding them and setting them on a stone bench. She undid his pants and realized he'd already taken off his shoes.

They stood naked, bathed in the colored lights. She wanted to look at his beautiful body, but she couldn't take her eyes from his. He took her hand and stepped down into the pool, drawing her with him. The water was so soft she could hardly feel it, other than its warmth. It swirled around her as she sank into its depths. Beneath her feet, the floor was smooth stone.

He pulled her into his arms and kissed her, slowly spinning them around. He got no more visions of her death. They'd tested it many, many times.

She wrapped her arms around his neck. "You're right. It is magical."

"It's not just this place. It's you."

"It's us." She placed her hands on either side of his face, so handsome, even with the bruise and healing cut. "Marry me."

"You must have been reading my mind."

"I was reading your heart, I think. You know, we've had this mysterious connection between us right from the beginning. Do you think it's because of our abilities?"

"They brought us together and created sparks

between us, but I think it goes deeper than that."
He lifted his hand out of the water and pulled a
ring off his pinky finger. The diamond glittered
in the lights.

She laughed. "You were going to ask me to
marry you here?"

He nodded, smiling. He slid the ring on her
finger and kissed the palm of her hand. "You beat
me to the punch. But that's okay. Because I have a
feeling nothing's going to go as planned with you.
And that's fine by me."

Since she was a kid, **JAIME RUSH** has devoured books on unexplained mysteries and psychic phenomena. She knew she would be published, marry a fabulous guy, and win a Toyota Supra. Missing the romance, relationship drama, and action of her favorite television shows—*X-Files*, *Roswell*, and *Highlander*—she created her own mix in the Offspring series. Kristy and Adrian don't know it yet, but they're Offspring, too.

Jaime loves to hear from readers (unless they're deranged or don't have something nice to say). You can reach her at PO Box 10622, Naples, Florida 34116 or through her website at *www.jaimerush.com*.

THE NIGHT HUNTRESS NOVELS FROM

Jeaniene Frost

✠ HALFWAY TO THE GRAVE ✠

978-0-06-124508-4

Before she can enjoy her newfound status as kick-ass demon hunter, half vampire Cat Crawfield and her sexy mentor, Bones, are pursued by a group of killers. Now Cat will have to choose a side…and Bones is turning out to be as tempting as any man with a heartbeat.

✠ ONE FOOT IN THE GRAVE ✠

978-0-06-124509-1

Cat Crawfield is now a special agent, working for the government to rid the world of the rogue undead. But when she's targeted for assassination she turns to her ex, the sexy and dangerous vampire Bones, to help her.

✠ AT GRAVE'S END ✠

978-0-06-158307-0

Caught in the crosshairs of a vengeful vamp, Cat's about to learn the true meaning of bad blood—just as she and Bones need to stop a lethal magic from being unleashed.

At Avon Books, we know your passion for romance—once you finish one of our novels, you find yourself wanting more.

May we tempt you with . . .

- **Excerpts** from our upcoming releases.
- Entertaining **extras**, including authors' personal photo albums and book lists.
- Behind-the-scenes **scoop** on your favorite characters and series.
- **Sweepstakes** for the chance to win free books, romantic getaways, and other fun prizes.
- Writing **tips** from our authors and editors.
- **Blog** with our authors and find out why they love to write romance.
- **Exclusive content** that's not contained within the pages of our novels.

Join us at
www.avonbooks.com

AVON

An Imprint of HarperCollins*Publishers*
www.avonromance.com